The commander raised his hand and shouted, and the horn's screaming ululation was echoed in men's war cries as the deghans kicked their horses into a gallop.

The archers lined up as planned, with the precision the commander had struggled so hard to create. The chargers passed between them and swept down the remainder of the field like water from a broken dam.

The deghans still shouted, but the thunder of the chargers' hooves swallowed their cries, swallowed the world. If the drums still beat, Jiaan couldn't hear them. He yelled himself, just to hear the sound torn to shreds as it left his lips. He'd heard the crashing rumble of the charge before, but never from within it, from the very heart of it. The earth shook, and even the pounding of his own heart was lost in it. It was impossible to be afraid.

Also by Hilari Bell

THE FARSALA TRILOGY BOOK 2:
RISE OF A HERO

THE FARSALA TRILOGY
BOOK 1

FALL OF A KINGDOM

HILARI BELL

Simon Pulse

New York   London   Toronto   Sydney

This book is a work of fiction. Any references to historical events, real people, or real locales are used fictitiously. Other names, characters, places, and incidents are the product of the author's imagination, and any resemblance to actual events or locales or persons, living or dead, is entirely coincidental.

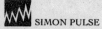 SIMON PULSE

An imprint of Simon & Schuster Children's Publishing Division

1230 Avenue of the Americas, New York, NY 10020

Text copyright © 2003 by Hilari Bell

Maps drawn by Russ Charpentier

All rights reserved, including the right of reproduction in whole or in part in any form.

SIMON PULSE and colophon are registered trademarks of Simon & Schuster, Inc.

Also available in a Simon & Schuster Books for Young Readers hardcover edition.

Designed by Greg Stadnyk

The text of this book was set in font Cochin.

Manufactured in the United States of America

First Simon Pulse edition January 2005

20 19 18 17 16 15 14 13 12 11

Library of Congress Control Number 2003114815

ISBN-13: 978-0-689-85414-9 (pbk.)
ISBN-10: 0-689-85414-5 (pbk.)

Originally published as *The Book of Sorahb: Flame*

For Debra

Sister in truth, as well as in law

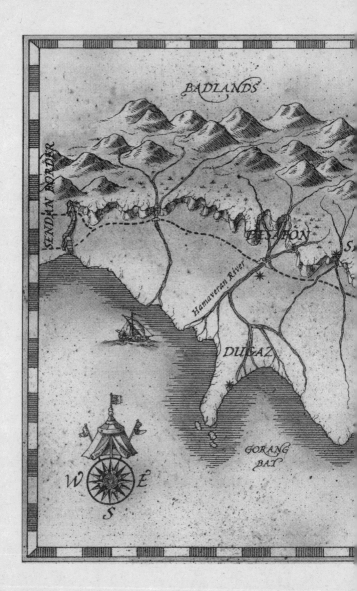

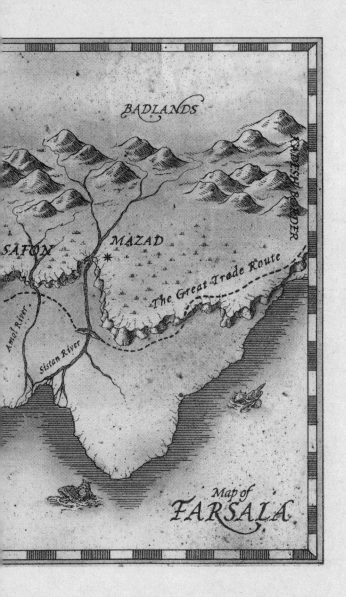

BADLANDS

KADESH BORDER

SAFON

MAZAD

The Great Trade Route

Amal River

Sistan River

Map of
FARSALA

OUTSIDE OF HIS ORIGINS *in the time of ancient legends, little is known of Sorahb. We know that he was a brilliant military commander, a shrewd ruler, and a mighty sorcerer—but how can a man so young have been all of these things? Was he a noble deghan? A peasant? Even, as some speculate, a Suud sorcerer in disguise? All this has been claimed, and more, but the one thing all agree upon is that he was a great hero, greater even than his father, Rostam. At least, if the legends are to be believed. . . .*

CHAPTER ONE

JIAAN

JIAAN DUCKED, and a bronze cup shaped like a ram's horn crashed into the wall behind him. It didn't clatter on the floor, since the thick carpets that had already absorbed its contents muffled the sound. He hoped the carpets wouldn't be too hard to clean. Jiaan knew that some people found it harder than others to fight off the djinn of rage. But he didn't think the lady Soraya was even trying.

"Lady, if you'll just lis—"

"I *have* listened," the girl snarled. Her grip tightened on the second cup. Her loose hair—the straight, black hair of the noblest of noble lines— was disheveled. The tight vest she wore beneath her loose, silk overrobe rose and fell with the force of her breathing. At fifteen, she was probably the most beautifully feminine creature Jiaan had ever seen—so what djinn-cursed fool had taught her to throw like a shepherd boy?

"I have listened," she repeated. "But all I've heard is that my father—my own father!—seeks to cast me out like some peas—like broken rubbish!"

Like some peasant-spawned bastard. It was an insult so familiar that Jiaan's heart hardly flinched. At least she hadn't said it aloud. That surprised him; most deghasses wouldn't have given a moment's thought to the possibility that he might be offended. But Jiaan's father hadn't cast him out. Far from it. And High Commander Merahb didn't intend . . .

"He doesn't intend to cast you out." Jiaan made his tone reasonable, despite the way her lovely, dark eyes narrowed. "He only means to hide you away for a time, in order to—"

"Away in some peasant sty . . ."

The second cup flew, and Jiaan sidestepped nimbly.

". . . in some dung-sucking outland while . . ."

Her groping hand found a niche, carved into the outer wall between the arched windows, and came to rest on a goblet whose glass bowl glowed as blue as the heart of a flame. Its base was chased in gold. Its worth was probably ten times that of Jiaan's sword, and his sword was more costly than all his other possessions put together.

The goblet hurtled toward the wall. Jiaan leaped, cursing the carpets that hindered his feet. He caught the goblet with the tips of his fingers, fumbled with it for an endless moment, and settled it into a secure grasp.

The plate it had rested on, thrown like a discus, struck him full in the chest, bruising him even through the padded silk layers of his armor.

"Ow!" Had she distracted him deliberately? "He's only trying to save your life, you . . . Lady Soraya. The gahn rules all of Farsala. Even the high commander has to obey him."

"Dung!" she shrieked. The incense burner her hand fell on next—small but solid stone and bronze—made a dent in the heavy panels of the door at Jiaan's back. "The armies of Farsala haven't propitiated the war djinn since Rostam cast down the last djinn emperor. Centuries ago!

And he thinks he's going to exile me for however long it takes to win his stupid war? Well, I won't—"

The door behind Jiaan opened. "You won't have any choice," said a woman's voice coldly. "And if you're overheard by the wrong people, your choices will become fewer—and even less pleasant than exile."

Jiaan stepped aside and bowed, the goblet still in his hands. Commander Merahb's wife, the lady Sudaba, moved gracefully into the small solarium.

Soraya froze, her hand clenched around the carved wooden horse she'd been about to throw. "Madam my mother, have you heard of this . . . this outrage? What about my marr—"

"I imagine everyone has heard." Sudaba took the goblet from Jiaan and crossed the room to return it to its shelf. "But I see no reason to give them any more information about our family's private affairs." Her ironic gaze rested on Jiaan.

He bowed himself out of the room, but not before Sudaba seized her daughter's ear and twisted it.

His own peasant-born mother had twisted his ears, and paddled his buttocks as well. But along with occasional—and usually deserved—punishment, there had been warmth, laughter, and love. Not only from her, but even from the farmholder to whom Jiaan's father had given her, when he was required to wed a deghass and produce a noble heir. His mother had died of a fever two years after the commander had outraged everyone by taking a peasant-born bastard into his household as a page, instead of as a servant. Jiaan still missed her.

Jiaan looked around the second-story gallery on which he stood. Intricately carved rails, sanded, waxed, and polished, encircled the courtyard below. Summer was ending; the leaves on the ornamental bushes looked dusty, almost ready to turn and fall, but a handful of late roses still bloomed, and the splash of the fountain calmed his ruffled nerves.

The home in which he'd lived till he turned ten had rough, log walls, and the plain, plank floors had never seen a carpet—yet he thought he'd been luckier than the lady Soraya.

On the other hand, all she had to do was go quietly and be patient for a while. Was that too much to ask?

The door behind him opened, and Sudaba emerged. "Soraya will depart with you tomorrow morning," she said calmly.

"Yes, madam." Jiaan bowed. She was eight inches shorter than he, but the assurance in her eyes made him feel as if he were the smaller.

"You should have pointed out that her father is plotting to save her," Sudaba murmured. "At some risk."

The crash of priceless glass against the door made Jiaan wince.

Sudaba didn't even twitch. "And however inconvenient it may seem, it's much better than the alternative."

In fact, Jiaan had pointed out all those things. Soraya hadn't cared. "Yes, madam."

"This is just a ploy." Sudaba leaned on the gallery rail, gazing down at the garden with unseeing eyes. "Another move in the game. But a good one."

Jiaan settled back to wait with the ease of long practice, till she noticed his existence long enough to dismiss him. The late-afternoon sun lit the expensive, brocaded silk of her overrobe and the almost equally expensive, fine-woven linen

underrobe beneath it. Gold on brown, to honor
the approaching harvest. Her hair, as straight and
black as her daughter's, was caught up in a complex coil, twined with silk ribbons knotted with
glowing glass beads and the hawk feathers only a
deghass, a lady of the noble class, could wear.

Jiaan's hair was brown and curly, like his
mother's . . . and his father's. Many of the deghans
had peasant hair. But not Sudaba. In her youth,
the poets had said, she'd been as lovely and imperial as the moon. *And as distant,* Jiaan thought now,
watching her calculate the political implications of
her daughter's fate. *As indifferent.*

But then a black-haired boy, his brown skin
as naked as the day, burst shrieking into the
courtyard and toddled toward the fountain. Two
nursemaids, armed with trousers and tunic, hurried after him.

Sudaba's frown faded and her eyes lit, her
face suddenly, warmly maternal. Merdas, the
long-awaited heir, had finally confirmed her status, eliminating the danger that she could be set
aside allowing High Commander Merahb to take
another wife. But still . . . Jiaan had served in the
high commander's household for seven years —

as page, as squire, and now as the commander's aide—and he had never seen Sudaba's face soften like that for Soraya.

On the other hand, her father loved her best. "The commander of the army must sacrifice the being he holds most precious in all the world," the priests had said. "Or the djinn of war will give their favor to the armies of the Hrum, who will roll over Farsala like the darkness of the pit itself."

Jiaan wondered uneasily which of the commander's enemies had bribed the priests to say it. And why. No, he didn't envy his half sister. Even if she was a silly, spoiled she-bitch.

CHAPTER TWO

SORAYA

SORAYA WENT ALONE down the stairs to the courtyard. The sun still crouched below the horizon, though the sky to the east was bright with its approach. It was light enough for her to see small puffs of steam when she breathed out. The cold weather was coming; rain, mud, and chills, and she was to be imprisoned in some sty in the outlands? She was fifteen this year—it was time for her to wed! She shivered.

She'd snarled at the maids who had awakened her to dress by candlelight, but she hadn't dared to refuse them, for behind the mouse-timid maids loomed her mother's shadow—and Sudaba was anything but timid. But it wasn't fear of Sudaba that was making her go. Not really.

Soraya crossed the garden and stalked down the stone-flagged walkway that passed under the servants' wing and out to the stables. Her escort waited there, his horse already saddled, his face pale in the gray light. Two of her father's armsmen, in the black-and-gold tunics of the House of the Leopard, accompanied him—not that all of them together could take her anywhere she didn't choose to go. Especially when she was on horseback. Jiaan smiled tentatively. Soraya scowled and turned away. She wasn't going because of him, and it probably wasn't fair to blame him for being the bearer of bad news, but she didn't feel like being fair. Particularly to the peasant-born bastard her foolish father had insisted on bringing into his household as a page, then as his aide, just as if he were a noble-born second son or an impoverished cousin.

One of the mousy maids brought up Soraya's pack, to be added to the load the mules carried. She waited while the grooms fussed with the ropes, trying to exude regal dignity and not shiver. If she looked regal enough, the servants, at least, might be fooled into thinking the whole thing was her idea.

Small bare feet made no sound on the stone floor, but Soraya caught a glimpse of the blue-striped nightdress, and she abandoned dignity to swoop down on Merdas just before he darted behind one of the horse's heels. It wasn't a charger, but even a placid horse might kick if startled.

"Merdas, don't run behind horses! You know better than that."

He squirmed in her arms to face her, warm and toddler-firm, pouting, because he really did know better. But Merdas never believed any horse would hurt him. Her brother. Her father's son.

"Djinn did it," he pronounced. At his age she had claimed the same. "Raya, horse!"

The nursery window overlooked the stable yard—he must have heard the hoofbeats. He had ears like a lynx where horses were concerned. And if there was a djinn who governed slipping past one's nurses, Merdas had it firmly under his control.

"I can't take you riding today, imp," said Soraya regretfully. "I'm going a long, long way. You'd get tired."

"Horse," said Merdas, who didn't believe he could get tired, either. Sometimes Soraya agreed with him.

"Sorry, no horse today. But if you're good, I'll bring you a present when I come back. How about that?"

The dark eyes turned thoughtful. Merdas liked presents, but . . . "Horse!" He squirmed again, kicking her in the stomach.

Where were his nurses? She could hand him over to the grooms, but she hated the thought of riding off with him howling behind her. "Horse, horse, horse!"

"I'll take him." It was Sudaba's voice.

Soraya spun, astonished. Her mother returned her gaze calmly, every braid in place, as if she always rose at dawn. She was dressed for riding, a modest split skirt beneath her overrobe—unlike Soraya.

"I didn't realize you were coming with me, madam." Soraya transferred Merdas into her outstretched arms, and he settled on her hip, reaching for the feathers in her hair. But for once he didn't have Sudaba's full attention. Her lips tightened as she took in the baggy men's trousers Soraya wore for riding. Not ladylike. Not proper for a deghass.

But making a scene in front of the servants wasn't proper either. "I thought it best to accompany you, daughter, in this difficult time."

To support Soraya in her troubles? No, to make certain her orders were obeyed. As if Soraya were an infant. Soraya scowled, but there was nothing she could do. The jumped-up page boy, Jiaan, looked startled, but Sudaba would care even less for his wishes than her daughter's.

Sudaba's maids brought out her baggage—far more than Soraya had brought—and several more mules were added to the caravan. Merdas' nurses scurried out and took him from his mother's arms.

"We're ready to depart, madam," Jiaan told Sudaba respectfully. He didn't even look at Soraya.

Sudaba mounted and set off, the armsmen trotting after her. But Soraya went to Merdas and covered his face with big, smacking kisses that made him giggle.

"A present when I come back," she promised, and then turned swiftly to her mare. The groom's cupped hands caught her bent knee and tossed her expertly up into the saddle. Soraya wrapped her legs around the mare's broad barrel and took her out without a backward glance. More regal that way. For if she looked back and Merdas reached for her, she might weep. And if he was indifferent to her departure—a perfectly normal reaction for a toddler, who had no idea how long she might be gone—she'd feel cheated. Besides . . .

She snickered, and Jiaan, who was trotting up beside her, stared, his annoyed scowl fading into curiosity.

If he'd been impertinent enough to ask why she laughed, she wouldn't have said anything, but he just watched her and let the silence stretch. And he looked almost embarrassingly like her father.

"I was just thinking that any grief Merdas showed would have been for his vanishing horseback ride, not for me."

Jiaan grinned, but his pale, greenish eyes—lighter than her father's, his peasant blood showed in that—were full of speculation.

Soraya knew what he was thinking. She'd heard it for almost two years—whispers in shadowy stalls, in the bushes in the courtyard, behind her back: "She really loves the boy. Or seems to. How can she when her mother . . ."

But Merdas couldn't take away affection that

Sudaba had never given her in the first place. If anything, she'd come to understand her mother better since Merdas had been born, for the need to be mistress of her own house, to be the first woman in it, had been setting its heels to Soraya's sides lately as well. And her father's recent letters had hinted that marriage, a fine marriage, was under consideration. So what was this ridiculous sacrifice business? Certainly the priests demanded sacrifices of gold, but the sacrifice of life, of blood, hadn't been demanded since the days folk truly believed in the power of the djinn. Soraya sighed. She had to discuss this with her father. Sudaba needn't have worried that she'd rebel; in fact, Soraya would have gone even if her mother had forbidden it. This was the first important thing her father had asked of her.

THEY TOOK THE ROAD that followed Little Jamshid Creek, which flowed eventually into the Jamshid River. Sudaba rode at the head of the party, as a high-ranking deghass should. Soraya kept her horse back, but she maintained her dignified silence, answering Jiaan's occasional conversational attempts politely but not expanding

17

on them. He soon gave up and stopped talking.

That suited Soraya. It was almost a full day's ride before the farms of the first village disrupted the sweeping plains of her father's estate, and silence was the proper greeting for windswept grass and the huge, open sky.

At dusk they began to encounter the kind of fields you weren't supposed to ride over—though sometimes, in the heat of the hunt, you did. When that happened, her father would send a groom to find the farmholder, with a small purse of copper stallions or a few silver falcons to set it right, but Soraya knew most deghans wouldn't bother to do the same. You had to eat, of course, but most deghans regarded plowed land as a waste of good pasture.

The inn at the small village was crude, but Soraya had stayed there before, and she knew it was clean and had a decent bathhouse. She frequently accompanied her parents on the six-day journey to Setesafon. It was Farsala's capital city, because the gahn's palace was there.

Soraya tossed her reins to the groom and slid off her horse. It had been a long ride, even for someone accustomed to the saddle. The innkeeper was already bowing Sudaba through the door. Soraya followed, waving over the first maid she saw to command a bath. Her escort would pay the tab.

AROUND MIDDAY THE HORSES picked their way down the shallow cliffs that separated the upland plains from the near-solid farmlands—the flatter, wetter country where the lesser noble houses held land.

Then a short canter across country brought them to the Great Trade Road. No matter how many times she'd seen it, the wide, dusty tracks always intrigued Soraya. The carters who drove it tried to move their carts around, to keep any one set of ruts from becoming too deep, but after a while they deepened anyway, and the road shifted a bit to the north or south to make new tracks. Over the centuries it had become not one road, but dozens of twining trails, weaving their way from the Sendar Wall at the western border of Farsala to the invisible line in the east where the border deghans held back the Kadeshi.

Some of the laden carts on this road had come from even farther away, carrying second-rate steel and mechanical creations from the Iron Empire of the Hrum, to trade for glass, spices, and dyes from the savage lands of Kadesh, for even the Hrum's second-rate steel was better than anything the Kadeshi could produce. Some traders from both directions stopped in Farsala to trade for Farsalan silk, which was so strong that armor could be made from its gathered layers, like the padded tunic Jiaan was wearing—armor both stronger and lighter than the leather armor most folk used. Sometimes they traded for horses, too. Farsala's horses were the finest in the world, and even the culls from their herds were worth much in other lands.

Traders liked Farsala, Soraya's father said, and paid their travel tax willingly because the deghans kept the road free of bandits. Soraya had never met anyone willing to pay taxes, but the traders were a cheerful lot, calling out greetings and talking of the lands they'd visited as you rode beside their carts—though they wouldn't unwrap the mysterious bundles and crates of their loads unless you had coin in hand and were interested in buying more than a trinket or two.

On past trips Soraya had talked to the traders

for candlemarks, to her father's amusement and her mother's disapproval. Sudaba would never permit casual conversation with such low-born men on this journey, just as Soraya's trousers had been taken away by her mother's maid and replaced with the voluminous, awkward split skirt.

Soraya sighed again. When she married, she would choose a man who let her wear what she pleased and talk to whomever she wished, like her father did. When she was married . . .

THE WEATHER HELD GOOD for two more days. The harvest was beginning, the fields full of peasants in their vulgar, brightly dyed clothes. Even little ones, barely older than Merdas, were fetching empty baskets for their elders or chasing off the birds. But midafternoon, on the fourth day of their journey, the clouds to the south began to build and darken.

Jiaan scowled at them—her father's scowl— the rising wind ruffling his curly, peasant hair, and he asked Sudaba if they could stop at the next village.

Soraya bit back the urge to argue. She might love a thunderstorm, but she knew the horses wouldn't.

So it came about that Soraya found herself, in the late afternoon, with time and energy to spare, cooped up in a bedchamber that was too small even to pace in. There were peasant designs painted on the furniture, and the painted shutters of the single, small window opened onto the inn's kitchen yard. The trees on the other side of the yard's wall rustled in the wind, their upper branches beginning to toss; but the window faced north, so that was all of the storm she could see.

At home Soraya had a south-facing room. She could sit at her open window, blanket wrapped around her, and watch the winter rains rush in, spitting lightning and growling like a lion, as the wind clawed at her hair. Sometimes she didn't close the shutters when the first drops struck her face. Sometimes she even went out in the storms. . . .

There was a shed roof not four feet below the windowsill. *Why not?* Her mother's maids had only taken away *one* pair of trousers.

Soraya pulled her next pair from inside one of her shifts, where she'd concealed them on the first night of the journey. She pinned her over-robe tight, grateful that it was split up the back for riding. It was the work of moments to swing one leg over the sill and pick her way down the shed's roof, rope-soled riding boots secure on the rough slats. Off to one side was a wood bin, conveniently placed for a girl who wasn't tall to reach with one toe and then wobble down to the ground.

Soraya grinned at the startled cook, who'd stopped pulling loaves from the oven under the shed's roof to stare at the source of the overhead footsteps. Then she turned and made for the gate that would lead to the inn's garden and, hopefully, to some open place where she could watch the storm come in.

Yes. Once she passed the trees, she saw a small rise that began where the garden ended. She'd almost reached it when a hand fell on her shoulder.

Soraya squeaked and spun, one hand clenching into a fist, as her father had taught her, the other reaching for the small eating dagger she wore at her belt. But the dagger went undrawn, for her fist smacked into a warm, strong palm, and a warm, strong voice said, "That's my leopard cub! But you should have the dagger out by the time your fist hits, girl."

"Father!"

A second later she was in his arms, a big man's hug that lifted her off her feet.

"How's my girl?" he growled into her hair.

"Angry with you," Soraya muttered into his shoulder. "And if you think I'm going off to rot in some hole while all the other girls my age make the good marriages, then—"

"Hush." Her father let her go; his expression was so serious that she did fall silent. Thunder rumbled. He glanced around the deserted garden, looking for all the world as if he feared to be seen with her. *What in the name of all the djinn . . . ?*

"This is too open." Taking her arm, he led her toward a small shed—no more than a lean-to with a thatched roof, half-buried in the trees. "Besides, we're about to get wet. Still, I'm glad the storm brought you out. With the inn this busy, I'd have had to wait till nightfall to sneak in without being seen."

Soraya felt a chill that had nothing to do with the storm. "Why don't you want to be seen talking to me? And who would see us?"

"I'm pretty sure one of the armsmen with Jiaan is in Garshab's pay."

A gust of wind sent leaves whirling, and her

father reached into the shed and began pulling out hoes and pitchforks, making them a place to sit, since the roof was far too low for them to stand. Soraya pulled her overrobe around her. She knew that Garshab headed the House of the Raven, one of the twelve great houses, just as her father was head of the House of the Leopard. This made Garshab one of the most powerful men in Farsala, and a powerful commander in her father's army too, but . . . "Why would Commander Garshab care if you talk to me? Why should anyone care? You outrank him—in the army, anyway."

"Ah, but he's trying to change that." Her father crawled into the dusty shelter without any visible thought for dignity or spiders. "That's the point of this whole ridiculous mess. How much did Jiaan explain to you?"

"That I'm supposed to be sacrificed to propitiate the djinn," said Soraya, scowling down at him. Thunder cracked and fat drops began to fall.

"And . . . ," said her father patiently.

"And that I'm supposed to hide out somewhere to avoid it, until you win the war. Which could take years! It's ridiculous. The temple never asks for blood sacrifice—not for centuries. I won't . . ."

The rain thickened suddenly, and she gave up and scrambled in to sit beside him.

"I'm afraid you'll have to," said her father. "Garshab's cozened the priests into demanding your sacrifice, and they've stirred up the soldiers. Even some of the deghans. I've been trying for years now to convince the gahn and the others that the Hrum are a real threat; now it looks like I may have succeeded too well. Anyway, if I don't agree to sacrifice you or Merdas, Garshab will argue that I'm unfit for command. He's got enough support in the deghanate that the gahn will be forced to agree to him replacing me."

For the first time Soraya felt a chill of real fear. The heads of the twelve great houses formed the gahn's council. Technically, they were all equal, but Soraya knew her father had the support of the majority there. The deghanate, on the other hand, was comprised of the heads of all noble houses, even if they owned no more than one village and a single charger. They quarreled constantly among themselves, but when they pulled together, they could overthrow gahns. If the majority of the deghanate supported Garshab, the gahn wouldn't dare ignore them.

"Don't worry," said her father, reading her expression. "I won't allow any harm to come to my leopard cub. Unfortunately, Garshab knows that. His plan—his real plan—is to catch me in the process of saving you."

"But wouldn't Commander Garshab have to make some sort of sacrifice too?"

"He's probably prepared some way to get around it." Her father's lips twisted in disgust. "But I swear, Garshab might sacrifice one of his children for real, if it was the only way to get command. He has a hunger for power that . . . Well, I wouldn't want him in command at the best of times, and now—"

"Now, if the Hrum come, he'll get the glory of defeating them," said Soraya indignantly.

"I'm sure that's what he thinks," said her father. "And by Azura's arm, if it were just the glory, I swear I'd give it to him. But the Hrum have conquered every land in their path for almost two centuries, leopardess. And despite what Garshab believes, he isn't Sorahb reborn—not even close. I don't think he can beat them. So I *have* to retain command, and that means you—"

"Have to be sacrificed." She understood; she just didn't like it. "But if Garshab has the temple and the deghanate behind him, how can you—"

"Don't worry about that. I'll see that no harm comes to you, and as soon as the Hrum are defeated, none of this will matter."

"But the Hrum might not come for years!"

"They're in Sendan now." Her father's voice was very soft. "Some of the deghans think they'll need time to conquer it, but Sendan is hardly putting up any resistance. The Hrum army mostly consists of infantry. The soldiers won't want to campaign in the winter, but when spring comes, they'll come for us."

Soraya decided to blame her shudder on the leaking thatch. "All winter in exile? And then the time it will take to fight a war as well? Besides, there's a wall between us and Sendan. We can stop them at the Sendar Wall."

"The Sendar Wall is Sendan's wall," said her father dryly. "Now it's the Hrum's. We can't exactly turn it around and use it against them."

Soraya frowned. "Why not?"

Her father laughed softly. "Sometimes I forget that you're a girl."

"Woman." Soraya scowled. "An *unwed* woman. Isn't a wall the same on both sides?"

"Not this kind of wall." Her father was still grinning. "The arrow slits, all the defensive structures, face the other way. Don't worry. The defense of Farsala lies in the strong arms of its deghans, and against the Hrum those arms had better be strong and well wielded. Because, frankly, looking at the Hrum, I wish the previous gahns had built us a few walls."

"But you can beat them?" The Hrum might have conquered half the world in the last few centuries, but no one had been able to conquer Farsala for thousands of years. And many had tried. And her father was the best commander—

"Of course I can." His frown vanished in a grin. "Don't fret about that, girl. You'll have enough on your plate, trying to act like a proper sacrifice."

"I have no clue how to act like a sacrifice," Soraya told him gloomily. But she knew protest was useless. And Merdas was too young. She wouldn't sully her dignity by even mentioning his name.

"You'll bring it off, when the time comes," her father told her. "You're no fool, girl, any more than your mother is. You can lie better than any scheming deghan, if you put your mind to it."

29

Soraya sighed. "I'll try." But she wasn't happy about it.

Her father laughed. "Just keep sulking, like you have for the last few days, and that'll do."

"I haven't been . . . How do you know what I've been doing?"

"I started following you late this morning," her father confessed. "I had to catch up with you before you reached the capital. We'll both be watched there. My aides are covering for me now, but I wore out three good horses getting here, and I'll wear out as many more getting back to the city before dawn."

"I haven't been sulking," said Soraya. "How are you going—"

"Soraya?" Her mother's voice sounded, not quite an unladylike shout, but loud enough to carry. Soraya's absence had been discovered. And the rain was letting up. The maids would begin searching for her soon.

"Time to go," said her father. "I only came to be sure that you weren't fri—that you knew what was really going on."

"But I don't know what's going on! Not nearly enough." Soraya grasped his sleeve. "Doesn't Mother know you're here?"

"She knows all she needs to. And so do you now. Don't worry." Her father kissed her temple. "I won't let any harm come to you."

"I know you won't," said Soraya. "But what about—"

Her mother's summoning increased in firmness, if not in volume. This would cost her another set of trousers.

"That's my leopardess." Her father pulled free of her grip, crawled out into the rain, and departed, amazingly quiet for so big a man.

If she had nothing to fear, why did he keep reassuring her? Could she really be in danger? Of being sacrificed? Nonsense. She was a deghass of the House of the Leopard, and her father would protect her. Still, she wished he'd had time to explain more. Soraya suppressed a shiver and raised her voice to answer her mother's call.

CHAPTER THREE

KAVI

THE PERFECT GOLD SURFACE of the bronze pot glowed under Kavi's hands. He studied it with his fingertips, as much as with his eyes, seeking shallower spots in the new coating, places in the design where he'd not quite . . . Ah, there was a section that should be a bit sharper. He reached for the stylus with his right hand, then switched it to his left and pressed the blunt iron point into the gold-filled indentations, working them just a bit deeper. The soft gold spread and then flattened as he tipped the stylus to smooth it. Cold, and still it yielded to the muscles of hand and arm alone. Kavi despised gold—no strength, no temper, no worth but to adorn things. Like the deghans who wore it.

It was the only metal he could work now.

"Be done with it, lad," said Nadi. "It's plenty fine."

"Can't be too careful," Kavi replied placidly, continuing to refine the pattern. "Some look closer at a bargain."

And some looked at a pretty little maidservant, selling her poor, impoverished mistress's valuables, and thought of nothing but how far they could bargain her down. Hama, who posed as the maidservant, liked cheating them.

"I know, I know. But at least you're finished layering?" At Kavi's nod Nadi began boxing away the wafer-thin sheets of gold. He knew it was hard for her, watching him apply coat after coat of leaf, knowing what her girl had risked to get it.

Kavi grinned. "Craft, Nadi. You never skimp on craft—it'll bite you on the ass every time. Stealing a bit more melting gold is a far smaller risk than if any little dagger nick showed bronze. And as it is . . ."

He held up the pot he'd been working on, giving it another inspection. It was heavy, for Kavi purchased only hollow shells and then filled them with lead so their weight would feel right to potential buyers. The undercellar in which he was working was as well lit as lamps could make it, but he'd take a look by sunlight, too, before handing it over to Hama. Time's Wheel spun all things, from the Tree of Life down into the Flame of Destruction, but there was no sense in tempting it to turn.

". . . as it is, this'll pass any test and wear like solid gold for centuries, like as not. By the time the fraud's found out, if it ever is, we'll all be long dead. And we'll have died fat, and of old age, too."

The sound of the door banging open echoed down the chimney and silenced Nadi's chuckle. Kavi frowned. Only a deghan, a family member, or the guard would burst through a door like that, without asking permission to come in. And Hama and Sim would have taken care for the little ones sleeping in the loft. Unless . . .

Rapid footsteps pounded down the stairs. Nadi's husband's family had been stonemasons for generations. The chimney in this hidden cellar was linked to the ones above it so cleverly that you couldn't possibly tell by looking at the hearths that it even existed. But sound from all the upper rooms came down clearly—and traveled up as well.

Kavi's heart was beating faster, but he softened his breathing as he listened to the light footsteps cross the floor of the laundry in the cellar above. They went straight to the well-concealed trapdoor.

"It's Sim," said Nadi just before the trap lifted and a young, freckled face peered down.

"Mam, I think there's trouble. A guard got Hama, but he's a new one, and he says he wants to deal with the man of the family."

"What, you're not man enough for him?" Kavi started to reach out as Sim came down the ladder, but he stopped. Sim, at eleven, felt he was too grown up to have his hair tousled.

Nadi looked grim. "Well, he'll have to be making do, won't he? Wonder why he wants a man. I'd think if he wanted to bargain, he'd be happier with a child—or a woman."

"Maybe he knows that women bargain best," said Kavi. "Stop looking so worried. You've got the bribe money put by, don't you?"

"Fifteen gold eagles," Nadi confirmed.

"More'n double the going price. Otherwise, I don't let Hama go out." She knelt to press the pivoting floor stone as she spoke. One of the pivoting stones. Who knew what there might be in a house built by generations of master masons?

"That's half a year's salary for a town guard," Kavi reminded her. He gave the pot a final rub and picked up his cape. "Don't fret—all fishermen throw the sprats back in so that they can catch them again when they're bigger."

The purse clinked as Nadi lifted it. Her frown grew deeper. "Then why didn't he just send Sim back for five eagles? Seven, if he's being greedy or if Hama bit him. But she knows better than that, unless—" She turned and saw Kavi fastening his cape, and her eyes widened. "You're not the man of this family, lad, however much kindness you've shown us. There's danger here. Suppose this one's honest?"

Kavi snorted. "Suppose fire's cold. What's the matter?" He nodded at the purse. "Don't you trust me?"

He did his best to sound huffy, with a bit of hurt beneath it, but Nadi smiled. "With my children's lives, and you know it. But you shouldn't be putting yourself in harm's way, after all you've done for us already."

Kavi shrugged. "He wants a man. I'm the only man you've got."

"You're nineteen."

"Man enough," said Kavi. "If he doesn't like it, Flame take him. Besides, peddlers bargain even better than women."

Nadi scowled.

"Who else do I have to put myself in harm's way for?" he added softly.

Nadi's eyes filled. She handed him the purse. "Be careful."

"Ha. I thought that'd get you." Kavi dodged a clap on the ear with the ease of a lifetime's practice and climbed the ladder to the laundry, then the stairs to the big room. He let himself out into the early-autumn night, Sim following at his heels. It had been dark for several marks now, but the moon was rising.

Kavi had left Nadi snickering instead of worrying, but he knew that wouldn't last. In truth, he was concerned himself. The town guard's willingness to look the other way for a small (or large) consideration was so well established that there was almost a set price for it. And why "the man of the house"? Faking gold pots was a lucrative sideline, but Kavi was a peddler by trade—he knew that women bargained better than men, but he'd yet to meet the man who'd admit it.

No, he wanted to find out what was going on himself. He wasn't responsible for Nadi's family, but he'd been in business with them ever since the day, three years ago, when a twelve-year-old Hama had tried to cut his purse.

After a brief . . . discussion of the matter, she'd led him back to the newly opened laundry to meet her mother, a pregnant widow with three small children of her own and two more she'd inherited, the younger brother and sister of the apprentice who'd died in the same quarry accident as her husband.

Kavi made his living on the road—not that he had any inclination to adopt the small family, even if he could have. But even at sixteen, he'd spun around Time's Wheel often enough to know that many crimes were safer, and more profitable, than cutting purses. And he knew gilding, though it wasn't his favorite craft.

So one stolen gold pot became a heavy coating

of gold over several other pots or bracelets or buckles. And a cutpurse became a young servant selling family goods . . . and, unfortunately, a burglar.

Mind, Hama was a better burglar than she'd been a cutpurse. She'd case a house for weeks, even months, learning the routines, befriending the dogs. She had a gift with dogs. And if the guard did catch her, Nadi, on Kavi's advice, had money on hand to pay them off. But if the scheme went awry . . .

It was pure luck he'd been here. He stopped at Farsala's capital only twice a year, to do the metalwork none of Nadi's family were trained in.

Passing one of the sewer grates, he almost wished he'd come at another season. The sewer system was one of Setesafon's marvels, and in the winter rains, even in spring and midsummer when it rained occasionally, it worked as it should. But during the long dry spell at the end of summer, when the river levels dropped, the lesser drains frankly stank. Yet the smallest, poorest village, where the people hauled their dung out to the fields each morning, smelled as fresh in the dry time as in the rains.

The other marvels of Setesafon—the wide paved streets, the fountains and statues that decorated the public squares—were conspicuous by their absence in this dark suburb of shops and work yards. As was yet another boast of Setesafon's worthy citizens: the honesty of the town guard.

Sim led Kavi through the warren of twisting lanes with the ease of an urchin who'd grown up in this city. Not half a candlemark later, in an alley so dark that Kavi had to slide his feet forward to keep from tripping, Sim went up to a door and rapped three times, then twice.

It opened immediately.

"We'll talk outside." The heavyset man who'd opened the door looked grim and authoritative, but he stank with nervous sweat. The shadow of stubble on his chin showed he hadn't shaved this morning. Too worried to take care of himself? Or too broke to afford even a few tin foals for the public baths? Kavi's concern deepened.

The guard station's common room looked bright after the inky darkness of the alley. A couple of men, their scarlet tabards tossed over an empty bench, diced idly at one of the tables. In fact, it could have been the common room of any tavern, aside from the lack of a bar—that, and the fact that the row of wooden doors along the far wall had iron bars crossing their small windows.

"I see the girl before we talk," said Kavi. Both Sim and Hama knew better than to give the town guard their names.

The guard stiffened, studied Kavi's face, and then shrugged and led the way across to one of the cells. The other guards barely glanced up from their game.

The cell was almost as dark as the alley outside. Kavi could barely see the small form huddled in one corner. "Hey, girl," he called softly. "You all right in there?"

The huddled form shot upright with all of Hama's usual awkward energy, and Kavi's worst worry faded.

"What are you doing here?" Close up, the window shed enough light for him to see her face. She looked tense and angry, but there were no tears. Not from Hama.

"Come to buy you out. But I wanted to make sure you were all right first."

"Of course I'm all right. I know better than to be fighting the—oh, no, nothing like that. But,

Kavi . . . curse him with all the djinn in the pit, have you heard what he's asking?"

"No." Kavi suppressed a qualm. How much could it be, after all? "Don't worry. Whatever he's asking, we'll get it."

He turned away, nodding his satisfaction to the guard, who looked indignant. "You think I'd rape a child? Or anyone? You think even if I wanted to—which I don't!—the others would let me?"

"Not at all, good sir," Kavi lied easily. "But her mother told me to ask. You know how mothers are."

"Humph." The guard was herding him back toward the door to the alley. "Well, she's in no danger of that, but she might be getting a flogging— even lose a finger or two—if the magister's feeling nasty."

"That's a terrible thing for a girl so young," said Kavi, stepping out into the alley's cool darkness. "Surely a man like you, a good man, has enough compassion to keep a child like that from the magister's clutches."

It was the standard, reassuring opening to bargaining situations like this one. Depending on how deep a veneer of respectability the guard wanted to put up, he might bemoan the conflict between his compassion and his duty for quite some time before he named his price.

They'd reached the alley's entrance now, and the guard stopped. Moonlight glimmered on his perspiring face. "I want forty gold eagles."

"*What?* Forty *eagles*?" For once the outraged shock in Kavi's voice wasn't feigned. "That's absurd. That's insane! If her family had that kind of money, she wouldn't be needing to steal!"

"To support her poor starving mother?" The guard snorted. "Well, I got a poor starving mother too. I can give you nine days to raise it, but if I'm not seeing forty eagles by the fourth day of Ram, the girl takes her chances with the magister." His voice was inexorable with panic. And why nine days?

"Your poor starving mother has a fondness for the dice, does she?" Kavi guessed. "Or did she bet too much on the last flags-and-lances match?" A hiss of indrawn breath told him he'd struck the mark. "Azura's eyes, man! You must have been possessed!"

"Yeah, well, that makes no difference, does it

now?" said the guard grimly. "Forty eagles by fourth day is the price."

Sim tugged frantically on Kavi's sleeve. "We don't have that," he whispered. "We don't have it!"

"The boy speaks true," Kavi told the guard slowly. "Suppose you catch someone else in the next nine days—you could charge twenty eagles for them, and if we give you twenty for the girl, you'd be having your sum. Catch two, and you needn't ask more than thirteen. Folks might be able to pay that."

"Yeah, and suppose I don't catch anybody," said the guard. "It's not like fishing, you know. There's weeks, months sometimes, when no one happens along. Besides, there's this ceremony coming up in just a sevenday—sacrificing that commander's daughter, so the djinn will let us beat the Hrum. There'll be lots of people coming to the city for that. For the blood and all. Surely there'll be a way for you to get the money, all those new folks in town."

Kavi grimaced. "There won't be blood. Or, if there is, it'll be chicken's blood or goat's. That's just a ploy so we can't complain when they raise the taxes, to pay for this new war. 'Look what the commander of the army sacrificed—surely you can be paying a few more stallions.'"

The deghans never paid for anything.

"I don't care about the commander's daughter," said the guard. "But if you're wanting your girl back, unscarred with all her fingers, you've got nine days to raise the sum. All of it." He turned and headed back toward the guard station, swearing as he ran into something in the dark.

"Kavi, we don't have it!" Sim whispered furiously. "No one has that kind of money."

"Some do." Kavi reached out absently, tousling the boy's thick curls. He wondered what the men the guard owed had threatened to do to him. Broken joints, from the sound of it. But worse might come to Hama, at the magisters' hands. "Some do. It's just a matter of figuring how much we need and the safest way to get it."

THEY SPILLED ALL THEIR MONEY onto the table in Nadi's main room. The hearth fire glinted on stacks of copper, brass, and tin, a bit of silver, and fifteen gold eagles.

"Seventeen eagles short," said Nadi grimly.

"Seventeen and a bit." Her warm brown skin was pale.

"How much could we be getting for the stuff in your packs?" Sim demanded.

"Not more than four eagles, at the most," said Kavi. "Not here, for apprentice work. Even if I sold Duckie, she'd only bring a few falcons more."

"I could sell the house and the laundry," said Nadi. "That'd fetch it. But it would be hard to do, in just nine days." The flickering light picked out worry lines on her face. She looked old.

Kavi snorted. "And then sell yourself? And your daughters? You're still thinking honest, woman. We've got gold enough below to fetch the sum without adding in a single coin." He gestured to the pile on the table.

Nadi's breath caught. "Sold in just nine days? Never get greedy, you told us. Just one or two pieces in a month. Give them long enough to forget your face."

"And for you, who live in this city, that's true," said Kavi, faking a confidence he didn't feel. "But once I've finished the selling, I'll be gone for six months. No reason for me not to sell the lot."

"But what if someone up and cuts one of your deep-coated buckles in half? What happens to you?" Nadi's eyes were dark with hope and guilt, gratitude and fear, but she looked younger. Kavi's heart lightened to see it.

"Then I'll smile, bow, and run like a djinn was on my heels," he said. "Just like I taught Hama. My time for the Flame hasn't come yet, Nadi. I promise."

ANY ACCOUNT OF SORAHB—*at least, any that heeds the ancient legends—must begin with his father. Rostam was the greatest warrior Farsala has ever seen. He lived during the reign of Kay Kobad, and even though Rostam was as greatly blessed with the divine farr as any man has ever been, that very quality kept him loyal to his gahn.*

Others were not as noble. For many years Kay Kobad's cousin, Saman, had tried to take the Ghanate from him. But eventually Saman grew older, and Kay Kobad decided to try to make peace with his cousin. He chose Rostam to be his ambassador, for he trusted Rostam's honor in the face of any bribe or threat, and even Rostam's enemies respected him.

So Rostam came to the manor of Saman under flag of truce, riding at the head of his troop, as a commander should. His robes were silk, embroidered with gold that shone like Azura's own sun; his helm was chased with gold, and even the barding of his steed, Rakesh, gleamed in the sunlight. Only the mace at his side was of plain, battered steel.

But it was not the wealth of Rostam's accoutrements that caught the eye of the young woman who walked with her maid in the garden of her father's estate. It was the keen nobility of his features, the grace and might of his limbs, and, above all, the divine farr, which showed itself in everything about him, as if he were himself a gahn.

Tahmina, the youngest daughter of Saman, turned to her maid. "Who is this man?"

CHAPTER FOUR

SORAYA

THE ROBES WERE RICHER than any Soraya had ever seen, so crusted with gold embroidery that they could probably stand upright without her inside them. She gazed gloomily in the polished, steel mirror, watching the maids hustle about the small room, under Sudaba's vigilant gaze. Once, as a child, she had wiggled into her father's cuirass and put on his helm, which promptly covered her eyes. She'd been all but blind, staggering down the gallery to show off her finery. She swore these robes were even heavier.

But at least she could see. In fact, Sudaba had braided all her hair back from her face, dressing it even more elaborately than her own. Soraya thought she'd seen an eagle's drab feather among the hawk feathers her mother braided in, but that had to be wrong. Eagle feathers could be worn only by the gahn and his immediate family, those closest to Azura among men, just as the eagle was closest to him among birds. And Sudaba would never make such a mistake. Which could only mean her mother had done it on purpose. Defiance? Insult? But to whom? And *why*? Layers within layers.

Soraya unclenched her teeth and took a deep breath, trying to slow her pounding heart. She'd been in the city for over a week while this farce was being prepared, and she hadn't been allowed to see her father once. She'd become so desperate to find out more about his plans that she had approached her mother. Unlike her father, Sudaba took Soraya's marriage seriously. But the only time Soraya had succeeded in getting her mother alone, Sudaba refused to tell her anything except that her father had everything under control and that all Soraya had to do was obey. She had stressed the final word firmly enough to silence her daughter.

I could obey better if I knew more about what was going on, Soraya thought for at least the hundredth time. But perhaps she should look on the bright side: Once she was "sacrificed," in an outland hovel, no one would braid her hair so tightly that her scalp ached.

Yet another maid entered and approached Sudaba. "Lady, it is time."

In an ordinary household the maids would probably be half-blood children, like Jiaan, or the descendants of such — sisters of the men who provided the deghans with foot soldiers and archers when they went to fight. But in the gahn's household the maids weren't peasants, but the second, third, or fourth daughters of the poorer deghans. They had watched her, surreptitiously, as they helped her dress. Soraya wondered who *they* reported to. Layers within layers. She suppressed a shiver.

"Soraya?" said her mother.

"Yes. I'm ready." She turned from the mirror and faced them. She'd already decided she couldn't bring off tragic grandeur — how *was* a sacrifice supposed to act, anyway? — and decided to go for subdued pride. She should be proud. *I am proud, curse it!*

She would serve her father in this, and even Farsala itself, by making his plans come right. It was a deghass's duty. *Yes, that's the attitude. Proud and calm.* Her chin rose. "I am ready."

Sudaba leaned forward, dutifully presenting her cheek for Soraya's kiss, and Soraya dutifully kissed it. Then Sudaba grasped Soraya's chin and inspected her face for a moment before leaning down to kiss her brow.

"Make me proud, daughter."

Soraya barely managed to keep her astonishment out of her voice. "Yes, madam."

Acting for the maids, no doubt. It had already been decided that Sudaba would not be required to be present for her daughter's "sacrifice." Too hard for a mother's heart to bear. Little did they know. But if they knew Sudaba so little, they knew Soraya even less. So maybe she could bring this off after all.

The maid who had come for her led Soraya out of the wing where she and her mother had slept last night, one of dozens of bewildering wings in the gahn's palace, and through a wide court lined with fountains. They made it a bit cooler. Azura's sun was blessing the harvest, which was fine for the harvest, but Soraya's robes were as hot as they were heavy.

Fortunately, her guide didn't seem to be in a hurry, and all the steps they encountered led down. A deghass shouldn't arrive covered with sweat. *Proud and calm.*

The White Palace perched on the very edge of the cliffs that separated the plains from the lowlands, but here, beside the Amol Falls, the river had worn down the land. Here the cliffs were no more than a steep slope, and on that slope the Hall of Whispers had been built.

The arch of the hall's great dome appeared before her. Not so impressive from this side, about twenty feet tall, and only the back of the gahn's dais visible within. But on the other side the structure ran down the slope like water falling from pool to pool, its every wall open to the winds. The high, arched ceiling not only shaded the crowd within from sun and rain, but by some trick of the echoes it carried every word spoken in the great dome down to the deghans and deghasses who gathered there. In the past Soraya had stood on the second level down and marveled at it.

Now the words the arches carried would

be hers. She took a deep breath. *Proud. Calm.*

She passed between the great horse statues that flanked the entrance, signifying that the current gahn was of the House of the Horse. Her father's leopards were only two down in the row of sculptures that stretched away from the horses on either side. Only Jandal's gazelles and Garshab's ravens were higher in the gahn's esteem.

Soraya climbed the steps and took three paces across the marble floor. Her fourth step echoed, and she jumped like a frightened doe, her eyes flying to the dome above. So much for calm.

The maid who was guiding her shrugged and led Soraya around the back of the dais, her own steps raising not even a whisper. She'd shed her shoes at the entrance. *Curse the girl. She could have warned me.* If her failure to do so was some subtle attempt to throw Soraya off stride . . . well, it had worked. *Djinn take her. Djinn take them all!* Soraya stood where she was—the girl could hardly go on without her—and breathed deeply, relaxing her quivering muscles. She'd been hunting often enough to know how to soften her footsteps. She could do this. She walked across the floor without making the ceiling echo, but it took sufficient concentration that the roar of the crowd as she came around the dais startled her.

She'd expected to see the deghans and their ladies, filling level after level of the hall as it fell away. But she hadn't known that the slopes outside the hall would be crammed with people. The crowd stretched almost as far as she could see, and she realized that the men perched at each arched opening were stationed there to shout the words that came down from the high dome out to the mob—a crude version of the echoing ceiling.

The peasants loved a show—Soraya had heard that public executions drew a huge audience—but they must have emptied the whole city! Were they so eager to see her blood? So confident? Soraya's lip curled. The jackals would be disappointed today. Her father would protect her. She was certain. It was only the heat of the robes that made her sweat so.

The maid led her around to the platform directly in front of the gahn's dais. Soraya's gaze fled to her father's platform, where he sat with the heads of the other twelve high houses. He met her eyes—his steady gaze a greater promise of safety than a thousand empty words from another man. Soraya lowered her own eyes to hide her expression—the picture of a modest maid—but she couldn't suppress a sigh of relief.

The ceiling above her platform had been pierced; flakes of light flashed on her robes. Soraya resigned herself to becoming even hotter as the ceremony wore on—if she was sweating, no one would wonder why. Only when she'd stilled her expression completely did she look up at Kay Amin, the gahn.

He must be roasting, was her first thought. He stood in a shaft of full sunlight, his robes, even more heavily embroidered than hers, surrounding him with a glowing aura, as if the sun itself shone from him. Did the peasants, crouching in the dirt, mistake that glow for divine farr? Probably. But farr, the nobility of nature that showed in every thought and action, wasn't a glow of light. It was the weariness in her father's face when he sat up late planning supply routes, so his army could eat wherever the battle led them, without stripping the countryside. It was the way he grimaced in pain when the old wound in his thigh caught him as he mounted, but never uttered a word of complaint. *Maybe the gahn has farr too*, thought Soraya rebelliously. But watching his eyes shift nervously from one of the twelve high deghans to the other, Soraya doubted it.

The gahn stepped up to the edge of the dais. "Commander Merahb, is this the lady Soraya, your daughter?" Here, beneath the dome itself, his voice didn't seem to echo, but to swell, stretching farther and farther as if to encompass the world.

"Yes, High One." Her father's voice grew, just as the gahn's had, strong and somber. "As you see, she is as I described her: beautiful beyond compare, as courageous as a maid might be, and yet so warm of heart and gentle of demeanor that the very sun might envy her. She is without flaw . . ."

Soraya, recalling a certain childhood incident concerning honey, feathers, and horse dung, fought down a giggle.

". . . and her loss will grieve me sorely, for she is as dear to me as any living soul."

All desire to laugh vanished. Even through the formal phrases, you could tell he meant it. A murmur of sympathy rose from the crowd.

A thin man, his black robes trimmed in gold,

like a crow in barding, stepped up beside the gahn and the murmur died.

"So, good priest," said the gahn seriously. "Will she serve the temple's purpose?"

Soraya bristled. *He gets to decide if I'm good enough to sac—*

"Yes, High One," said the priest. Even his soft voice carried clearly. "Her blood is pure, as the djinn demand. She will serve."

Sincerity burned in his voice, and Soraya felt cold, despite the stifling robes. He sounded as if he really meant it—as if he intended to see her blood running over the marble floor. Hadn't anyone told him this was a hoax?

Soraya looked at her father; his expression, his posture were the same, but she could tell his muscles had stiffened in real alarm. And if her false sacrifice would increase Garshab's power, what would her true sacrifice do for the temple's? Her hands jerked to the stiff robes, to lift them up and flee, but that would be useless, worse than useless, for it might force her father's hand. He had planned for this, right? And the gahn himself knew it for a farce?

The sudden alarm that underlay the gahn's

expression of regal calm did nothing to steady Soraya's quivering nerves. The ruler of all Farsala looked, betrayingly, at the man whose platform was only one remove from the dais. Soraya had seen Garshab a time or two before, though never with his fit, stocky form so richly dressed. Garshab was too shrewd to meet the gahn's gaze. Did it matter to Garshab if her father was forced to save her here and now? It might even be better for him—a public betrayal of the high commander's unworthiness! Soraya sought frantically for something, anything to say.

"I would make a stipulation," said her father, a bit too swiftly.

The gahn turned to him, a flicker of relief in his frozen face.

"I would first remind you that the djinn have permitted our armies to win countless battles over the centuries since Rostam cast down Zahhak, without sacrifice of blood, and that Azura abhor—"

"It is for the temple to deal with the powers of both light and darkness," the priest hissed. "Thwarting the one and seeking the blessing of the other!"

"But in this case," said her father, "you plan to

propitiate the 'powers of darkness,' not to thwart them. And Azura abhors blood sacrifice."

The gahn laid a hand on the priest's arm, quelling him. "You are the one, Merahb, who insists that the Hrum are no ordinary enemy."

"Yes, High One," said her father respectfully. His voice was calm. But Soraya would have felt better if his hand hadn't been resting on the hilt of his sword. "I do not seek to defy the temple's will. But all acknowledge that Azura is mightier than any djinn, and we dare not forfeit his favor. I ask only that my daughter be exposed in the mountains, without shelter, food, or aid. If the djinn claim her, so be it. But if Azura takes pity on her, he himself might shelter her—as he did Rostam's father when he was a babe, exposed by his own father at the ancient temple's order because he was born with a djinn's white hair."

A noise like restless surf rose from the crowd. It was true; Azura had, in ancient times, rescued and sheltered sacrifices exposed in the mountains. It was generally held that this was Azura's way of telling the priests that they had gotten it wrong.

The priest flushed. "The girl is ours! The manner of her sacrifice is ours to choose. It is for the temple to deal with the djinn and to interpret Azura's will!" But his eyes now went to Garshab, who shook his head so slightly that even Soraya, who was watching, wasn't sure she saw it.

Her father's hand left his sword hilt.

"Merahb's request seems both pious and fair," said the gahn hastily.

The priest still looked angry, but Soraya could see her father relaxing. If this had been some ploy to force him to reveal himself, it had failed.

Soraya tried to stiffen her wobbling knees. She hoped her father's scheme was a good one; whatever it was, his enemies were ready for it.

"And you, Lady Soraya," said the gahn. "Do you understand the burden laid upon you?"

"Yes, High One." Her voice was high and breathless, for all she tried to control it. Then she thought of something to add and spoke more firmly: "I am willing to do this, if it will aid my father's victory over the foes who threaten our land."

The gahn winced, very slightly. *Yes,* she thought with savage satisfaction. *Let that remind them who will fight and risk his life and bleed in their defense.* Sweat ran down her back beneath the linen undershirt. It itched. She'd been too tense to notice it before.

"Then I accept your sacrifice, for the strength of Farsala's army and for the good of its people."

The sunlight glittering on her robe vanished, like a sign from the heavens. The crowd roared. Had a cloud passed over the sun? But the gahn was still bathed in light.

Soraya looked up. A blanket! Someone on the roof had pulled a blanket over the grid that had speckled her with light.

"Wait, there's—"

"Wait!" Her father's voice overrode hers, drowning it, even in the dome. "I would make one more request." His eyes flickered to Soraya's, urgent, commanding. She ground her teeth.

"I would be allowed to accompany my daughter on her final journey, to offer her the comfort of my presence."

"But what assurance do we have," said the priest swiftly, "that a father's love will not overcome your duty to do all that you may in defense of the land?"

A new sense of danger prickled down Soraya's

spine. Not for herself, not anymore. But what was the penalty for a high commander who was caught disobeying the gahn's orders? Who defied the temple?

She glared up at the blanket. *Lying bastards.* The clean heat of anger burned away her fear.

"I will go also," said Jandal suddenly. "As witness for Kay Amin that the maid is abandoned as promised."

Soraya barely listened to the gahn's reluctant agreement—she was watching the men who mattered. Garshab's brows jutted in a faint frown. Her father's face showed no change, but the tension in his shoulders eased. This was part of his plan then, not Garshab's. She wished, passionately, that she knew more details.

Jandal, whose gazelle stood next to the gahn's horse, was a powerful ally, but this was a more intricate pattern than any she'd stitched. And embroidery wasn't Soraya's best skill either.

"The temple would send a witness too." The priest barely waited for the gahn to finish speaking.

Jandal glared at him. "You doubt my word, priest?"

"No doubt is implied," said the gahn soothingly. He sounded far less regal than he should, in front of so large an audience. Was he frightened too? He probably had reason. How many gahns had been cast down by ambitious deghans who could manipulate the deghanate, their house statues moved to the farthest end of the line? "One witness for the temple and one for the deghanate. That is fair."

Now both her father and Garshab looked satisfied.

"We shall celebrate the assurance of our victory tomorrow," the gahn went on, "with a day of feasting and a flags-and-lances match. Leopard against Raven!"

The crowd roared again, with complete approval this time. Garshab wasn't the only one who could manipulate.

"And two days after that the lady Soraya will take her leave of us." He managed to sound sorrowful, the hypocrite. "But what of you, Lady Soraya? Is there anything in our power to offer you that might make your burden lighter?"

I want to get out of these robes and walk straight into the nearest fountain. And it wasn't just the honest sweat of a hot day, or even her own fear, that she wished to rinse away. "No, High One, there is—Wait." She remembered the maids' greedy, secretive gazes. "Could my cousin Pari accompany me on the journey?"

Sudaba disapproved of Pari, who talked too freely with commoners. Improper. Unladylike. Most of the younger deghasses were jealous of Soraya's beauty and her family's position, but Pari had become a friend.

"That is both modest and fitting; it will be made so," said the gahn. He did regal better now that he wasn't afraid. "We offer praise," he went on, "to the courage and nobility of a true deghass, and to the father who raised such a daughter."

Soraya lowered her gaze again. She was too angry to lie and too frightened to speak true.

Her father suffered neither temper nor fear. "I thank you for your praise, High One, but it is Soraya alone who deserves it. She is the treasure of my heart."

And that made it all worthwhile.

CHAPTER FIVE

JIAAN

THE MATCH WAS WELL into the second round of battle, and Jiaan could barely see the flags-and-lances field through the dust. Most of the mobile, potted forest had been placed at the ends of the field, and a maze of small hills had been constructed, but the center of the field was clear. In spring or midsummer the ground would have been perfect; damp but firm. In winter it would have been a sea of churned mud, but at least an anxious watcher could have seen what was going on. Now, between the dry earth and the dry grass, every pounding hoof raised a puff of dust, and the battle between Commander Merahb and Garshab's second aide raised so much of the djinn-cursed stuff . . . There!

A breeze swept the field, and the dust cloud dissipated.

Commander Merahb leaned forward, swinging the heavy wooden sword he used for flags and lances with all the strength of his powerful shoulders and arms. The sword met his opponent's with a crack that should have broken wooden blades, but both swords held.

The younger man's seat slid under the force of the blow, and Merahb launched another. But his opponent spun his horse away, so the powerful swing met only air.

A lesser horseman would have been unbalanced, as Garshab's aide clearly intended, but the high commander just gripped harder with his legs, and even twisted his body to block the blow that looped toward his helm with the lance in his left hand. Most men only hurled the light, blunted lances—it took an expert to use one as a shield. But Commander Merahb was an expert—and so was his horse. Rakesh had been only a foal when the commander had named him after Rostam's legendary steed, but he'd lived up to the name. Now he spun on his haunches, to give his rider another opening.

Dust rose again, obscuring the white sock on his off hind leg, which contrasted with his dappled chestnut hide. One white foot was thought to be unsightly, unbalancing a horse's beauty, but the commander swore he'd never have won a match or survived a battle without Rakesh. Jiaan might have believed it, except Rakesh was only five years old and the commander had been winning for over twenty years.

The swords cracked and cracked and cracked. The aide's bay mare sidestepped again. She was almost as good as Rakesh, Jiaan thought, but not quite, and the dust had risen so high now that it concealed the white blaze on Rakesh's face. Soon the riders would be invisible. Again.

Never taking his eyes from the duel, Jiaan moved across the open ground between the two sets of stands that served as both the commander's team's base camp and his enemies' goal.

When the great banner passed under the arches that spanned the openings at both ends of the field, the team that carried it earned ten points, and that battle round ended. The banner hadn't been touched in this round.

In the previous round the banner had been carried by the same lancer the commander now engaged, galloping through the arch not three yards from where Jiaan and the servants stood scowling. But Commander Merahb's team had fought so well, it had only given Garshab's team a three-point advantage.

The horses spun again, and the dust rose high.

Soraya, in the seat of honor just below the gahn's shaded dais, was on her feet and screaming, clutching another girl her age, who stood beside her. Unladylike, and not much like someone who was about to be sacrificed, either. The lady Sudaba, seated several rows away, was too far off to intervene, but her faint scowl promised retribution to come. Jiaan felt a pang of sympathy. Soraya would no doubt be hearing about her behavior after the match but at least she was high enough to see. Could Jiaan climb a few levels on the crowded stand? He shuffled toward it.

When his ankle first encountered a hard bar, Jiaan thought he'd walked into something, but the shove on his shoulder that sent him stumbling to his knees told him otherwise. The lance butt that had tripped him was whisked away.

"Clumsy bastard, isn't he?"

Jiaan glared up at the sneering faces—far up, for Markhan and Fasal were still mounted. The barrage of hoofbeats from the field had concealed the sound of their approach.

It was Markhan who'd spoken. They were the commander's aides too, younger than Jiaan was. Second sons set in service to another house, but true born. They'd been fouled out of the match early in the round: Fasal, only fifteen, because he'd been knocked from his horse by a much older and heavier man; Markhan, because he'd lost his sword and then had thrown all three of his lances, the idiot. He'd scored all three points on the man who'd disarmed him, but his opponent was still on the field, and he was here on the sidelines.

Both of them, and their horses, were covered with dust. Jiaan felt a stab of pure envy. "What's going on?" He scrambled to his feet. "This is the third time today someone's tripped me or tried to ride over me."

And that was unusual. The commander's other aides knew what Jiaan was—no more their equal than the peasant-born foot soldiers and archers, some of whom were probably their own half brothers or cousins. But they usually restricted their resentment to hard words, at least in situations where they might be caught at it. The commander had made it clear that he expected his aides to treat Jiaan with the respect due his military rank, regardless of his birth.

Jiaan had returned late last night. It had taken several days to take the farm family the commander had chosen to their destination, but the commander insisted Jiaan escort them himself. The fewer who knew where the lady Soraya was to be hidden, the better.

From the moment Soraya arrived in the city, the other aides had been jockeying for position like a band of cocks with one hen, but this morning all their animosity seemed to be focused on Jiaan. Why?

The crowd yelled, and Fasal's and Markhan's faces swiveled toward the match. Jiaan looked too, but Fasal's horse was in front of him. He swore under his breath.

The two turned their horses and rode off, ignoring him with the arrogant indifference that deghans seemed to learn with their first steps. Ordinarily, Jiaan accepted it. But this morning he was watching the most hard-fought flags-and-lances match he'd ever seen. He could have ridden, have fought, as well as any of them. But support troops weren't allowed on the field. Only full-blood deghans could compete.

Half a dozen running strides brought him up to his fellow aides. He grabbed Fasal's reins just above the bit, bringing his horse to a halt.

"I want to know what's going on," he repeated. He tried to sound polite, or at least reasonable, but he didn't think he succeeded.

"Get your dung-covered, peasant's hands off my horse." Fasal spoke through gritted teeth, his face flushed with anger.

Jiaan was so startled, he almost let go. *What in Azura's name is this about?* But he was half deghan himself, and his rank in the army was equal to theirs. The commander had decreed it. "Not until you tell me what's going on."

Fasal's horse stamped as his legs tightened, and Jiaan gripped the reins more firmly.

"I said, take your hands off my horse."

"No," said Jiaan. Was this what it felt like to

have the djinn of rage possess you? No wonder the lady Soraya succumbed so often.

Fasal's breath hissed. He snatched the short quirt that hung from his saddle, whipped it up, and paused.

Markhan's grin faded abruptly. Jiaan was just as surprised. Flags-and-lances riders were required to carry a quirt, but to use it on a horse was the mark of an unskilled rider—a shame no one would accept. There was no shame in using it on a servant, but if Fasal left a mark on Jiaan, they were all going to have to explain it to the commander.

Anger warred with uncertainty in Fasal's dark, young face, but he couldn't lower the quirt without yielding. Yielding to a half-blood bastard.

Ordinarily, Jiaan would have let go. For all his pride that the commander had advanced him so far beyond the rank to which he had been born, he knew better than to push. The sane, rational part of his mind urged him to yield. It was how he had gotten along as well as he had, all these years, with the commander's true-born aides. On any other day . . .

He set his jaw and tightened his grip on the reins. *Hit me. I don't care.*

Fasal's hand tightened on the quirt. "I'll say a djinn did it."

"That's a babe's excuse. You wouldn't dare." *Would he?*

"Problem, boys?" The high commander's voice was very mild.

All of the aides shied like startled foals. If the horses hadn't been more sensible, they might have ended on the ground.

Rakesh was so coated in dust, you couldn't have told what color he was. Sweat tracked through the dirt on the commander's face, creating mud. He should have looked absurd. He never looked absurd.

He gazed at Fasal, raising one brow in mild inquiry. Fasal paled and lowered the quirt.

Jiaan, not being an idiot, had already released Fasal's reins, so there was nothing to stop Fasal from riding after Markhan, who had already fled the field. The field . . .

"What are you doing here, sir?" Jiaan gestured to the match, which was in full, thundering charge.

"Young imp got me off balance," the commander grumbled. "Knocked me off on my ass. I had two lances left too." He didn't sound unduly disgruntled.

"Don't you care?" Jiaan asked.

"Why should I? That"—the commander gestured to the dusty field—"is just a game. In the match that matters I intend to win. The others hounding you, lad?"

Merahb turned Rakesh toward the wash tent, and Jiaan followed. A squire's duties still came naturally to him—only a few years ago he'd held that post.

"Yes," Jiaan admitted. "But I don't know why."

"They know there's something important afoot. After all, I have to choose someone to steal my leopardess off to her lair."

"Yes," said Jiaan. "But I figured you'd choose one of the lesser deghans who rides under your banner. An old—um, a reliable man."

"That's what I expect everyone to think," said the commander. "And I'm going to have to find out how those young fools figured out who I decided on. I can't afford leaks."

"I understand that, but—" Jiaan stopped in his tracks. Rakesh walked on a few steps before the commander realized his aide no longer accompanied him, and he reined in the horse.

"You want *me* to escort the lady?" Jiaan's voice was high with astonishment. "Why me?"

The commander frowned. "Attend me, Jiaan." He spoke as if to a shirking servant, and Jiaan flushed. No one *seemed* to be listening, but . . . Jiaan hurried to take Rakesh's reins and lead him, like a proper squire attending his lord.

"I'm choosing you instead of an older man," the commander continued softly, "because Garshab is working on the older men. Anyone who hasn't taken his money will be watched. I just wish one of the honorable ones had had the sense to take the money and then come to me. I don't think any of my aides have been approached. Garshab expects me to choose an experienced man, and he probably realizes that those young hotheads would never take a bribe."

"But why me?"

"Because I trust you to keep a—"

The crowd roared. The commander clenched his thighs on Rakesh's barrel and lifted himself in the saddle to see better. "Watch out, you idiot! No! It's too soon!"

Jiaan only saw the end of it. Gostan, another of the commander's aides, galloped through the dust cloud at the far end of the field, the game banner clutched in his hand like a lance, despite its weighted base. His sword was gone, but he still had two lances strapped to his saddle; the blue streamers that stabilized their flight and marked him for a member of Merahb's team rippled out behind his mare's laboring haunches.

Two lances weren't enough to save him from two older deghans of Garshab's faction, who swept down the field and knocked him from the saddle with less than half a dozen blows.

Seizing the banner, Garshab's men rode toward the grove at the other end of the field—presumably to try something smarter than charging straight into the men Merahb had posted to protect his goal.

". . . a level head," the commander finished grimly. "This is what I'm talking about. They're playing to impress me instead of playing as a team, to win. If you were out there, you wouldn't do that."

Jiaan bit his lip. He wasn't so certain.

"You're the steadiest of my aides." The commander turned Rakesh to the pavilion, where wash water and refreshment awaited him. "The most reliable."

I'm also your son. His commander had never said the word. *Do you think I don't know? That my mother wouldn't have told me?* But his father knew that he knew. It was why he had lifted Jiaan so high above his normal station. *So why not say it?*

"Tomorrow I'm sending every one of my aides off on some errand or other," the commander continued. "Garshab hasn't half enough servants to follow you all. I'll claim I'm sending you to the Sendar border, to pick up a report on the Hrum's movements. But that report is actually locked in my traveling desk right now, and I'll give it to you later, so you can return with it after the proper amount of time." The commander was speaking softer and faster. The pavilion was nearer now. "But your real job will be to join Soraya after we've left her and then get her to the refuge you know of, *without being followed.* That's the important part, lad. They'll know what we're doing, but as long as I can keep Soraya hidden, as long as they can't produce her, along with evidence that I preserved her, they'll have nothing but smoke and suspicions. And I'll be in command while we prepare for the Hrum."

Jiaan swallowed. His father had entrusted

him with important errands before, but this . . . this was a deghan's mission! A chance to finally prove himself. To everyone. But still . . .

"Do we have time for this, sir? If the Hrum are coming in the spring—"

"Don't worry about the Hrum," said the commander.

Why not? You are.

"Your job is to get Soraya into hiding, unseen. And you can do it. I have confidence in you, Jiaan."

The note in his father's voice as he said Jiaan's name transformed the words. *My son.* He didn't have to say it aloud.

CHAPTER SIX

KAVI

KAVI WAS ONE HARD DAY'S travel out of Setesafon, and the prickling uneasiness that had dogged him for the last week was beginning to fade. He'd walked for several candlemarks beyond the town at which most people stopped on the first night of their journey, and not just because he was too short of coin to put up at an inn. He wanted to put more than a day's distance between him and the city where he'd created such a stir by selling fifteen gold pieces in just eight days.

During the last few days he thought he'd seen several of his customers looking for him. They might only have wanted to purchase another piece. On the other hand . . .

No, Kavi was delighted to be out of the rich, teeming city. He'd left Hama and her family, and even the pathetically grateful guard, safe behind him, and he had three remaining gold pieces buried deep in his pack. To repay him for his trouble, Nadi had said. He'd offered to leave them with Nadi, for Hama could have sold them in seven or eight months with no danger— or, at least, no additional danger. But Nadi had refused, with a firmness that led him to suspect that a profitable partnership had come to an end. Ah, well. At least he was back on the road.

When he first became a peddler he'd hated making camp like this, in the rustling darkness of the open country, even though the blackened, stone ring and trampled earth told him that many had camped here before. Now the fire's crackle and the ripping sound of Duckie's teeth in the grass spelled home to him. Even the wind, rattling the leaves of the surrounding bushes, sparked no terrors. Not in these settled lands, where a gazelle would be lucky to survive—though he was no more afraid in the mountains, where jackal packs roamed, just a bit more careful.

Even the sound of hoofbeats on the road didn't worry him, for they weren't trotting, like a troop of guards trying to catch up with a miscreant; but plodding, like travelers who were using the full moon to push on an extra league or two.

It didn't surprise him when the sound of the hoofbeats stopped at the riders' sight of his fire. And reaching for his sturdy staff, transferring it from his right hand to his left, was a normal precaution.

"Hello, the camp." The deep voice was genial, even friendly, but the accent was pure deghan. Kavi stifled a curse. The last thing he wanted was to share his camp with a party of deghans—and they'd take his hospitality, whether he offered it or not. In all fairness, if their places had been reversed, the deghans would have offered him shelter without hesitation. Hospitality was a point of honor with them. Of course, it was easy to be hospitable when you had money.

"May we come to your fire?"

As if he had a choice? Kavi could see the rider who led the party now. His clothes were modest for one of his class, but only the richest of nobles could afford *that* horse.

"Come and be welcome." Kavi tried to sound friendly instead of resigned. Fighting with deghans was a losing proposition.

There were a lot of them too, he noted as they moved into the firelight. The servants had a somewhat military air, and several of the men looked very like soldiers; but there weren't enough weapons for this to be any sort of army troop, and the only charger present was the one the deghan in command was riding. There were even a couple of young deghasses, with their maids in tow, as well as an older man in the severe black robes of a temple priest.

The last two members of the party made Kavi's eyes widen. They were clad in bright-striped, hooded robes. With their hoods up, they might have been taken for lower servants—or even servants' children, for they were smaller than the teenage deghasses. But in the darkness their hoods lay around their shoulders, revealing skin as white as moonlight and hair as pale as their skin. As white as a djinn's. *Suud tribesmen. Or, rather, a tribesman and a tribeswoman.* Kavi had seen the Suud bargaining in the markets, trading exquisitely woven baskets for cloth and iron goods. The credulous said they had a djinn's powers, as well as their coloring. But that had to be nonsense—no one with magical powers would live that poor. Were they returning to their tribe in the desert beyond the mountains and had joined the deghan's cavalcade for an escort? It was none of his business, but Kavi had never had an opportunity to talk to a Suud, and he was curious.

In fact, the whole party was a bit odd. Kavi sat by the fire and watched pavilions go up, glowing like lamps themselves as lamps were lit within them. He couldn't help but notice, as the servants bustled back and forth, that his own humble bedroll was pushed farther and farther from the fire, till it lay beside the bushes under which he'd placed his packs.

Duckie, on the other hand, was added to the herd of lesser horses and pack mules and led off to be tethered where the grazing was better. The grooms just assumed his permission, Kavi noted sourly. Though when they added his mule to their herd, one of them had checked to make certain Duckie's hobbles weren't too tight and he had nodded his approval. And, in fact, Duckie now had access to better grass, better water, and the company of her own kind, and she'd be guarded by the groom who took the watch. It would be foolish for Kavi to object.

He mellowed a bit more when a servant woman, who'd set up a tripod over the fire and hung a teakettle, asked if he'd like to share the camp's meal. A good meal would be welcome after a day that had started before dawn and ended after sunset.

But it was cool enough that he clung to his seat at the fireside and was still sitting there when the two deghasses came up and held out their hands to the blaze.

The smaller, and prettier, of the two gave him the typical deghass you-are-beneath-my-notice-and-therefore-I-don't-see-you look, but the taller one smiled.

"Good evening, Master Peddler," she said. "At least, I assume you're a peddler, from the packs." She gestured toward the bushes where he'd stashed them.

"Aye, that I am," said Kavi, using the broad country speech that was even further from the way the deghans spoke than the city folks' accents. "But what's a pretty girl like you doing out on the rough road this time of night, instead of tucked snug in a good inn?" He had no doubt they could afford it.

The girl smiled. "Traveling from one place to another. Why else take to the road?" She was trying to sound mysterious and exotic, he guessed, but she spoiled it with a giggle. Under the beads and feathers and the subtle cosmetics, her face was as ordinary as any country girl's, but it was bright and lively—unlike that of her companion, who might have been a bronze statue. A disapproving statue.

"The truth is, we've taken two days to get here," the nicer one went on. "We had a couple of late starts."

Kavi smiled back. If she hadn't been a deghass, he might have flirted with her. But she was what she was—not for the likes of him. *Let it go.* "So tell me, why are the desert folk traveling with you?" He nodded toward the tribespeople, who were setting up their shelter in a corner of the camp. It wasn't even a proper tent, just a square of cloth stretched over a frame.

"Oh, they're just gui—" She jumped and blinked at her companion. Kavi hadn't seen the other girl move, but they were standing close together on the opposite side of the fire. Still, that kick to the ankle had been subtle. The haughty one returned his curiosity with bland indifference.

"They're just guides, going home after escorting a party of traders back from the desert." It would have been a smooth recovery if her cheeks weren't so flushed.

Were they up to something? None of his business. The business of any deghan or deghass was the last thing Kavi wanted to be part of. Peasants who got involved in such things usually came to nasty ends.

"So what are you doing here, Master Peddler?" The girl's desire to change the subject was a bit too obvious.

"Why, taking my goods down the road," said Kavi, as if he hadn't noticed anything. "I sell steel-work in the smaller villages, the ones off the trade routes that don't see peddlers often and sometimes don't have a smith of their own."

The haughty one spoke for the first time. "Can you make money there? I thought the smaller villages had no more than a few tin foals to stack together." Her voice was low and might have been pleasing if it weren't so cool—and if the question hadn't been so shrewd.

"Aye, but I'm not selling a master smith's work, just that of the lesser journeymen and some of the apprentices' better pieces."

The girl snorted.

"It's good work," Kavi protested, stung in spite of himself. "Strong and durable. But it's not pretty enough to sell in the city, where the masters' work and the older journeymen's goods compete. This way, the farmers get a better knife than their blacksmith can manage, since he only knows horseshoes and plowshares and maybe doesn't work steel at all. And they pay less than if they had to travel to a town to buy it."

"We know you're not cheating them," the plain girl soothed.

The pretty one snorted again, and Kavi glared at her.

"So you sell knives?" the plain girl went on.

"Aye, for the most part, and scissors and other fine steelcraft. Whatever bits I pick up. Though I got lucky in the city just . . . now."

Both girls looked more alert at his stumble, and Kavi cursed himself. What djinn had taken possession of his tongue? He couldn't sell these girls his forged gold—not this close to Setesafon and not this soon. Could he?

"What luck did you find?" It was the plain one who asked, of course, but even the beauty looked interested. Kavi suddenly realized that he wanted to sell her his gold. And if the plain one bought instead, well, she was just as much a deghass as the other! He'd been selling his gold work for days. Just one more time . . .

"Well, it was good luck for me, but I suppose it wasn't being so good for the man I bought from," he admitted. "A merchant, poor man, or so he had been. He said he lost interest in business after the death of his wife, him with no child or kin to leave it to, and that his competitors stole all his customers and he was too old to try to build up again. Selling off his wife's jewelry, poor man. Though he got a fair price for it. And it'll be giving me something I can sell in the next city, where my apprentices' work doesn't go so well."

He smiled cheerfully and didn't twitch the bait. He'd hoped to snare the beauty, but it was the nicer girl who said, "Jewelry?"

"A fine gold bracelet," Kavi said. No need to

show them the other pieces. Too many might make them suspicious.

In the end, they agreed to let him show them the bracelet in their tent. Kavi preferred to conduct this bit of business in private, and besides, the cook was beginning to glare at them impatiently. She could chase him off if she needed to, but she couldn't do that with the deghasses, and Kavi wanted to be fed.

Away from the fire it was colder, reminding Kavi that autumn was well under way. Lingering in Setesafon had put him behind his usual schedule, but the price of this bracelet alone would more than make up for it.

The ladies' small pavilion was bright with lamplight, and it was warmed by a charcoal brazier in one corner. The dusty, beaten earth was covered with soft rugs, and a low table held goblets of gold-chased glass, worth more than solid gold, and a silver pitcher. Kavi added a handful of falcons to his asking price. There were no chairs, but plump cushions surrounded the table and were scattered over the rugs. Two well-filled ticks lay near the brazier, covered with blankets of silk stuffed with loose wool. Kavi thought of his bedroll, and the ground on which it lay, and raised his price by a whole gold eagle.

"So what have you to show us, Master Peddler? What's your name, anyway?"

"Barmahn," said Kavi, pulling the silk-wrapped bundle from his pocket. He knew better than to expect even the nicer one to offer him a name in return. "This is the bracelet the old man sold me, Lady. In a way, I hate to sell, for I could see what it cost him to be parting with it. But I think it would please him to have it worn by someone as . . . sweet-natured as his dead wife."

He'd started to say *as beautiful,* but the taller girl had been decent enough that he didn't like insulting her intelligence. He wished the beauty would show more interest, but you took the fish that bit your hook.

The taller girl's face was alive with interest, sympathy, and a bit of greed for the slender, glowing bracelet he held out on its bed of dark silk. He'd been attracted to it in the market because it had been lovely even in bronze. Now, lamplight gleaming on its elegant curves, it was exquisite.

"It's beautiful," said the girl sincerely. The

haughty one closed her eyes in a faint wince at such bad bargaining technique. She'd be the one he had to watch out for, but Kavi wasn't worried. The gold coating was thick enough to pass any normal test, and if they got another late start tomorrow, why, no one would be surprised if he got an early one.

"Would you like to try it on?" He tried to sound reluctant, as if he hated to let the bracelet out of his possession, and as she reached for it he tightened his grip just a bit.

But before she could take it, a strong hand fell on his shoulder, and another plucked the bracelet effortlessly from his grasp.

"What's going on here? A sale?" It was the deghan in command.

"A pretty bit that I picked up from a man less fortunate than me, noble sir," said Kavi easily. The man had made no sound on the soft rugs.

"Aren't you a bit young for this trade, boy?" The deghan didn't look angry. There was suspicion in his expression, yes, but also amusement and a kind of wild cheer, as if he'd just received good news. It was only because Kavi, who wasn't short, had to look up to see his face, and the strength of the hand gripping his shoulder, that made him seem formidable.

"The road doesn't care if I'm young or not," said Kavi cautiously. "And my goods are worthy, whatever my age. The bracelet was just a stroke of good luck."

The deghan released his grip with a small shove that made Kavi stumble on the soft rugs.

"I hate to cast doubt on your good fortune," said the deghan, "but perhaps we should make certain you weren't cheated." He pulled out his knife and set the point casually against the bracelet's shining surface, his gaze intent on Kavi's face.

Kavi wasn't worried. This happened at some point in every sale. "Noble sir, if you damage it, you've destroyed its value!" The standard protest and true enough. It usually assured that the buyer made an even shallower nick than he'd intended.

"You're right, of course." The deghan turned the bracelet in his hand. "And it's a lovely thing. Look good on your arm, sparrow."

The plain girl giggled, but her eyes shifted curiously from Kavi to the deghan. The haughty one frowned.

"I won't mark it," said the deghan. His knife clicked into its sheath, but Kavi didn't mistake this for surrender. For the first time he felt a chill.

"What will you be doing, then?"

"Oh, don't worry, boy." The deghan took Kavi's arm and pulled him out of the pavilion. His grip wasn't painful, but it was too firm to break. Kavi began to be alarmed.

The girls followed them out into the night, even when the deghan moved away from the fire toward the chopping block the servants had set up at the edge of the clearing. The ax was still embedded in it. Kavi's breath caught. "Noble sir! You can't!"

"Ah, I told you not to worry. Well, if you're honest, you don't have to worry. If it's gold throughout, I'll pay you its full worth, with an eagle thrown in for doubting you."

He released Kavi with another of those little shoves. Kavi let his stumble take him closer to the bushes than it might have. His heart was pounding now. With any other man, he might have tried to bluff his way out, but one look at this man's shrewd eyes told him that would fail — and he knew better than to expect mercy from a noble. But he knew when the moment to flee would come. He could steal Duckie out of the deghan's herd sometime in the future. The loss of his pack . . . well, better that than his fingers.

"But if you're the one the city guard was talking about," the deghan went on, "well, that's another matter."

City guard? Definitely time to run.

The deghan pried the ax out of the block and set the slender bracelet where it had been. His gaze locked with Kavi's.

Kavi's shrug was a masterpiece. "As long as you pay full price. Perhaps you can have it mended."

The deghan laughed. "I think I like you, boy." He lifted the ax, eyes still on Kavi's face. Then his gaze flicked away, perforce, as he brought the ax down.

Now! While the deghan was looking away and all eyes tracked the fall of the ax, Kavi spun and darted for the bushes. If he could just—

He ran headfirst into a warm, muscular body that oofed at the impact. But that didn't stop the hands that clamped down on Kavi's shoulders.

He couldn't afford to be taken. He hooked one foot around the other man's ankle and pulled, reaching out to shove him back at the same time, planning to run right over his fallen body. It was a good move, one he'd taught Hama.

It worked this time too, except the man grabbed Kavi's hands as he pushed him, dragging Kavi down on top of him when he fell.

Kavi tried to pull his wrists free, then he twisted them, and the tight fingers began to yield. But suddenly the ground heaved and the world flipped around. Kavi's head struck the earth with stunning force; when it cleared, he was lying on his back, with the other man seated on his stomach, reaching for his wrists again.

Kavi flung his right hand out of reach, but the man captured his left wrist in an iron grasp. Kavi tried to grab his opponent's wrist, but the weakened fingers of his right hand betrayed him, as they always did. The man pulled out of his grip as if it were a babe's and grabbed Kavi's other wrist, pinning him. Before Kavi could twist his wrists free again, the man rolled to his feet, bringing Kavi with him, but with a skillful twist that pulled Kavi's left arm up behind his back in such a way that it would break if Kavi tried to flee. The man knew what he was doing, djinn take him, even down to recognizing the weakness of Kavi's right hand and pinning his left instead. A soldier? Someone trained in wrestling, for certain.

Kavi staggered forward, bent almost double by the ache in his shoulder, and ended on his knees before the chopping block. The bracelet lay there, cut neatly in half. Lead gleamed dully inside its casing of gold-coated bronze.

When in doubt, lie. "I didn't know, noble sir, truly I didn't. The man deceived me."

The deghan snorted. He hadn't moved an inch from the block, curse him. His expression no longer held the manic amusement that had brightened it before, but at least he didn't look murderously angry. "Weak, very weak," he pronounced. "If you thought it was gold all through, why did you run?"

"I knew you'd not be willing to pay full price for a broken bracelet, and I feared you'd turn your anger against me," said Kavi quickly, though this lie was weaker still. He fought to control his expression. "Mercy, noble sir, my mother is a widow, and—"

"Be still." It was an order, for all its softness, and Kavi fell silent as the deghan reached out and lifted his right hand, so the light of the distant fire highlighted the scar on his palm. "Let's get ourselves inside. No use letting more see you than need be."

The deghan's eyes were on the man who held Kavi—a man who evidently wasn't supposed to be here. But without knowing why he wasn't supposed to be here, Kavi couldn't think of a way to blackmail them.

The deghan led the way back to the ladies' pavilion, which happened to be nearest, and lifted the flap with ironic courtesy as Kavi's captor dragged him inside. The two girls trailed behind, but the deghan, as Kavi craned his neck to see, gestured to someone outside. A few moments later he came in, absurdly quiet for such a big man. "Let him go, Jiaan. If he runs, he won't get far."

The iron grip on Kavi's wrist vanished, and he fell forward, catching himself on his hands. He considered scrambling to his feet and bolting, despite the deghan's words, but the noble was between him and the entrance. Rubbing his wrist, he turned to look at the man behind him. Not a man, he saw now, but a youth near his own age. He looked a lot like the deghan, but he wasn't dressed richly enough to be a son. At least, not a legitimate son. Whoever he was, his hands were open and ready to grapple.

The deghan came forward and squatted to take Kavi's hand again, studying the scar. It took all of Kavi's self-control not to snatch it back. "What's your real name, Barmahn of wherever?"

"Naru," said Kavi reluctantly. "Of Desafon."

The noble snorted. "If you insist." He nodded toward Kavi's hand. "This was bad, boy. How did it happen?"

The cruel master or the accident at sea? Either would do. Kavi took a breath.

"Never mind," said the deghan, rising to his feet. "You'd only lie. And I suppose the cause matters less than the consequence. Did you know the Setesafon guard is looking for you? They've found three pieces of your false gold so far. Soon anyone who bought anything from a young peddler with a scarred hand will be coming forward."

Kavi's heart beat like a hammer, fast and hard. This was disaster. But at least they weren't looking for Hama. Beneath the fear curiosity stirred. "How did they find out?" He'd have sworn his gilding was deep enough to pass any test.

The deghan's lips twitched. "It was Gorahz who undid you. Man got into a fight with his wife, and when the djinn of rage seized him, he picked up the new gold pot she'd been bragging about and threw it at the hearth. It hit the edge of the stone and dented deeply enough that they could see the bronze. You've performed one good service, boy. They're now united as close as any couple could be, in howling for your blood. It'll be up to the magister, of course, but the guards are suggesting one finger for each piece you sold. How many did you sell, anyway?"

Kavi's fingers curled into protective fists, despite himself. The deghan grinned. "That many? Not that it would take many to cripple you, if they started with your left hand."

"Are you enjoying this?" Kavi demanded. If he was, then Kavi was coming back for the bastard someday. Assuming there was enough left of his hands after the magister got through with him for him to do anything but beg. Kavi didn't believe in Sanglak or in any other djinn—that was a deghan's excuse—but he now understood why the nobles might believe in him, for surely despair this pure couldn't have been generated solely in Kavi's own heart.

"No, I'm not. Stop looking like that." The deep voice was stern but oddly gentle. "I've no intention of turning you over to the guard; I have use for you myself. I just wanted to make the penalty for disobeying me very clear."

Hope stirred. If this business was as dirty and desperate as it sounded, Kavi might gain some leverage for counterblackmail after all.

The deghan snorted again. "Don't think you can use what I'm going to tell you against me either. You might cause me trouble, but if you do, I'll take you down with me. And I think you'll lose more than I."

No doubt. A wealthy deghan could buy or influence his way out of anything short of assassinating the gahn. But when had Kavi's face become so revealing?

"What do you want from me?" If the deghan's plans were too vicious, Kavi could always run later and take his chances. Though this deghan didn't seem as vicious as some.

"Nothing dreadful," said the noble, reading Kavi's face with annoying ease. "Where do your rounds run, and how often do you make them?"

Kavi blinked in surprise, but at this point he

had little to lose by an honest answer. "I go to the small towns and villages north and south of the Trade Road. I'm usually getting through them twice a year. Sometimes faster."

"How far north?" The deghan made it sound like a casual question, but Kavi heard the youth behind him stir nervously.

"I follow the foothills," said Kavi. "Into the mountains sometimes. Mining towns and camps." He preferred to avoid the high, grassy plains that held the deghans' herds and manors.

"Excellent." The big bastard almost purred. "I want you to add a stop to your rounds, Master whatever-your-name-really-is. You'll go twice a year and give the folk there anything they need. If they want something you don't have, you'll get it for them. Then, when you come near the army, you'll find some excuse to contact me and bring me any news."

"Twice a *year*?" It was the haughty girl. Kavi had all but forgotten the girls' presence. "How many years?"

At the same time the youth, Jiaan, murmured urgently, "Commander, how can you trust this man? He's a criminal to start with!"

"Not many, cub." The deghan answered the girl first. "Probably not even two. But this way, you'll be able to get supplies, and I can get news of you from a source no one will suspect. It's the only thing that was lacking.

"And trust," he said turning to Jiaan, "has nothing to do with it."

The deghan's searching gaze returned to Kavi, who wished it hadn't. "Tomorrow you'll take an early departure, just like you probably planned. Jiaan, who you will never admit to having seen here tonight, will pick you up later somewhere on the road. After a few more days the two of you will meet with the lady"—he nodded toward the haughty girl—"and go to the place that you'll make part of your route. You will never mention that place, or the lady Soraya's existence, to anyone. You'll stop there twice a year until I give you leave to quit.

"If you do these things, I'll pay you generously for all the goods you deliver there; and when your service ends, I'll reward you handsomely. If you fail to obey any of these orders, in word or in deed, I will dedicate all my forces to hunting you down and then turn you over to Setesafon's magisters.

And a peddler your age with a crippled hand"—he nudged Kavi's fingers with the toe of one boot— "won't be very hard to find. So I advise you to keep a still tongue and make your stops, peddler."

"I never skip stops," said Kavi grimly. "I won't be starting with this one."

What choice did he have?

ROSTAM AND TAHMINA *spoke seldom, and only under the eyes of her parents, but still it was enough. She came to love him, not only for the divine farr he possessed in such great measure, but also for his courage and his honor. And he came to love her, not only for her beauty, but also for her spirit, which was not meek, and for her merry heart.*

Thus came the night that Tahmina sent her maid to Rostam, to bring him in secret to her room, and they joined together and brought each other joy. As the dawn was breaking Rostam rose and dressed. Then he returned to the bed where Tahmina watched him, and knelt before her.

"You are the most wonderful and precious of

women," he told her, "tender as the spring, bright as Azura's sun. I will never love another woman as I love you. If our negotiations go well, if peace can be made between your father and my gahn, I will seek your father's consent to our marriage. If that is your wish."

Tahmina sat up, more glorious wearing nothing but the beauty Azura gave her than in gold and jewels, and she took him in her arms.

"I will never love another man as I love you," she said. "And it will be a great honor to be your wife, though the greatest honor is to hold your heart."

So their troth was plighted, and Rostam gave Tahmina the gold amulet he wore about his neck, which had belonged to his father, in token of their pledge.

CHAPTER SEVEN

SORAYA

ONLY THREE DAYS LATER, despite all Soraya's attempts to slow their journey, they reached the parting of the ways.

It had rained the night before, long and cold, though it was early for that kind of rain. The oiled silk of the pavilions and the braziers had kept them dry and almost warm. But the morning was cool and cloudy, and the Trade Road was a sea of mud. Her father had finally lost patience with it, and the party had climbed the low cliffs at the first path they found. They'd ridden over the grasslands till they reached this small, muddy trail that meandered over the plains toward the mountains, just visible in the distance.

Soraya sighed and pulled the warm, woolen robe tight around her. Her father had insisted on rough, practical clothes—almost as if she were truly going to be abandoned and he wished to give her the best chance of survival. In truth, silk, or even fur, would be ridiculous on this cold, muddy ride.

Soraya had resolved to face this moment with the same proud dignity she'd managed so far, but it was dificult, under the gaze of the witnesses and the hard-eyed armsmen the gahn had sent to actually escort her into the wilderness. These men had joined the others this morning, since her father had refused to travel with them for the whole journey. Right before they arrived, the two Suud tribespeople, with their corpse-pale skin and strange light eyes, had stolen away, just as Jiaan and the young peddler-forger had done earlier.

The plan is *working*, Soraya assured herself. She had nothing to worry about but boredom and loneliness. *Years* of boredom and loneliness, with no marriage in sight. On the other hand, her mother wouldn't be there. Soraya sighed again, but resentment stiffened her pride. She cherished that pride as the wide-eyed servants, who hadn't been let in on the secret, touched their heads, their hearts, and gestured to their bodies as they bowed, indicating that all those things were at her service. Her father's armsmen, who knew at least part of the truth, were brisker about it. But they looked sober enough to keep up the act.

Pari's warm, teary embrace almost undid Soraya and would have convinced any watcher that Pari hadn't a clue what was really going on. *She's not faking either,* thought Soraya grimly, patting her cousin's shoulder. Pari's emotions were open to the world. She would laugh at flowers or weep over a dead bird. It was something Soraya liked about her cousin, except when she had to deal with the storm. "Come now, there's enough water around without you adding to it."

Pari sniffed, giggled, and pulled her horse away. Soraya mustered all her control, turned to face her father, and instantly realized that despite the gravity of the long-term situation, the farce of the moment had overtaken him.

"Be brave, daughter." His voice was somber, but his eyes laughed. "Azura will surely shelter the innocent, as he did so often in ancient times. Your heart is pure." His lips twitched, and Soraya had to hide her face in her hands, maidenlike, to conceal her expression.

"Stop laughing," she muttered. "I hate this."

She pulled herself together and met his gaze. She tried to think of something ridiculously maudlin she could say to get back at him, but nothing came to her.

"I go at your bidding," she said. Pari and the others might take it for acting, but it was true. So true that tears stung her eyes. Soraya reined her horse around abruptly and set off down the track at a trot. If they had any decency, they'd leave her alone for a while. Forever.

But she'd not gone more than a hundred yards when she heard a horse thundering up behind her at full gallop. *Boors.* They could have given her a moment. Anger flared. She turned to tell them what she thought of their courtesy, their manhood, their ancestry, and anything else that might occur to her, but then she stopped, open-mouthed, as Rakesh galloped up in a torrent of splattering mud.

Her father reached out and swept her off her saddle and onto his lap, hugging her hard. "Did you think I'd let my leopardess go without a proper good-bye?" There were tears in his eyes.

Soraya hugged him. Her own eyes were damp. "It makes a good show too," she mumbled into the fur of his cloak. "Like that cursed blanket on the echoing dome. Why didn't you let me reveal the truth about that?"

"Ah, there's truth and truth, and revealing that one might have gained you an enemy that neither of us needs right now. There's little enough of magic in the world, cub. Small blame to the temple for making its own."

"It's still a cheat," said Soraya, straightening to look at him.

"I know." Her father shrugged. "But since I'm planning another cheat, with you in the center of it, I can hardly complain. Keep a stout heart, daughter. I'll take the Hrum apart and come for you as soon as I can. And there you'll be, a beautiful maiden, sheltered by Azura himself. They'll be tripping over themselves to marry you!"

Her arms went round him again, hard and warm and true, however the world might cheat. "I know you'll come."

Even if it took *years.* Soraya sniffed, but there was no point in complaining.

"I love you, leopard cub."

"I know."

He sighed and put her back into her saddle with an ease and strength other men could only envy. Then he turned Rakesh and cantered off.

Soraya turned her horse the other way, wiping frantically at her tears. She'd never be able to remove all the signs of grief before those cursed armsmen caught up with her. And curse the man for oversetting her, for sticking her with this whole impossible mess. She was glad she'd said "I know" instead of *I love you, too*.

AS THE NEXT FEW DAYS PASSED the flat plains near the cliffs gave way to rolling hills, then the tree-covered foothills of the mountains themselves, for Soraya no longer tried to delay their journey. Her blankets—no longer quilted silk, but coarse sheep-skins and wool—were warm enough. But the small tent the hard-faced armsmen pitched for her each night held no temptations to linger. *Get it over with.*

She shivered as they passed into the forest and the road began to climb more steeply. Soraya disliked being surrounded by trees. Their dense, towering shadows concealed Azura's sun, and she couldn't see more than a dozen yards in any direction. At least she didn't need to imagine enemies behind them—her enemies rode beside her.

Only Jandal spoke to her at all beyond the necessities of the journey, and even he, for all his courtesy, kept a distance between them. The temple's witness, who'd seemed friendly enough when traveling with her father, had turned stern and silent in the presence of the gahn's guards. It was all part of the act, and she knew it, but Soraya had never before been surrounded by people who ignored her. *By all means, get it over with.*

Once into the mountains they kept traveling deeper, higher, and Soraya thought they were heading west, though it was hard to be certain surrounded by trees. She'd never gone much past the foothills; she hadn't realized the mountains were this vast. Or this high. It grew colder, and the very air seemed thin and useless.

They made too much noise to see any game, but Soraya saw the scat of gazelle and wild goats on the trail, and the days were filled with birdsong and the squirrels' scolding chatter.

She might have thought they were riding in circles to confuse pursuit, but they kept going up and mostly north until the morning of the sixth day after they'd left her father, when they started down.

The track, small to begin with, had narrowed to a trail, then to something that could barely be described as a path. Now her guards left it altogether and turned east, traveling through groves and across the rock-strewn meadows of the high country.

In the early afternoon they reached another meadow, running down a long slope with a shallow ravine to one side. Beyond it rose a series of dark-clad, rugged peaks that looked as if the ocean's waves had been cast in stone and made giant upon the land.

"Here," the leader of Soraya's guards pronounced. "Get off the horse, girl."

Soraya sat and looked at him, with the pride of twenty generations of the House of the Leopard in her eyes. They could abandon her here, without ceremony or dignity, but no common armsman could call her "girl" and order her about. And he of all people should realize that someday she might be coming back.

His face remained expressionless, but his

horse snorted and stamped as his grip on the reins tightened. Did his weather-beaten cheeks darken a bit?

"If you would please to dismount, Lady Soraya?"

It was no longer an order. Soraya snorted and slid from the saddle.

"Take her back to my father," she instructed Jandal regally. "She's a fine mare."

"Very fine," he agreed. He looked as if he wanted to say more but couldn't find the words. He turned his horse and cantered off in the direction of the track.

The priest made the signs for protection from various djinn over her heart, her forehead, and her hands. Ironic, since she was being offered to the djinn. Or was it some subtle message? Who cared?

Finally the priest and the guards mounted and followed Jandal, without a backward glance. Almost as if they were enticing her to follow.

As if she weren't huntress enough to have retraced their route back to the path at any time. In fact, if she'd really been abandoned, that was probably what she'd have done. The last town they passed was in the foothills, three days' ride back. It would have been a long walk, with cold nights and no food except a handful of late berries. But Soraya could have done it, if she'd had to. If the watchers wouldn't have followed her.

She hadn't been aware of them until she reached the foothills, though she didn't know if that was where they started trailing her or if they'd been there all along.

It was her own guards who'd betrayed their presence. She'd seen her warders cast too many searching glances over their shoulders. Then she'd noticed the way the last man in the troop would dismount at any fork in the trail and, under pretext of checking his girth or his horse's hooves, overturn three stones in a line or point a stick in the direction they'd taken. It was almost insulting, how obvious they'd been.

So Soraya had no doubt, as she settled herself on a rock in the middle of the meadow and wrapped her long robe around her, that she was being watched. She wondered how Jiaan would get past them, but that was his problem. All she had to do was wait.

Time passed. The view palled. Throwing small stones at a bigger rock a few yards away palled.

Combing out her hair and rebraiding it didn't take nearly enough time. *Where is the djinn-cursed fellow?*

And more important: *What will I do if he doesn't arrive?*

He would come eventually, of course, to take her to the refuge her father had spoken of with such careful vagueness. But how long would it take him to get past the guards? Candlemarks? Days? No one had told her how long she should wait — only that Jiaan would come to take her away. If he hadn't come by nightfall, she would have to find shelter and food, but she had no idea how to build a shelter — that was servants' work. Soraya scowled. She could hunt if she had her bow, but as soon as she'd left the company of her father, the guards had taken even her eating dagger from her. She had no weapons and no shelter — only the hope that a peasant-born boy little older than she would be able to smuggle her past . . . how many spies?

All she could do was wait.

The morning wore into afternoon. If Jiaan hadn't arrived by evening, Soraya resolved, she would find some shelter in the woods and start walking back at sunrise. Playing at being a sacrifice was all very well, but she had no intention of turning herself into one because that incompetent peasant couldn't do his job. She could make her way back to town . . . if her watchers allowed it.

The sun was warm, but it was worry that pushed Soraya to her feet. If she was going to wait till dusk, she would need water. At least they'd had the decency to leave her near a stream. The ravine's banks were several yards deep, but only the first yard or so was sheer; the rest was a steep slope of loose gravel. Nothing her boots couldn't handle. Soraya swung her feet over the edge and slithered down in a small avalanche of pebbles and dirt. At the bottom she brushed off her buttocks and went to kneel by the stream. Her cupped hands had just touched the water when a soft, fierce voice whispered, "What in Azura's name took you so long?"

CHAPTER EIGHT

JIAAN

THE IDIOT BRAT JUMPED, looking wildly around. "Don't do that, Lady," Jiaan hissed. "I don't think they can see you, but I can't be certain."

At least she had the wit to turn her motion into a twisting stretch before she bent to drink.

"Where have *you* been?" she whispered, her face inches from the water. "I've been waiting for *marks*."

It hadn't been marks, but Jiaan felt that way too.

"I've been waiting for you to get your . . . self off that accursed rock and get into the trees. Or at least somewhere I'd have a chance to reach you," he muttered. "Did you expect me to gallop into the meadow and pluck you up under half a dozen eyes?"

The girl looked startled. "Six of them?"

Jiaan snorted. "Three of them. Two eyes each."

There had been eighteen of Garshab's spies when they'd started out, three bands of six. The commander's huntsmen had lured twelve of them off, changing the markings on the trail, making themselves visible and suspicious—though they had excuses for their presence ready, if they were caught. "It doesn't matter what anyone suspects," the commander had said. "As long as no one actually sees Soraya in the company of any man of mine."

"How was I supposed to know you wanted me to head for the trees?" the girl complained. She'd spotted him now, in the prickly bushes where he'd been lurking under the assumption that she had to go to the stream sometime. Azura be thanked, she wasn't looking at him. She pulled off her coat and dipped her hands in the water again, bathing her throat and forehead. "If I'd just gone wandering off, I'd probably have gone in the wrong direction. If you wanted me to go somewhere, you should have told me so back on the road when we were planning."

"How could I tell you what direction to go when I didn't know where they'd . . . ? Never mind. Please, Lady Soraya, just get your drink and go back to the rock. Give me enough time to get out of here, then head for the woods to the north. That's toward—"

"I know where north is."

"Pretend you're going to relieve yourself," Jiaan went on grimly. He wished he dared to say all the things he'd been thinking up for the last mark. "It won't give us long, but they'll assume the man they posted there is watching you."

"How boorish." Her lips barely moved. She stood and stretched again. "Will he be watching me?" She started toward the bank.

"No. He tripped over something and hit his head. He's not dead, but he won't notice much for a while."

"Killing him would be safer." She scrambled up the slope, almost on top of him. Gravel rained through the leaves, onto his hair.

"He's just doing his job, you . . ." He didn't say it loud enough for her to hear him.

JIAAN CRAWLED ON HIS BELLY up the ravine, and any rocks his battered knees and elbows had missed on the way down they found on the way back. He didn't dare to stand, even bent over. From where he was, he could just see the tops of the trees to the southeast and southwest, where the other men had stationed themselves. If he couldn't see them, they couldn't see him, but if he stood . . .

Only one band of six had been trailing the lady for the last four days, and just yesterday one of them had broken his ankle when a stone turned underfoot—a simple accident, but it was almost enough to make Jiaan believe that Azura was listening to his prayers.

The commander had told Jiaan that his best chance to steal the lady Soraya away would be just before dawn. He hadn't dreamed it might be possible in the bright sunlight of midafternoon—and evidently, Garshab's watchers hadn't either. As soon as it became apparent that the fool girl had settled in the meadow for the duration, two of them had gone off to set up a temporary camp, leaving the other three to watch. The man to the north had been stationed where he could see into the ravine as well, but there was no one guarding his back — and Soraya wasn't the only one the commander had instructed in woodcraft.

Jiaan had seen his opportunity and seized it — just like the commander, like a real deghan, would. Now, as the ravine passed into the cover of the trees, Jiaan made certain he was deeply within the forest before he scrambled out and over to a bush where he could look back into the meadow.

The girl was sitting on the rock again. She had picked some flowers and appeared to be trying to braid them, but she was failing. To Jiaan's nervous eyes, she seemed far less relaxed than she'd been earlier, but perhaps her other watchers wouldn't be so critical. She picked another flower. And another.

Jiaan gritted his teeth. She couldn't know how quickly he had scurried up the ravine. It was *sensible* of her to wait till she could be certain he'd made it out. She plucked a flower, discarded it, and reached for another that suited her better. Jiaan swore and went to check on the armsman he'd hit over the head.

The man still lay in the bushes where Jiaan had dragged him, near to his post, so that his fellows would find him once they began to look.

He had moved a bit, lying on his side now, with his legs curled toward his chest. He moaned softly with each breath, but at least he was breathing. The blood on his face had dried, and no fresh blood was flowing. According to the weapons master, he would recover, Azura willing, if he was well cared for. If assistance reached him in time.

It might be better for Jiaan's mission if he was never found, but Jiaan couldn't bring himself to be that ruthless—a weakness of his peasant blood, perhaps. But even the commander had said it would be better if no one was killed.

Jiaan took several deep breaths, hoping to quiet his twisting stomach. This was the first time he'd struck a man down in earnest.

He crawled back to the edge of the trees and saw that the idiot . . . the lady Soraya was finally moving, picking her way up the meadow with a casual ease that was . . . *sensible*. He ungritted his teeth, but they soon clamped together again.

Nothing stirred to the south as she entered the woods, looking around as if for a likely spot.

"Over here," Jiaan whispered. "Farther in."

"In a moment," she said, though she moved

toward him. "I really do need to relieve myself."

"Piss in your pants," Jiaan hissed—the djinn take proper respect! He would not fail his father for this girl's whims. "How long do you think it will be before they decide you're taking too long and come to investigate?"

Soraya glanced over her shoulder, then walked more briskly. The moment there was enough cover between them and the meadow, Jiaan leaped to his feet and grabbed her wrist, dragging her through the whipping branches at a dead run. She scrambled after him, one arm raised to shield her face, but she was quick and surefooted and didn't slow him down.

"Where are the horses?" she asked softly.

"Just over this rise." Jiaan was already pulling her up the low slope. He was certain the trees were thick enough to conceal them. He thought they were. Besides, Garshab's spies shouldn't even be looking at this slope . . . yet. "I left the peddler holding them."

"The peddler? Why did you bring him along?" Her tone was decidedly critical.

Jiaan ungritted his teeth, again. "I didn't have enough time to take him on a tour of the countryside, in the opposite direction from where you were heading, rent horses for all of us, and keep in touch with our trackers, who were dealing with their trackers! We had no way of knowing where they were going to leave you until just now, so we didn't dare let you out of sight."

"Oh."

He bent down, hauling her with him as they pounded over the low crest. Then he let her go, scrambling as quickly as he could down the slope to where the peddler waited with three horses and his mule.

The peddler was already tightening loose girths when Jiaan reached him. He'd said very little during the last eight days. Jiaan hadn't been with him the whole time; he'd had to rent the horses and had preferred not to bring such an . . . uncertain man with him when he met the trackers. He was young — hardly older than Jiaan himself — but Jiaan had seen enough of him to know that he wasn't a fool and that his weak hand hindered him very seldom.

There was only one girth left; Jiaan tugged it tight while the peddler hoisted himself into the saddle and took up the mule's lead rein. He'd refused to leave the beast behind, though Jiaan had pointed out that it was rare for the jackals to take a full-grown mule, even if it was hobbled.

Jiaan tossed the lady up to the saddle as soon as she came gasping up behind him, and then he grabbed her reins to stop her from cantering off. "No! We don't run till we're well away. I don't want them to hear the hoofbeats."

The girl glowered, but, unlike Fasal, she had no quirt. After a moment she nodded curtly, and he let go of the reins and leaped into the last empty saddle.

In fact, Jiaan sympathized with her. The need to run, to send his horse careening through the trees and flying over the meadows, set its spurs to him as well. But the longer Garshab's spies took to realize she was gone, to search the woods, to find their injured companion, the longer their own lead became.

Over a quarter candlemark passed before the distant shout echoed among the hills. They'd found their colleague.

Jiaan looked back at the rise that lay between them and pursuit. No movement. Another meadow lay before them, and it would take a long time to go around it, through the trees. It would take the spies some time to figure out where they'd gone, and the echoes confused the direction a sound came from. Jiaan grinned and urged his horse to gallop through the open space, avoiding the raised burrows of the ground squirrels with practiced ease.

The horses the inn had rented to him weren't the pride of the commander's herd, but they weren't nags, either. His mare's dark mane whipped back into his face as she ran.

The girl drew level with him, her legs wrapped tight around the barrel of the dappled gelding. She rode like a deghan, like she was part of the horse, and she flashed him a triumphant grin as she passed him by.

She reined in, sensibly, as they entered the trees. Jiaan did the same and then looked back to see the peddler trotting slowly over the field, bouncing in the saddle like a sack of grain, the mule trailing behind him.

Jiaan's mouth tightened with annoyance, but all he could do was wait and pray the watchers didn't make it to the top of the rise anytime in the next day or so.

"Is he going to fall off?" The lady's voice was coolly amused.

"Probably," said Jiaan grimly.

In fact, it was only a few moments before the peddler trotted up to them, panting and flushed with the effort of staying in the saddle.

"You have to keep up," said Jiaan in his best imitation of his father's command voice.

"Duckie's not being a charger," said the peddler, in the stubborn tone Jiaan had come to know well. "And I'm not breaking her legs, galloping over rough ground like a . . . deghan." His voice went expressionless on the last word, making it ten kinds of insult.

The girl scowled.

Jiaan sighed. "Let's go."

Perhaps another quarter mark later they came to a thinner grove, and Jiaan looked back at the rise. Three of the watchers stalked slowly over the low ridge, paying careful attention to the ground. Tracking. Garshab would have sent his best huntsmen for this task, but as the men continued down the slope and no one followed, Jiaan realized he'd eliminated two of them with one blow. "One of them is staying with the man I hit. Good."

The peddler's brows lifted. "With just three coming on"—he gestured to the bow and quiver that hung from Jiaan's saddle— "couldn't you be leveling the odds even more?"

"Not without giving them proof that someone came to the lady's rescue," said Jiaan. "The whole point of this is to get her away without being seen—and especially without being identified as the commander's men. Later he can claim that Azura shielded her or some such thing. As long as they can't prove he had a hand in it, it doesn't matter. That's why he wants to use you, since you have no previous connection to him."

Jiaan turned his horse and set off again, and the others followed. The peddler was frowning. "But those fellows you said were witnesses, they saw me in the camp. That'd be a connection."

"Don't get your hopes up," said the girl dryly. "They're on Father's side. They're sworn to tell the truth if they're asked, but who'd ask them about you?"

The peddler's soft snort expressed a world of contempt for deghan politics, but he kept his horse and the absurdly named mule within the shelter of the trees, which was enough for Jiaan. He knew even the most skilled hunter couldn't track them as fast as they could ride, though three horses and

a mule left a trail even the peddler might have followed.

It soon became clear that the gap between
them and their pursuers was widening. The brat
excused herself, with a glare Jiaan didn't dare
challenge.

"Why shouldn't she?" the peddler asked, seeing his frown. "Even I can see that we're pulling
away."

"Yes, but we have to be able to keep out of
their sight when we get there."

"And where would 'there' be?"

"You'll see," said Jiaan shortly. The lady came
back, straightening her clothes. Jiaan started to
dismount, to help her up to the saddle, but she
grasped the pommel, along with a handful of reins,
and sprang up like a boy.

It seemed to take forever, but the sun was only
half down the sky when they came abruptly out of
the forest and stared into space. The peddler's
horse shied as his rider recoiled, and even Jiaan,
who'd seen the site before, swallowed. "I told you
you'd see."

See, indeed. The cliff was half a dozen yards
from their feet, but with a cliff that high, yards

weren't nearly enough. Beyond it the world fell away into the badlands, a maze of reddish rock pillars with only space between. So much space. Looking outward made Jiaan feel like he was standing in the sky, and his stomach grew hollow.

He had escorted the farm family to the lady's refuge on ordinary mountain roads, but the commander had sworn that the desert was the best possible place to elude pursuit. Jiaan began to understand why; he didn't even want to think about traversing that cliff, guided or not.

The girl dismounted and went to the edge of the abyss. Her arms lifted, almost as if she intended to take flight.

"Get back!" said Jiaan sharply.

Her dark gaze was reassuringly ironic. Earthbound. "Why? Don't we have to go down?"

"Yes, but not here." Jiaan swallowed again at the thought of descending that cliff, even on a trail. A good trail, the tribesman had assured him. He looked for the landmarks the Suud had pointed out. The huge, twisting spire to his left looked familiar. Sort of. "That way."

A candlemark later Jiaan wasn't so certain, for the spire's appearance altered with every change in his angle of view. He tried to conceal his doubts from the others, like a real deghan would.

Sometimes they were able to travel in the trees, but sometimes they were forced onto the cliff edge, and that worried Jiaan for more reasons than the height. They were too visible. If the trail down was equally visible, they'd surely be . . . There!

The slight figure might have been a child, against the towering backdrop of the badlands, but the red-striped robe that concealed the woman's vulnerable, white skin had become very familiar. The commander had had to double his price when the tribespeople had learned that this might take place in the daytime.

The tribeswoman sprinted up to them. "Good good!" The long sleeves, uncuffed and tied shut at the bottom to protect her hands, didn't stop her from reaching up to lift her hood, carefully keeping out the direct sunlight as she did so. Her bizarre, pale eyes were bright with excitement. The irises were actually gray but hardly darker than the whites, and her pupils were little larger than pinpricks. She looked blind, and Jiaan wondered with a stab of worry how well their guides could see in the daylight.

"Man much long back," she went on eagerly. "Down path, not see. Good come now."

"How do you know where he is?" Jiaan asked.

She struggled for words and failed. "Tell. Know. Come now!" A small foot stamped impatiently.

Was that gesture universal? Jiaan smiled. "Very well. Good. Take us to the trail." He looked around for some ravine or canyon that might give access to the desert so far below, but for as far as he could see the cliff was unbroken. "Is it far?"

The small woman snorted—another universal gesture, which she'd demonstrated often over the last week. She took a handful of strides to the edge of the cliff and turned back. Her face was hidden in the hood's deep folds, but her voice was clear. "Here."

"No." Jiaan sighed. He hoped achieving communication wouldn't take as long as it sometimes had. Gestures might help. He dismounted and went to join her. "Not the cliff, the trail down. Show us the tra—"

It opened at his feet, as if a djinn's concealing spell had been banished, though Jiaan knew it had only been hidden by an angle of the rock. He peered over the edge.

The path tumbled down the rock face, turning back and forth on itself like the track of a hunted hare. It was about four feet wide where Jiaan stood, but the bottom looked no wider than a piece of string.

"No. It's too open. They'll see us. The horses won't be able to make it."

The small foot stamped again, raising a puff of dust. "Trail good. Horses good. Man back, us come now!"

The others dismounted and came to see for themselves. The peddler exclaimed in astonishment, and even the crazy . . . the lady Soraya seemed taken aback. But she was the one who looked up to meet Jiaan's eyes.

"This was the plan. Do you have a better idea?"

IT WASN'T AS BAD as it had looked from above. As long as Jiaan kept his eyes on the trail and didn't look down or out, it was better than he'd expected.

The trail was generally three to four feet wide, though it narrowed in a few spots, until Jiaan worried about the horses. But, secure on their four feet, they were calmer than the humans who led them. Even the peddler had agreed to lead his horse and leave Duckie to follow on her own. Watching the surefooted mule pick her way down after them, Jiaan understood why.

It wasn't always a life-threatening drop either, he told himself firmly. As you neared the sharp turns you could probably survive a fall to the next level of the track, and sometimes the slope softened, supporting a bush that a desperate hand might snatch. There were really only a dozen places where it felt as if they clung to a wrinkle in the rock's ancient face and its slightest frown would pitch them off.

Finally his feet touched the earth of the desert floor. Jiaan looked up, stretching tense neck muscles. The cliff appeared almost as high looking up as it had looking down. In fact, it looked to him like they'd descended half a league, but that was surely impossible. Though, judging by the sweat that soaked his undershirt, he might have been running twice that far.

The peddler, the last to clatter off the trail, sighed and went to stroke his mule's damp neck and whisper into her ears. He didn't seem to be sweating as hard as Jiaan.

And except for the dust on her boots, the girl might have come from a stroll in a spring garden. "Shouldn't we get out of sight?" She gestured at the cliff overhead. "Or were you planning to take a nap? Our hunters could come along at any time."

Jiaan grimaced and let her mount on her own, since she did it so well. She was right. There really wasn't time to kiss the ground.

THEY MADE CAMP that night at the base of a sandstone tower greater than any raised by man. At first Jiaan refused to let the tribeswoman make a fire, for fear their pursuers would see it from the cliff top, but soon she pointed to the glow of fires illuminating several rock faces in the distance, and Jiaan realized that there was no way to distinguish their fire from those of the scattered . . . hunting parties? Surely there couldn't be that many tribes so close, in an area so barren.

"Besides," the peddler pointed out, "after what

happened today, they'd have to be stark mad to be coming down in the dark."

All three of them grinned, united in delighted memory.

They had made it into the rocks before their stalkers reached the cliff top. Their guide had kept them out of sight, weaving through the maze like a shuttle through the warp, till suddenly Jiaan saw a formation he knew he'd seen before and looked down at their own tracks.

"Hey." He said it softly, so as not to wake the echoes. "We're going in circles."

The woman, whom he'd mounted on the saddle behind him, gave him a look that made him grateful her vocabulary wasn't up to much. "Look," she said, as if speaking to a not-very-bright child. She pointed at their tracks, which they were now riding over. A bit later she led them round a bend; then she tugged his tunic and pointed behind them. "Look now."

They had turned in a different direction than they had the last time—one set of tracks went left and the other right. Both sets were so recent, the hunters wouldn't know which to follow.

After that Jiaan left the matter of eluding

pursuit entirely in her hands. His favorite moment
was when they'd reached the base of a spire, and
she'd directed him and Soraya around one side
and sent the peddler and his mule in the opposite
direction. When they met on the other side, she
signaled for them to keep going and meet back
where they'd started. Then they rode back over
their trail and got off on a dry riverbed they'd
already taken so often that one more set of tracks
would hardly show.

It wouldn't take a skilled tracker long to figure
out, but the sheer, artistic exuberance of all those
backward and forward tracks still made Jiaan
chuckle.

When they'd finally left the maze, it had been
very simple. The tribeswoman had guided them
along a central trail they must have taken half a
dozen times, then they turned abruptly, going
down a sandy defile. But as soon as they had
rounded a bend in the narrow canyon, the woman
jumped from Jiaan's horse. He started to protest
but then watched in astonishment as she cut several twiggy branches from a nearby bush and
wove them into a broom with which she swept
away their tracks. Then, after checking carefully

to be certain the rock shadow would keep the setting sun from her skin, she had pulled off her robe
and swung it over the sand in windy, sweeping
arcs, erasing even the thin lines the broom had
left. Given a few moments for the surface sand to
dry, it would be impossible for anyone to tell that
three horses and a mule had left the trail there.
They never crossed their own tracks again.

Jiaan looked up now and met the woman's
odd, light eyes. She had taken off her robe in the
warmth of the fire and wore only a thin shift,
which revealed far too much of her moon-pale
skin. Her hair looked like curling corn silk—
unnatural. Jiaan smiled. "You are good," he told
her sincerely. "Good good!"

She grinned back at him—another universal
human gesture. There were those who said the
tribesfolk were djinn, or at least a djinn's get,
because of their pale skin and hair. Even that they
had a djinn's powers. Jiaan had scoffed, but he
hadn't *known;* now he did.

"My father said the Suud were the best trackers he'd ever seen," Soraya told the peddler. "He
took a troop into the badlands once, looking for
some miners who'd gone missing, and they led him

141

in circles for days. He said he'd never have gotten out if they hadn't finally taken pity on him and led him to a trail up the cliff. He sent his men back and stayed on as their guest for several weeks."

Jiaan suppressed a pang of startled jealousy. The commander hadn't mentioned staying with the tribes to him, though he had told Jiaan that he thought the miners were dead. The only reason he'd been allowed to escape, he said, was because soon after he entered the desert, he'd come across a hunting party and had offered them neither violence nor insult, nor had he allowed his men to do so. He feared the miners hadn't been so restrained.

"But why would miners come here at all?" Jiaan wondered aloud. It wasn't quite as desolate as it had looked from above; there was grass, in scattered brown clumps, and bushes and even small trees by the stream not far from their camp. The desert obviously supported life, for the Suud tribes lived here, but he saw nothing that might lure anyone from more verdant lands. Unless . . . "I've never heard of the Suud trading anything but baskets. Is there gold here? Gems?"

The peddler snorted. "Nothing so useless. Probably nothing at all, but the mining camps are full of rumors that there's iron ore in the desert that makes better steel than anything we get out of the mountains. A few fools go looking for it every year."

"That's right," said Jiaan. "You sell in the mining camps. But why call them fools? A sword that won't break is worth its weight in gold, and might sell for even more, if it's well proven."

"Oh, I've nothing but respect for good steel," said the peddler. "I'm calling them fools because most of them don't come back, and there's no treasure of any kind worth dying for."

A true peasant attitude. Jiaan looked at the lady, hoping she wouldn't spoil the moment of amity by saying so. She pressed her lips together and looked down. The firelight revealed nothing in her smooth, sculpted face, but it occurred to Jiaan that she also might not be coming back.

THEY REACHED THE OLD CROFT around midday. The tribesman had joined them when they awoke, and his command of the Faran language was good enough to convey that their pursuers had left the badlands and were waiting for them to come back up the trail they'd used to descend. The other two huntsmen had joined them, even the man with the

143

broken head. Jiaan was glad to hear it, and he was even more relieved when they left the desert by a different trail, which led up a small canyon and made him fear for his life in only a handful of places.

The croft was tucked into a snug mountain valley. The commander had discovered it on his expedition to the desert, but it had been abandoned even then. He didn't think it was remarkable enough that any of the men who'd been with him would remember it.

Abandoned it might have been, but the farmhouse was built by miners. It had stone walls and a slate slab roof that only leaked in a few places, which Behras had assured Jiaan he and his sons could patch. It looked far better than it had when Jiaan had taken the family there just a few weeks ago.

Having lost their own farm to a flood that shifted a riverbed over their fields, they were delighted to do a favor for the deghan who'd supported them by employing Behras with odd jobs.

From the look on the lady Soraya's face, this would be a job and a half.

"I can't stay here." Her eyes were wide with shocked disgust. "It's a hovel."

In fact, the farmhouse was much the same size

as the house where Jiaan had grown up. Two big rooms, with a fireplace between them, and two rooms under the eaves that would be heated by the chimney. Behras and his wife, Golnar, had cleared away the signs of disrepair and had even painted the shutters red, with gold suns and dark blue moons on them. The privy, tucked into the grove to the right of the house, and the bathhouse in the yard to the left were built of clean, new wood. To Jiaan, it looked snug and almost prosperous. . . . But he wasn't a deghass. Reluctant pity mingled with his exasperation.

Still, he had a duty to perform.

"Lady Soraya, these are Master Behras and Madam Golnar." Their sons hovered behind them, but Jiaan judged it wiser not to push things. "They will share this place with you, protect you, and see to your needs."

The girl said nothing.

Golnar smiled nervously. "Don't you be worrying about a thing, Lady. We've supplies laid in to last two winters, with more promised in the spring, and soon as the ground thaws, we'll be putting in a bit of garden."

"Thaws," Soraya repeated.

Had she ever seen snow? Jiaan wondered.

"Aye, we'll be growing our own, fresh, as soon as the season permits. We've made a room ready for you, upstairs. Proper stairs too, not a ladder. Quite separate and private from the boys."

The lady looked at the boys in question, who stared back, wide-eyed.

She grimaced and slid from her horse to the ground, tugging free the straps that held her pack. Behras took a step as if to help but then stopped, warned off by a wall of anger as thick as any besieged city could boast.

She had the pack in her hands in moments. Then she stalked into the building, banging open the door and not bothering to close it. Jiaan wished she had more of her father in her. The commander asked permission before entering even the humblest peasant's home.

"She's had a bad week," he offered Behras, whose face had darkened.

A man's shirt flew past the open door, then a woman's bright skirt, which settled in a crumpled heap on the floor. Evidently, the lady preferred the downstairs bedroom the older couple had claimed. A man's boot thudded onto the skirt. Jiaan winced.

"If she's wanting the lower room, she's welcome." Golnar sounded bewildered. "We thought she'd be happier upstairs. It's more private, without noise coming through the fireplace and footsteps overhead and all."

"She's had a very bad week," Jiaan repeated, knowing that it was true and that it still didn't excuse her. "She'll be . . . feeling better tomorrow. You'll do fine." He wondered if he was lying. Or, rather, how badly he was lying.

Still, he'd gotten her to safety, leaving the commander to fight with a clear mind and an easy heart. And the other aides would know it, know that Jiaan had been chosen and had succeeded. No full-blooded deghan could have done it better.

Fine or not, the lady would survive and be well, and that was all that was necessary. But Jiaan still felt sorry for her.

CHAPTER NINE

KAVI

THE YOUNG MAN REPEATED the deghan's threats for the final time, possibly the sixth, and set off down the track to the lowlands. It was late afternoon now, and it would have made more sense to go up the road to the big mining camp—almost a small town—that worked a vein of tin only half a day's ride from the deghass' hideaway. But the youth, Jiaan, obviously wanted to report back to his commander; he was heading down the road at a trot.

Kavi was torn between putting all the distance he could between himself and the whole mess, and common sense, which told him that visiting the miners now would give him an excuse to come up this road again in six months' time. It would take him out of his way, for he preferred not to venture this far into the mountains, but perhaps the deghan would follow through on his promise of a generous reward. And it could have been worse—he could have lost fingers.

Or, almost as bad, *he* could have been set to mind the she-bitch. Losing her temper with servants came as easy as breathing to that one.

Kavi sighed and turned Duckie uphill. It angered him, having his life preempted so casually, but when you worked for your bread, common sense had to prevail. Besides, this far into the mountains, the miners probably never saw a peddler. He'd picked up some salt and plenty of spices in Setesafon, but his load of ironmongery was light. Sometimes the miners did a bit of forging, and a few of them were as good as the better apprentices. If nothing else, they'd be glad to see a new face and hear news of the outside world. He could even tell the public tale of the sacrifice of the high commander's daughter; it had been the talk of Setesafon when he was there. Kavi had been terrified when he realized what a dangerous intrigue he'd stumbled into, but he seemed to have gotten out of it with a whole skin.

Unlike his last encounter with a deghan.

Kavi forced the thought away with the ease of long practice. He could hate them into the pit and back—it would do him no good and them no harm at all. That was what his old master had said, and Kavi knew it for truth. Still, telling those miners the tale of a beautiful, courageous maiden offering her life for Farsala, when he'd just watched her expel honest folk from their own room, might challenge even a liar of his skill. He pitied her keepers.

Would living like the rest of the world for a while teach her some compassion? Probably not. And she really wasn't living like the rest of the world. She still had servants to dress her and feed her and clean for her. She still didn't have to pass her life away in work and see ten to thirty percent of her profit going to put gold and glass beads on the bridle of some deghass' horse. She still wouldn't see some arrogant noble stride into her master's shop as if he owned it and pick up a newly forged sword . . .

No, Kavi didn't feel sorry for her. He wished all deghans could share the same fate.

THE MINERS WERE GLAD of Kavi's spices and even bought a set of glass game markers he'd picked up on a bargain and despaired of selling, since they were expensive and could easily be replaced with tokens of carved wood.

He told them Soraya's public tale and managed not to snicker at their appreciative pity for the fate of the tragic heroine. He talked more seriously of the rumors that the Hrum were actually coming— and coming soon. But to the miners, in their mountain fastness, that mattered less than a good story. How many times had the deghans beaten back Kadeshi invaders? They'd defeat these Hrum, too.

Kavi left the camp pleased with his profit and not too unhappy at the prospect of returning. He was running almost a month late at this point, and he endured the good-natured gibes in the camps where he usually stopped with equal good nature. In some cases fear that "their" peddler had passed them by made the miners even more welcoming, though they bargained as hard as ever. Still, by the time he neared the western border, Kavi had sold almost all of his spices and many of the luxury bits he carried. And even better, the last few months of autumn had been drier than usual, so he'd made good time and caught up with his schedule.

Usually he cut up to Desafon from Bulak on the canal boats, which gave him and Duckie a welcome break from walking, and he returned to his route the same way. But with the roads this dry, and with his pack light of all but cutlery, might it be worth his while to take the Trade Road into Desafon?

That was the most pressing question on Kavi's mind as he made his way to his usual campsite in the foothills and saw a wisp of smoke curling up against the dark pines.

He pulled Duckie to a halt, though her ears twitched in annoyance. She knew that this place, between the rocks and a bend in the stream, was where he took off her pack, and the grazing was good there.

But why was someone else there? It wasn't far from the main road, and it was right off the track that led to the last mining camp, but none of the miners had mentioned that they were expecting visitors. Kavi knew that other people stopped there. It was just that he'd never encountered them.

A mule's bray shattered the silence. Before he could reach for her nose, Duckie inflated her lungs and sang back to it, revealing their presence to anyone within leagues. Kavi sighed. But why should he care if their presence was revealed?

"Hello, the camp." He and Duckie clattered forward, in the open way of honest travelers.

"Hello, the road," came the standard reply. Just a beat too slowly? Nonsense.

There were eight of them, Kavi saw as he approached. Six men and two women, all wearing brightly embroidered vests over bright shirts and, in the case of the women, skirts. *Good, no deghan's hunting party here.* A small herd of mules grazed in the rope-and-stake corral they'd set up by the stream, so Duckie would have company too.

"You're a peddler, I see," said one of the men, stepping forward to grasp Kavi's wrist. His smile was friendly.

"Aye," said Kavi cheerfully. "With a load of cutlery and iron goods, if you're needing such things. I'm just back from a loop of the mining camps, and I picked up some of their work. It's not city fancy, but it's strong and serviceable."

"Mining camps?" The man's eyes narrowed

with interest. "Yes, I'd like to see some of your goods."

"Well, I'm pleased to be showing you," said Kavi. "Though you don't seem much in need of knives."

In fact, every one of them bore a dagger, longer than the knives most men used for eating — four inches longer than the knife at Kavi's belt.

One of the women went to help him put Duckie in the makeshift corral, but she didn't say much. She might have been shy, but the few times her eyes met his, her gaze was bright and keen. She was surely a peasant, though, for her hands were callused, her whole body as strong and lean as a hunting wolf's.

In fact, they were all lean. Lean and wary. They had no packs that Kavi could see, beyond their bedrolls and traveling gear. He might have wondered if they were fleeing a bad master, but with eight mules? And did none of them walk?

They had a pot on the fire; salt-pork stew, said the man who seemed to do all the talking. It was often made by travelers who had time to cook a hot meal, but the spices smelled odd to Kavi.

It was still early, so he sat down and told the

spokesman the news of the mining camps: a tin vein playing out, a rich copper vein rumored to have been found, though no one seemed to know where. There was some concern that the snow would be too deep in the passes for supply wagons to get through, but they always worried about that. . . .

The spokesman let the talk go where it would, but he never mentioned what he and his fellows were doing on the road or asked to see Kavi's wares. Though, as Kavi had noticed, they'd no shortage of knives, and their bedrolls had a rigid look, as if they might have been rolled around short swords.

Kavi smiled through the ebb and flow of the conversation with the ease of a man who sold for his living, but the back of his neck prickled. If he'd been near the eastern border, he'd have taken them for Kadeshi bandits slipping over to raid. But Kadesh was on the other side of the realm, and Sendan was almost as orderly as Farsala was. Unless the rumored Hrum invasion had begun driving folk off their land? But why would Sendar refugees disguise themselves as Farsalan peasants? For it *was* a disguise, Kavi realized. The bedrolls, each wrapped around some long, rigid object, were all composed of similar blankets, as if they'd all been purchased at the same time. And all their boots were new, with just a few months' wear on them.

He had to get out of here. Not too soon, though, or they'd become suspicious. Kavi made a casual comment on the warmth of the evening and how dry the roads were for late fall. He let the conversation turn again, but soon he would mention that adding a new camp had put him behind schedule. After sunset, when the nearly full moon rose in the clear sky—*please, Azura, please keep the clouds away*—no one would think it strange if he decided to press on to the next village. He hoped.

The stew pot took forever to boil, and the vegetables still had to cook. Kavi's face was stiff with smiling. He told them the official story of the high commander's sacrificed daughter, then the most recent rumor that someone had found superior iron ore in the Suud's desert. The latter topic seemed to interest them more, though when Kavi told Soraya's story, their gazes met in a look he couldn't interpret.

The man who was tending the pot—and why was a man cooking, with women present?—went over to stir the thrice-cursed stew yet again and lifted a ladle to taste. To Kavi's dismay, he wrinkled his nose, and after a bit of fishing in their supply bag, he pulled out an onion and drew his knife to slice it.

Sunset and firelight glowed on the blade, highlighting a pattern of rippling dark waves that flowed through the steel like captured smoke. *Watersteel? But only the—*

The earth seemed to heave up and crash into his chest, but it was the spokesman, leaping onto his back, slamming him to the ground. For the second time in a few months Kavi's arm was wrenched up between his shoulder blades.

"You idiot, Arius," the spokesman—no, the leader—snarled. "He sells knives. You think he's not going to notice your blade?" He still spoke Faran, but the accent was different. The other man replied in a language Kavi didn't know, crisp and regular, not at all like the slithering rasp of Kadi.

The conversation went on in that language, oddly formal, for all its acrimony. The language wouldn't have given them away—Kavi knew only a handful of words in that tongue—but their steel did. Only the Hrum made watersteel, and they never sold it or let it past their empire's borders. Kavi had only seen one stolen piece, long ago, when the proud owner had showed it to his former master, but no one could forget the look of it.

The Hrum were here, closer than anyone had dreamed. They must have taken Sendan already or be on the verge of doing so.

Kavi had thought he was frightened when the high commander caught him, but he now realized that he hadn't begun to be afraid then. The high commander would only have turned him over to the guards. There was no way these men would let him live, unless . . .

"I'll talk," said Kavi. "I'm a peddler. I hear everything. I know where all the villages are. Back roads. Trails. I can be telling you lots of things. And . . ." The qualm he felt startled him—he owed nothing to the she-bitch, and her father had taken over his life and threatened to have his fingers cut off if he didn't obey! No, he owed nothing to any of *them*. "And I know what really happened to the high commander's daughter! She wasn't sacrificed. I know where she is."

"Brave, isn't he?" said one of the women in heavily accented Faran.

"Be quiet, Morra," said the leader. "He knows courage will only get him killed."

She replied in Hrum, but Kavi could guess what she said, and despair filled him.

"All right, maybe talking won't save me," he said. "But if you kill me, you're playing the fool. You should never waste resources. Not in war. And you'll be fighting a war here. Our deghans have never been beaten. Never. You'll need all the help, all the information, you can get." Even if they tortured him, as long as they left him alive, perhaps he could escape, even if only into slavery. He'd heard the Hrum kept slaves. He'd thought it the most horrifying fate short of death that could befall a man. He now realized that it was a *lot* better than dying.

The leader snorted. "Bring me a strap."

Panic flooded Kavi's veins. Would they strangle him? He wrenched at the grip on his wrists, but it was hopeless. He tried to think of something else to say, to offer, but his throat locked closed, and his thoughts were fixed on the coming strap.

The leather loop fell over his hands, not his head, and breath shuddered into his lungs as his wrists were cinched together. They weren't going to kill him now, or they wouldn't bother to tie him up. Would they?

The leader's hard weight lifted off his back. "Sit up," he commanded. "But don't try anything." The metallic slither of a drawn sword reinforced the order, but Kavi's knees were too wobbly to run, even if he'd been that stupid. He sat up and turned to face them. How had he ever imagined they could be anything but soldiers?

"The problem with keeping you alive as a source of information," said the leader, "is that you'll probably lie, at least some of the time. Sorting out scraps of truth from the rubbish will be more trouble than you're worth." His voice was quiet, almost conversational, but Kavi knew his life hung on the edge of that exquisite, gleaming blade. Even now, the pattern caught his eyes.

These people weren't amateurs. If they intended to kill him, they'd have done it already. Kavi took a shuddering breath. "If you want to make sure I don't lie, then check what I tell you against some other source. This doesn't have to be a short-term deal."

The leader's eyes narrowed. "Deal. Are you trying to bargain with me?"

Kavi shivered, but a peddler recognized the time to push. "Yes. I have something you want, and you have something I want. If we trade, we're both getting what we want. If we don't, neither of us gets anything."

"You'd betray your people for your life and a whole skin?" The leader's voice was very gentle.

It was Kavi's turn to snort. "Betray? I don't owe the deghans anything. My people are peasants and craftsmen. Why should I die to prevent a change of masters? And I was thinking of money, in addition to life and a whole skin." There, the bait was on the hook. He knew he shouldn't twitch it, but he couldn't resist adding: "Though I'd take the secret of making that steel even over gold."

The wistful note in his voice was sincere. The leader laughed. "You sound like a smith."

"I was. Once. The deghans put an end to it."

Kavi rose with careful slowness to his knees

and turned, twisting his hand in the strap to show them his right palm. The tip of that beautiful sword touched his fingers, nudging them down. Then the sword withdrew, and he turned back. "I have no loyalty to them. I'll give you the high commander's daughter on a platter, if you want her." Could they hear the truth in his voice?

Eyes of a lighter brown than most peasants' searched his. "We don't kidnap the children of enemy commanders—that's a weapon that cuts two ways."

"But I do have something you're wanting," said Kavi. "Or you'd have killed me the moment you saw that I recognized your steel." He held his breath, praying he was right.

"Maybe," said the leader. "And maybe not. Tie his ankles, Morra. We're taking him with us."

ON THE DAY AFTER *their union neither Rostam nor Tahmina could conceal their love; it glowed about them like the sun, illuminating each touch of their hands and meeting of their eyes. Saman, who had always been first in his daughter's heart, saw this and grew bitter.*

After the midday meal he took his guest out to hunt wild boar, a prey too fierce for the women to accompany them. Rostam and Rakesh were among the first in the field, riding the boar down. Rostam himself crushed the beast's hind leg with a blow from his great mace, while Rakesh danced aside to save him from the lashing tusks. But once the boar was crippled, and not so dangerous,

Rostam rode aside to give other men the honor of the kill.

Seeing in his generosity yet another sign of divine farr, Saman's jealousy grew blacker still, and he spoke roughly: "I wonder that so great a champion would fear to dismount and meet a crippled boar on the ground where his tusks might find you. But then, I suppose anyone on a great horse might be a great champion."

All men turned to stare, amazed at the injustice of the charge.

Rostam was pricked with anger and his cheeks flushed, but he remembered that this man was Tahmina's father and replied graciously, "Rakesh is indeed half my strength and the friend of my heart. I thank you for your praise of him."

Saman grew angrier still at his restraint. "So your courage dwells in your horse's hooves rather than in your own heart? I'm surprised to hear you admit it, for a man of honor would take insult at my words. Of course, the answer for slighted honor cannot be found upon horseback, so perhaps it isn't strange that you ignore it."

At this bold insult the others gasped, for there was no man present who doubted Rostam's courage or his skill, and this was an insult that could only be answered with steel.

But Rostam bethought him that he had come as an ambassador, under banner of truce, and to sunder that would be a greater stain on his honor than to pass the insult by. "I think, Saman, that you forget the courtesy owed a guest, much less that owed an ambassador, sworn upon my gahn's honor to keep my steel sheathed within your house. For were this not so"— his voice rumbled now like distant thunder—"you must answer to me for what you have just said."

Saman laughed. "And so the greatest champion of Farsala hides behind a banner of truce and his aged gahn's skirts. It shouldn't surprise me that Kobad, who all men know to have become a coward in his dotage, would choose as champion a hollow man such as you."

Rakesh reared as Rostam's hand tightened on the reins, and Rostam cried out in a great voice, "It is you who are a dotard, Saman. My gahn sent me to try to end this conflict between you, which he never sought. But I see that Arzhang and Gorahz have their claws sunk fast in your heart, and there can be no answer for you but war. The insults to myself I would ignore, but you cannot insult my gahn. You should thank Azura, with whatever shred of your heart remains your own, that my oath to honor the truce lies between us. That, and one other thing."

Then he gathered his followers and rode straight away from the lands of his enemy, not even returning for his baggage or his servants, seeking only to flee before he lost his own battle with Gorahz and slew Saman, to the despite of his gahn's honor and his love.

So he did not say farewell to Tahmina, who wept for him most sorely, and he never knew that the brief night of their union had borne fruit. ∴ . .

CHAPTER TEN

KAVI

THE HRUM KEPT TO THE FOOTHILLS and Kavi saw no one he could have asked for help. Not that screaming for help would have resulted in anything except another prisoner. Or a corpse.

Kavi rode on Duckie's back, bound and uncomfortable during the day, and he was shackled to a tree or a stone at night. They did him no harm, and they even shared out the contents of his pack among them so he could ride, but Kavi didn't deceive himself about their ruthlessness. A ruthlessness, he slowly realized, that sprang mostly from fear. They knew what their fate would be if they were captured, so in the end . . . "We're pretty much plowing the same field, aren't we?"

He spoke softly, mostly to the stars trapped in the pine boughs overhead, but Alen, one of the handful of women who were part of the troop, was on watch tonight.

"I don't know about that. For one thing, you're chained up and we're not."

"That's so," Kavi admitted. On the first days of their journey he'd been afraid to speak to them. He'd picked up a few words of Hrum from chance meetings on the Trade Road; he'd hoped to travel into the empire himself one day and take another look at their famed watersteel. He'd heard that the empire was a just and lawful land—safe for travelers and traders. But his scant vocabulary was useless for translating the soldiers' flashing, idiomatic conversations, and men whose lives were in danger cared little for law or justice. On the other hand, they must have some reason for keeping him alive. Soon Kavi started talking to them in Faran out of sheer boredom. He'd been cuffed for it once or twice by the more irascible ones, but most of them answered—or ignored him if they chose not to answer. Alen was one of the friendlier ones, so he went on. "But I think you're almost more . . . nervous than I am. Especially when you're going off."

They didn't always remain together. In fact, the group was actually composed of ten; two of them had been off scouting, or spying, or whatever it was they did, when Kavi first found them. They usually left in groups of two to four and almost always took one of the women with them—trying to look more harmless, Kavi supposed, though these women were far from harmless. *Women warriors.* They didn't seem to be nobles either, for they carried water from the stream, cared for the animals, and shared in the other camp chores just as the men did. *Peasant* women warriors. The mind boggled.

Yet she wore the same rank marks as the men—at least, Kavi assumed the slashing diagonal bars that all the Hrum bore on their right shoulders were marks of rank. Alen had three bars. Only Raiban, the troop's leader, had more.

"You can say that we're scared," said Alen amiably. She sat in the shadow of a tree trunk, her eyes searching the darkness. "Who wouldn't be scared, in the midst of enemy territory?"

"It must be important," said Kavi, "for them to risk so many of you." With some of the others, this attempt to learn what they sought might have earned him a kick, but Alen grinned and said nothing.

Kavi sighed. "It's not as if I'm going to be able to tell anyone."

Which was true. The Hrum hadn't been unduly brutal, but neither had they given him any chance to escape, and by now Kavi knew that they never relaxed their guard. A thoroughly professional attitude. He sighed again.

"If you can't tell anyone, then why do you care?" Alen murmured.

"Because if I knew what kind of information you were looking for, I'd know what to offer."

A jackal howled in the distance, and they both stiffened, but the reply was more distant still. Besides, jackals never took on a party this big unless they were starving.

"You're right to be afraid," said Kavi softly. "Djinn come out in the night too. And they don't make any noise. That's why we only go abroad in the day. The sun is Azura's, but the night is theirs."

Alen chuckled. "Sorry. Not buying."

Kavi shrugged. "Worth a try. Some people really do believe in them, you know. At least, some deghans do. That's what the temple is for, to combat djinn. If you're a deghan and you're bribing them with a big enough donation, you can get off a criminal charge by claiming that a djinn possessed you, and the temple will swear they exorcised it."

"You're kidding. An actual, legal charge?"

"Aye. It's only for deghans, of course. The rest of us answer for our own temper or greed or whatnot."

"But you said the high commander's daughter was actually sacrificed. Left in the wilderness to propitiate your djinn or the temple or something."

"Ah, but that was political. They're hoping to catch the commander shielding her; then they can claim he's unfit to lead the army and replace him. The deghans never have to pay for what they do. Not really."

"Unfit? Because he refuses to sacrifice a child to some idiotic, ancient superstition?" She leaned back against the tree with a soft snort. "I don't think we'll have much trouble taking your army, peddler."

Kavi was beginning to wonder about that himself.

WHEN THE TROOP FINALLY EMERGED from the foothills, everything looked the same as it did on the Farsalan side of the border. Even the Trade Road, close to the mountains here, where the land narrowed, looked the same. But now the Hrum soldiers rode down it openly, with their swords belted at their waists instead of rolled in blankets. The traders they passed pulled their wagons aside and nodded respectfully. All their swords were watersteel, Kavi noted. Straight blades, sharpened on both sides, unlike a Farsalan blade, which curved.

"You've taken Sendan," Kavi muttered to Favius under the cover of the mules' pounding hooves. Not that anyone would care what he learned now. His wrists were tied to Duckie's pack frame, and guards rode in front, behind, and to either side of him. Favius, on his left with Duckie's lead rein tied to his saddle, was the one who had padded the pack frame with blankets so it wasn't quite so uncomfortable to ride.

"Pretty much," Favius replied, not bothering to lower his voice. "There are still some pockets of resistance and a few large towns to take, but we've all the cities now, and the farmers are beginning to figure out we're not so bad. It'll be settled by mid-winter, if you ask me—months ahead of schedule."

They had a schedule for conquest? From what little Kavi had heard of the Hrum, that wasn't impossible. Their empire had conquered dozens of countries in the last few centuries.

Kavi had been racking his brain over the last weeks for any information about them, but all he remembered, aside from their possession of the secret of watersteel, was that traders liked passing into their empire. Not just because they kept the peace as well as any civilized land, but also because inside the boundaries of the empire the whole length of the Trade Road was raised and paved with stone slabs. Kavi found that so improbable that he hadn't entirely believed it, even though he'd heard it from several men. Certainly the road here was the same winding, muddy mess it was on the other side of the border, for the first of the winter rains had started a few days ago, and it had rained every afternoon since.

THE STORM THAT DAY arrived on schedule. Alen fastened up Kavi's cloak for him, but soon the hood blew back, and rain soaked through his hair and ran down his neck to wet his back and shoulders. He had seldom been more grateful to see the walls of a town looming out of the thin, gray drizzle.

The gate guard was clad in the scarlet cloak of a Hrum soldier, with a fitted steel breastplate, and a crested helmet whose peaked brim kept some of the rain off his face. He spoke with Raiban and examined a set of documents that had been stitched into the lining of Raiban's saddle till that morning. But soon he signaled the gatekeeper to open for them.

Mazad, where Kavi had grown up and learned his craft, was walled too—the only walled city in Farsala. He was familiar with the way stone caught the ring of iron-shod hooves and intensified it. On this dim, dripping evening the streets were all but empty. Even in the inn, where they lodged warm and dry for the night, the folk spoke only Sendan and made no move to help him, though he caught flashes of guilt or pity in their eyes before they turned away. Conquered people minded their own business. Kavi shivered, despite the warmth of the hearth fire.

The morning dawned fair, though the road was

muddy enough to make Kavi grateful he wasn't walking. If the soldiers complained, they did it in Hrum. But with or without complaints, they set a fast enough pace that they reached the rise that overlooked the Hrum camp just before midday.

When he first saw it, Kavi thought it must be a town, but no town he'd ever seen was laid out in squares like a game board. As they drew nearer he saw that the neat rows of peaked roofs were not houses, but tents, all of the same design, made with the same, drab canvas. His view was obscured as they rode down the hill to the staked palisade.

Raiban showed no papers here, for the guards recognized him and waved him on with a grin and a comment that sounded like a jest. Kavi was getting very tired of Hrum.

Inside the palisade the resemblance to a town was even greater, despite the lack of permanent buildings. The straight, muddy streets were full of people, and not all were dressed as soldiers, for some wore the leather of craftsmen or the drab cotton and wool of Sendar shopkeepers. There were also women among them who obviously weren't soldiers, though Alen called greetings to a few of them. How many soldiers did the Hrum have here? Thousands? It was larger than any Farsalan army camp that Kavi had seen.

Raiban led them straight to the central square, where he was intercepted by another man, a superior officer, judging by the swirling bronze decorations on his breastplate and by the way Raiban laid his clenched fist over his heart at the sight of him.

The rest of the troop went off, taking Duckie with the other mules and leaving Kavi with Favius and Alen. Unlike most of the camp, which was filled with the soldiers' tents, the central square was empty in the middle and surrounded by larger tents, whose function Kavi could often guess. The clang of a hammer identified the smithy, just as the domed ovens behind a long tent that ran down one whole side of the square told of a bakery and probably the camp's kitchen. That guess was confirmed when a word from Favius to an old man, who wore only a rough drab tunic under his cloak, brought out half a loaf of bread and three bowls of bean soup. Was he a servant? A slave? The man wore no shackles and bore no marks of punishment, but a chill passed down Kavi's spine. Even the deghans didn't keep slaves. It was probably their only virtue.

Kavi's captors untied his hands to let him eat. He considered refusing the food, but going hungry would do nothing to help the old man. He recognized the flat brown beans that formed the soup's base, but the Hrum cook had added potatoes, beef, and pepper, where a Farsalan would have used onions, cumin, and perhaps raisins to enliven it.

When Kavi's bowl was empty, Favius bound his wrists again and replied to Kavi's protest with a single curt word: "Orders."

A limping soldier supported by two of his fellows told Kavi the location of the surgeons' tent; the number of men exiting the tent beyond it with new boots revealed the cobbler. As time dragged on Kavi developed guesses for all the tents on the square and was beginning to grow bored. The way everything was arranged in squares and rows was as tedious as it was alien. Even the latrines, when Favius took him there, were laid out in a straight line.

He was reduced to trying to guess the contents of the crates, barrels, and wagonloads that had been stored outside—what were those covered bundles that emerged from both the front and back of the carts that carried them?—and was almost grateful to see Raiban approaching with a couple of armed and armored Hrum, whose attitude proclaimed: *Guard*. Almost grateful.

Alen patted his shoulder before she left, but no one said anything in Faran until Raiban gestured to the guards. "They'll take you to Substrategus Garren," he told Kavi. "Don't try anything."

After almost three weeks together, Raiban should have known Kavi wasn't that stupid, but saying so would be equally stupid. Kavi crossed the square meekly and went down the street between rows of tents. They were much larger than the common troopers', though of the same cut and made of the same drab canvas—utterly unlike a deghan's bright, luxurious pavilion. Officers' quarters?

The tent he was taken to wasn't the biggest, which stood at the end of the row, but the tent directly to its left. *Sub*strategus Garren.

His escort announced them loudly, and yet another guard gestured for Kavi to enter. Inside, the tent was divided into several rooms, with the front clearly for official business. Enough light came through the canvas that the brass lamps affixed to the support poles weren't lit. A table covered with scrolls, with chairs around it, numerous chests, and what looked like a traveling desk occupied the room—all plain and sturdy, with neither a peasant's bright paint nor the polished grace a deghan would have insisted on.

Judging by the way the chairs were pushed back from the table, there'd been a meeting here recently, but only two men remained. One was stacking papers on the table; the other lounged in the largest chair, which also had the only cushioned seat.

The guards thrust Kavi forward, hooking his ankles neatly from under him so that he fell to his knees before the chair. The earth beneath the canvas floor was cold and hard. Kavi looked up and met the seated man's gaze. "So you'd be Substrategus Garren?"

The man's eyes, a dark, cloudy gray, narrowed. "And you would be a foolish peddler, who'll lose that impudent tongue if you're not careful." His Faran was deghan accented, but fluent.

Kavi cursed himself. Favius and Alen had made him careless. He said nothing.

"Not a total fool, I see. Good. I have no use for fools. Free his hands. If he tries anything, kill him."

It would have been a fine, dramatic gesture to cut his bonds with a single stroke of one of those lovely, watersteel blades, but the Hrum were too practical to waste good leather. The substrategus waited while Kavi's wrists were untied, with the patience of a serpent.

Kavi rubbed his wrists and said nothing. Garren's thin mouth twitched in a semblance of a smile. "Decimaster Raiban says you might be able to provide us with information."

"Aye." Kavi took a breath. They both knew what he was bargaining for. "I'm a peddler. But my wares aren't city fancy—journeymen and apprentice pieces. So I sell in the countryside, north and south of the Trade Road. I know the back roads, the trails, the shortcuts. Terrain."

Soldiers cared about terrain, didn't they? He hoped he wasn't babbling.

Substrategus Garren's face gave nothing away. The other officer had come to stand behind him. His expression was somber, but Kavi saw a shadow of pity in his eyes. Not a good sign.

"There's something else I know. About the high commander's daughter. And it's political information too. . . ."

He told the lady Soraya's story from the beginning, bringing out any aspect he thought might interest them. Garren was paying attention now. Or, at least, he was frowning.

"Do your people actually believe in these djinn?" he asked when Kavi finished.

"Not my folk," said Kavi. He was sweating, despite the cool afternoon. The light had gone dimmer as he spoke. Soon it would be raining. "Not even the deghans, really, though I think they did long ago. Now it's just a . . . an echo from the old times. Or a convenient excuse."

"Your folk. You're different from the deghans?"

"So the stories say," Kavi replied. "They say in the ancient days we made a pact: our ancestors to serve and farm, and the deghans to fight and rule. To protect us." Sarcasm bled into his voice, despite his care, and he bit his lip. This man was too dangerous for sarcasm—or any other form of wit.

"Hmm."

Judging by his lifted brows, Garren heard it anyway. Not a stupid man. Pity.

"So you feel the deghans are not 'your folk.' I notice you betrayed this Soraya to me very lightly."

Am I having a choice? "I don't care about her," said Kavi. "I care nothing for any of them." The truth of it rang in his voice. Could they hear it? Would it save him?

The other officer, a younger man than Garren, perhaps in his thirties, spoke for the first time. "What happened to your hand?"

One look at their faces told Kavi that prevarication would cost him his life. He swallowed. "I was a journeyman smith. Usually working with iron—like I said, just a journeyman—but my master was a weapon-smith. The best in Mazad."

"Mazad. That's the walled city, isn't it?"

That had caught the bastard's interest, right enough, but Kavi set his teeth. Mazad, he wouldn't betray. But telling them things that were common knowledge could do no harm—and might save his life.

"Aye, Mazad's walled. Whenever one of the high nobles takes a fancy to become gahn himself, first thing he does is seize Mazad. It's where most of the metal is worked, just like Desafon works wood. You can field an army without furniture but you can't without swords or javelins and arrowheads or armor. So one of the old gahns walled Mazad, and the governor makes sure that whatever craft strays outside the walls, tanning or weaving or whatever, the smithies are all inside."

Garren and the young officer exchanged a glance that Kavi couldn't interpret. "I see. Go on."

"Well, I was a smith, like I was saying, but one day this deghan came to the shop."

Walking in without a knock or a call, as if it was being his place and not another man's. Of course, a lot of them walked in without asking permission, but there was something about this one. He moved all tense and edgy, and his eyes glittered like a man in fever, though he didn't seem to be ill.

"I was minding the counter that day; my master was back in the forge, working with the younger ones. This deghan came in and said he needed a sword. The best we had."

They all asked for the best. Kavi hadn't wanted to bring the sword out, but the man had done nothing wrong by his own lights, and Kavi knew his master would be rightly angry if he missed a sale because the man *felt* wrong.

"I brought out the best sword we had. A good one."

Kavi's master had worked over it for months, not just the gleaming, perfect curve of the blade, but the flaring bronze guard, the perfect fit of the hilt to a man's hand. Kavi sometimes felt he'd learned more from watching him make that one sword than in all the years that had preceded it.

"He wanted to be testing it, of course, so I showed him the proving block, and he struck with the blade, the point, even the flat. I wasn't worried. It had been proved before. But he tried the blade over and over."

Hacking chips from the block like he wanted to kill it, like the battered log was a deadly enemy. Like that beautiful sword was just an ax.

"I got worried then, so I went and stood by the door, so he couldn't just walk out."

Garren's face was still indifferent, but the young officer frowned, seeing where this would lead. Any fool could have seen it. Why hadn't Kavi?

"He said it was good enough, that he'd be taking it," Kavi went on. "I told him the price was twenty-two gold eagles." Kavi had to stop and swallow, for his mouth was dry, just as it had been then. He'd barely been able to name the price.

"He said he'd come back later with the money. I said he could get the sword then. That we'd hold it for him."

A flare of anger had suddenly made it possible to speak and move. Not even a deghan should be able to walk into an honest man's shop, take what he pleased, and walk out without paying. Not while Kavi was there.

"He said he needed it now and that we'd get paid soon enough. I said no, I'd see his money before the sword left the shop."

He'd thought of calling his master and the boys, the neighbors, but he'd feared for them. He was too angry by now to fear for himself.

"Then he laughed, like he'd just been bluffing. Like he didn't care. He said, 'Take it, then,' and he held out the blade. I grabbed it, hard, meaning to wrench it away before he could do anything."

He'd been strong in those days, from swinging the heavy hammer. He'd been so certain he could twist the sword from the man's grasp.

"But he was ready for me. As soon as I grabbed tight, he pulled the sword toward him."

Kavi opened his hand and held it out. Even in the dimness, the scar showed, ridged and vivid, though it was white now with the passage of years. He had looked at his palm in astonishment then, seeing yellow bone at the bottom of the cut before blood welled to hide it. Before the pain hit and he began to scream.

"He took the sword. Seems he and a cousin both expected to inherit from some uncle, and the cousin did. He said the cousin forged the will or something. I don't know. But he'd been left without a tin foal. I think there was something else between them as well. He killed the cousin and then paid the temple enough to 'exorcise Gorahz.' He came back and paid for the sword. Said it had done good service. He even threw in three extra eagles. 'For your trouble,' he said."

It had happened almost four years ago, but the anger still burned—forge-fire hot. The tent was silent, except for the patter of rain on the roof. When had it started raining? Kavi could have gone on, but he knew these men wouldn't care about the painful stitching and the long, slow healing that ultimately hadn't healed enough.

"So you lost your living?" Garren asked.

"Aye." Kavi flexed and curled his fingers as far as they'd go—not quite fully open and not fully closed. "I got some movement back, but my grip's too weak to hold either hammer or tongs. But my master didn't abandon me. It was his idea for me to take some of the lesser goods around the countryside, instead of throwing them back in the melt. It's mostly from his shop that I get what I sell."

His master had offered to pay the surgeon's fee from his own pocket, and to support Kavi through his healing, but Kavi had refused. If his master wouldn't let him go after the bastard and throw his money in his face, it might as well be put to use. There had been enough left over to buy Duckie and to pay his master for the first load of goods.

"I can see why you've no loyalty to the deghans," said Garren. "So perhaps you could be trusted to serve us."

"How much are you paying?" said Kavi with well-feigned interest. "Good service costs —"

Garren's face darkened.

"All right, serve you how? I might be willing, but it depends on what you want me to do."

And whether it will give me a chance to escape.

"What we want is simple," said Garren. "We need information about the Farsalan army: their numbers, movements, and plans. It appears that through your link to the girl, you'll have access to their commander."

"Access to speak to him, maybe," said Kavi. "But I'm not a warrior, and he—"

Garren held up a hand. "We aren't asking you to serve as an assassin. If nothing else, that kind of thing has . . . limited value. All that killing the high commander would achieve is the appointment of another commander. One whom our spy would have no excuse to approach."

"Your spy," said Kavi slowly. "You don't think I'm young for that?" Most Farsalans thought him young to be a peddler, on his own.

"Our soldiers come to us younger than you," said Garren calmly. "And if you're not our spy, then you're nothing but a liability. You claim to have no love for the deghans. If you serve us well, bringing true and timely information, we will pay you. But be warned, we have other spies, and anything you tell us will be checked against other sources. If you lie, you'll be killed. But the Iron Empire knows how to reward those who serve it— and in one year from the time of the first battle, Farsala will belong to the empire."

Kavi shrugged. "I don't have much choice, do I?"

"No," said Garren. "You could flee, in the short term, but once the empire conquers your land, be assured we would find you."

And a peddler with a crippled hand would be easy to find. Curse the nobles, did they all think alike, no matter where they came from? Of course they did. To them, a peasant was just something to be used.

"But the empire rewards loyal service," said the young officer suddenly. "In any man, of any rank. That's why . . . Do you know that in many of the lands we've conquered, the common citizens, your 'folk,' I think you'd call them, have welcomed us? Even risen to fight their rulers in our support?"

Kavi grimaced. "I'm sure they have." Given the same choice he'd been given, who wouldn't?

"No," said the young officer, seemingly reading his thoughts. "It's because they know that in the empire the law is the same for all, rich or poor. What happened to you"—he gestured to Kavi's hand—"well, it might have happened; but in our lands the perpetrator would have been charged with theft and assault. If he was found guilty, he'd have been heavily fined and beaten or maimed himself. For the murder of his cousin, he'd have been executed. And as one of his victims, you would have been compensated."

Substrategus Garren rose to his feet. "I'll leave him to you, Patrius. Come back tomorrow and tell me his decision—and your estimate of his sincerity."

"Yes, sir." The younger officer, Patrius, reached down to help Kavi to his feet. "This way, peddler."

He stopped at the doorway to fasten his cloak and pull up the hood, and Kavi did the same. The rain was coming down with dreary steadiness. It was cold.

"Where are we going?" Kavi asked, following Patrius obediently. He was very aware that his hands and feet were free, but in the middle of the whole Hrum army it wasn't going to do him much good. Dozens of scarlet-cloaked figures bustled through the muddy streets, despite the weather.

"My tent, I think," said Patrius. "We can find both dryness and quiet there."

Patrius' tent was only a bit farther away, multi-roomed, like Garren's, though smaller. It was still far larger than the tents of the common soldiers.

"You talk fine about just laws for the . . . common citizens, but you're not exactly being one yourself, are you?" Kavi looked at the well-made chairs and a traveling desk that looked very like the one belonging to the substrategus.

Patrius shrugged. "I'm a tactimian. That means I lead a company of a thousand men. This is what the army provides for tactimians. But my father was a wool merchant, and his father was a butcher."

Kavi felt his jaw drop. He almost exclaimed in disbelief, but the leader of a thousand men was blowing up the coals in his brazier and adding more charcoal as if he did it every day.

"How does a merchant's son become a warrior?" he demanded, shedding his damp cloak.

"By rising in the army," said Patrius. He seemed to be trying for Garren's cool indifference, but he couldn't quite bring it off. There was a man under that officer-to-spy demeanor. Perhaps a good one. "I should tell you that everyone qualified to serve is required to enlist in the army from age eighteen to age twenty-three. I understand that's not true of your Farsala."

Qualified to serve. Well, that leaves peasants out. "Only the deghans fight," Kavi confirmed. "And their half-blood bastards and their descendants serve as foot soldiers and archers. My folk don't have it in them to be warriors. But there were women in the troop that brought me in, and that's something even deghasses don't do. Though I've met one who had the temper for it," he finished ruefully.

"Women aren't required to serve in the army," said Patrius. "Though they aren't turned away, as long as they can pass the physical challenges. If they can fight, and want to, the empire sees no reason not to let them."

"That seems . . . odd to me."

"There's a lot about the empire that may seem strange to you," said Patrius. "At first."

At first it did. Miracles of engineering, like league after league of raised, paved roads. Aqueducts that carried streams through the air and even furnaces that poured hot water through pipes inside a house were marvels, true enough. But a tax system that was consistent and fair to all? Laws that applied equally to the imperial governor and the lowest beggar?

Kavi was peddler enough to recognize a pitch when he heard it. But he'd heard some of the same things from the traders he'd spoken to—and, unlike Patrius, they had no reason to lie to him.

"The laws even apply to conquered people,"

Patrius added. "The moment we establish sufficient control of the countryside to begin collecting taxes, you become a citizen of the empire, with all the rights, and obligations, that entails."

"Aye," said Kavi skeptically. "But I've heard of how armies go 'collecting taxes' unofficially, before law comes. And they do things worse than looting, too." He met Patrius' eyes directly—no army in the history of the world conquered without rape. If Patrius claimed that the Hrum never raped conquered women, then Kavi would know he was lying.

Patrius sighed. "Some looting goes on, but it's illegal; if the person who's been robbed goes to the unit commander and complains, his goods will be restored to him and a fine levied. As for rape . . . I can't say it never happens, but first offenders are beaten and fined. Second offenders are beaten again and cast out of the army, and a third offense of that nature is punished by death."

Kavi rubbed his chin. "Among my folk it's much the same. Among deghans . . . well, they don't approve it, but they can get themselves off of charges by claiming that Drazan possessed them."

"Drazan?" said Patrius curiously.

"The djinn of violent lust," Kavi told him. "They've a djinn for every crime, the deghans."

Patrius shook his head. "I can't imagine basing any kind of legal system on . . . Well, there are different customs among many of the lands of the empire. Your deghans' djinn may survive as a local custom or faith, but they'll have no more force in law."

"But if a man's been cast out of your army, how could you recognize a third offender?" asked Kavi.

Patrius snorted. "You won't ask that when you know us better. First, we tattoo them. There's a different mark for every crime for which keeping track of offenses matters. And we find out a lot about anyone's legal history, even if they're not marked. The empire keeps more records than any people in the history of the world. They say that the empire rests, not on the swords of its soldiers, but on the pens of its scriveners. When I'm signing five sets of requisition forms, I curse them for it."

"You said some local customs survive," said Kavi. "Tell me, how do the Hrum feel about entering a man's house?"

"What do you mean?"

"Do you rap on the door or just be going in?" Kavi knew his voice was too intense, but it mattered.

Patrius frowned, obviously not understanding why the question was important. "We follow local custom in such matters. In the army you stand outside the tent and announce yourself, but outside . . . In some of the empire's lands people open the door and call to the inhabitants; in others they just enter. In Brishat they hang a stick on a hook beside the door, and you tap the door with the stick. They've got a code: Two raps, pause, two raps means it's a business matter; three without pause indicates a social visit. People who come to a house often will devise a personal knock, so the inhabitants know who's there. Outside of our own camp we follow the local cus —"

"Tactimian Patrius?" called a voice from outside the tent.

Patrius responded. Kavi recognized the Hrum word for "yes," though the babble that followed defeated him. But for once he was to get a translation. Patrius turned toward him in bemusement. "They're looking for you," he said. "It seems there's a . . . problem with your mule."

"YOU HAVE A DUCK POND?" said Kavi incredulously. "In the middle of an army camp?" He stared at the lapping water and the flapping, quacking inhabitants.

"We keep them for eggs," murmured Patrius absently. "If they've got a pond, they scatter less than chickens do. Your mule thinks she's a duck?"

"Near as I can figure it." Kavi sighed, eyeing the one inhabitant of the pond who wasn't quacking. The square pool was obviously artificial. Duckie was only belly-deep in the water, though perhaps the rain made up for it; she looked ridiculously content, ears flopped forward, as she watched the fleet of ducks maneuvering around her. Three perched on her back.

"A local custom?" Patrius' face was commendably grave, but his eyes were alive with laughter. The scarlet-cloaked soldiers who'd braved the rain to see the show were grinning.

"No." Kavi sighed again. "It's just her. Or, no, it's not just her. Watch."

He pulled off his boots and waded into the pond, knowing from long experience that not even honeyed oatcakes could tempt Duckie from the water. The mule waited till Kavi was almost within reach of her halter, then she spun and splashed away, followed by a flotilla of chuckling admirers.

At least the pond's bottom was level and regular. Kavi managed to corner Duckie and catch her lead rope without falling in, though in this rain it hardly mattered. He led Duckie out amid a chorus of indignant quacks and sloshed up the muddy bank to pick up his boots.

"Where do you want her?" he asked the snickering herdsman.

The man gestured for Kavi to follow him. Most of the ducks abandoned the parade as the pond fell out of sight, but four of them, deeply smitten, followed the mule right into the corral. One determined duck, with brown-and-white speckled feathers, maintained its perch on Duckie's rump, complaining loudly about the motion.

"Hold," said the herdsman in heavily accented Farsalan. "Will not they be stepped upon?"

"Not likely," said Kavi. "Most mules and horses just avoid them. They sometimes get kicked. You can chase them back to the pond if you want, but they'll just be coming back—and bringing a friend or two, like as not. Your best bet is to let them be."

"You sound as if you've had this problem before?" Patrius turned to lead Kavi back to the tent. Kavi was glad to go. He was soaked top and bottom by now, and the mud was cold on his bare feet.

"Oh, aye. Every village where there's a duck pond. Folk are mostly used to her by now, so it's not much of a problem. The worst is if we're near a swamp or a lake. It can be cursed hard to catch her there, and the ducks . . . Have you ever been pecked by a duck?"

"No." Patrius gave up the battle and started to laugh. "No, I haven't."

"Well, it hurts," said Kavi, beginning to grin himself. "They like her as much as she likes them, you see."

"I begin to think," said Patrius, holding the tent flap aside for Kavi to enter, "that Farsala will be an interesting addition to the empire."

PATRIUS SENT A MAN — a *slave*? — for a basin of warm water and dry clothes. As Kavi cleaned up and dried off, Patrius explained that the Hrum didn't attempt to banish or change local customs in any matters except those covered by the law. Customs of marriage and courtship, of inheritance, of religion and holiday, would all remain the same, and the Hrum occupying force would be forced to conform to them. The exceptions, in which imperial law prevailed over local custom, were crimes of theft or violence, which Patrius said were generally held to be crimes in all the lands the Hrum had conquered. They had taken twenty-eight countries and independent city-states in their centuries of expansion. Patrius went on to talk about how these countries had thrived under the empire, how their trade had expanded, and how their people—now citizens of the empire—had been endowed with all the rights, duties, and taxes that citizenship entailed.

"Taxes aren't always low," Patrius admitted. "But they are fairly levied as a proportion of a man's wealth. They may rise in those years that the empire needs more funding, but they usually fall in the next. And they're never high enough to cripple a business or a farm—the emperor knows full well that money begets money, and the government only consumes it."

"So all citizens pay your taxes," said Kavi. "Rich and poor?"

"Yes, and in the same percentage. It's one of the obligations of being a citizen."

"What about those who aren't citizens?" Kavi asked. "At least, I'm told your folk keep slaves." And surely that was a thing no righteous folk could justify.

"We do," Patrius admitted. "It's how we deal with those we capture in battle. They're enslaved and sent to other lands. But even though they aren't citizens, the law still protects them. There are legal limits, strictly enforced, regarding how much labor can be required of them, how they can be punished, and no child can be taken from its mother before the age of thirteen."

"We send boys to be apprenticed at twelve often enough," Kavi murmured. Could there be differences in slavery? Hrum slavery sounded very different from the tales told by escaped Kadeshi slaves, who were often horribly abused and had no protection at all. And the Kadeshi peasants weren't much better off. From the sound of it, a Kadeshi peasant might welcome the life of a Hrum slave.

"They can also earn their freedom," Patrius added. "Though it takes years and much labor, and many never do. And even if they win their freedom and become citizens, they're never allowed to return to their own land. It sounds harsh, but removing those who might rebel is our way of keeping the peace for those who remain. Can you understand that, peddler?"

They went on to talk of how the Hrum governed. Kavi wasn't pleased to learn that the commander of the army who conquered a land became its governor and that Garren, as substrategus, would command the army that would march into Farsala.

"There are reasons for it," Patrius explained. "It's held that in order to conquer a land within the time allowed, a commander will be forced to learn to understand the people. And if a commander, or even an imperial governor, abuses his power, the emperor will appoint another in his place."

Kavi shrugged. Farsala had had bad gahns in the past. And those gahns hadn't been checked by any law.

Patrius questioned Kavi as well, about his past, his feelings toward his country, but Kavi thought the questions he asked the tactimian revealed more about what he was thinking than any answer he gave.

The lamps were guttering when Patrius yawned and rolled out a bedroll on the floor, leaving Kavi to think things over.

Rain pattered on the canvas roof. It had been a fine job of selling, no question, Kavi acknowledged, staring into the darkness. But try as he might, he hadn't caught Patrius in any contradiction or in any statement that went counter to what little Kavi knew of the empire from the traders' tales.

And Patrius had freely confirmed the worst thing Kavi had heard of the empire: The Hrum kept slaves. But according to Patrius, they treated them far better than the Kadeshi did.

Did that matter? Even the deghans didn't keep slaves. But sometimes they treated their own peasants almost as badly.

Kavi could still escape. For all Garren's threats—and the bastard had meant them, no doubt of that—Kavi could escape. The villagers knew and trusted him. They'd hide him from the Hrum without hesitation.

But did he want to escape? The Hrum kept slaves, but they would only enslave the people who fought them—the deghans. Was it worth risking his life just to prevent a change of masters?

Especially when the Hrum might be better masters?

Garren wouldn't be a good master.

Kavi turned onto his side, trying to get comfortable on the hard earth beneath the canvas floor, though he'd slept soundly on harder ground than this.

In the deep silence that comes before dawn, Kavi faced the truth: Whether the Hrum would make better masters or not, they would take down the deghans. Those haughty, ruthless bastards would be humbled. They would pay, for once, for all the wrongs they'd done—and not only to Kavi himself. He had dreamed of vengeance for years but had pushed the thought aside, knowing that vengeance would destroy him long before he could really harm the deghans. The thought that he could actually bring them down made him dizzy with desire.

He had to be careful, he knew. He'd seen Garren's like before—Kavi's life meant less to him than the rugs beneath his feet. He came cheaper than the rugs, Kavi realized with a rueful grin. But that didn't mean he couldn't get what *he* wanted out of the bargain.

AFTER JUST A FEW MARKS of sleep Kavi was wakened by a soldier and went to give Substrategus Garren his answer.

"Aye, I'll spy for you. Do you want me going for information now? It'd be less suspicious if I go on my regular rounds and make contact with the high commander when I'm supposed to."

"As long as we get the information we need before spring, that should be adequate," said Garren. He'd showed neither surprise nor pleasure at Kavi's choice. He'd be Strategus Garren soon. A chilling thought. "You may work out the details with my aides." There were several in the tent today. Garren's gaze fixed on Patrius. "Take him out and mark him as ours, Tactimian. Then send him on his way. You may go."

Patrius led him from the tent.

"Mark me?" Kavi asked.

"A tattoo," said Patrius. "Here, on your shoulder. Show it to any Hrum, and you'll be identified as our agent. It will also gain you instant access to an officer, if you say your news is urgent."

"Aye, and identify me as a traitor in every bathhouse."

"So avoid public baths," said Patrius. "No, seriously, it's not a mark that many associate with the empire. No one in your land should recognize it for anything but decoration. And later on, you'll be proud of it. It's similar to the mark we award any civilian who performs a special service for the Empire. Like our rank marks in the army, only for people who aren't sodiers."

He pulled up his sleeve to show his own shoulder. He bore the same slashing bars that had marked the Hrum who captured Kavi, but there were other marks above them, squares and diamonds, in increasingly elaborte patterns that no doubt proclaimed "tactimian," if you knew how to read them.

"We decorate our houses and furniture," said Kavi, "not our skin."

"So . . . ?" Patrius prompted.

His first test as a spy. Kavi sighed. "So I must have met a trader from a distant land who talked me into trying it."

He would be lying a lot in the future. But he'd always been a good liar and never for a better purpose. Time's Wheel would tip the deghans down into the Flame, and as for his folk . . . In the long run his folk would have laws that protected them from their rulers, instead of the other way around. In the short run . . . In the short run Kavi would lie for all he was worth, and when they paid him, maybe he'd give the money away to some poor family who'd been harmed by the war. Maybe. Some of it.

CHAPTER ELEVEN

JIAAN

RAIN DANCED ON THE ROOF and dripped off the eaves, but the smith had kindled the forge for his morning's work before the high commander had commandeered the smithy for this meeting, so inside it was warm and dry. The smith had been resigned to giving up his workplace for the afternoon, even before Jiaan had paid him; afterward he'd gone home whistling.

Most of the villagers of Alberz had responded that way when the Farsalan army descended and took over their homes for an unknown number of weeks. Yes, it was awkward living in the barn, but the high commander had not only ordered compensation for all whose houses were occupied, he had set the payment high enough that most of the villagers were philosophical about it. The poorer folk were delighted.

Even when Jiaan encountered those who resented the army's presence, he couldn't feel too sorry about the situation. The winter rains had been falling for about two months now, and the thought of living in pavilions in this weather made him cringe. A brazier could only do so much.

And Jiaan should know. The commander's household had spent most of the last several months living in pavilions as the commander went through the land slowly gathering his forces — drilling them when he could but mostly bringing them together in this out-of-the-way village near the border so that this first meeting could take place.

"Attend to me, deghans." The words were formal, but the high commander's voice was relaxed, for all its firmness. He had once told Jiaan that controlling a tactical conference among deghans was like trying to herd sheep who had a bull's temper and a leopard's armament. "Get them upset, they'll do nothing but mill in circles and snort. Get them angry, and they'll claw you to ribbons. The trick," he'd said, "is to make them want to follow."

They're following now, more or less, Jiaan thought as they came slowly from the warmth of the forge over to the long worktable that the smith and his apprentices had cleared under Jiaan's direction. He took his place behind the commander, with his pen and parchment, and prepared to take notes. The deghans had all been told to bring only one aide to this conference, so, of course, some of them had brought two.

At least the rest of the commander's aides were absent. Jiaan had hoped that the success of his mission might win him . . . well, not their liking. And their respect was far too much to hope for. But perhaps some tolerance? Some acknowledgment that he was, if not their equal, at least competent in the rank to which his father had promoted him. If anything, his success had intensified their dislike. If it hadn't been so absurd, Jiaan would have thought they were jealous.

Most of the aides at this meeting were the oldest sons of the deghans they served—near strangers to Jiaan, which was good. But it did make Jiaan's resemblance to his father a bit embarrassing.

If the commander noticed, he didn't care.

"As you all know by now," the commander began, "the Hrum have taken Sendan."

"I heard the fighting's still going on," put in Gafrid, his deep voice rumbling over the words. "It'll be a long time, surely, before they actually hold the country, even if they're said to be winning now."

At least with Gafrid, it was an honest objection, not a challenge.

"In part, that's true," said the commander. "But in part, it's not. My information is that the Hrum have taken all the major cities. There's some resistance in the countryside, but not enough to stop them from leaving occupying troops behind and moving on Farsala when they choose.

"And that brings up the most critical point of all: our need for accurate information about when the Hrum plan to come into Farsala and where they'll go once they've done so. The first battle between us is absolutely critical, because —"

"What do you mean, where they go once they come into Farsala?" It was Barmayon, stubby and truculent. But he wasn't part of Garshab's faction either, Jiaan knew. Perhaps that was because he was so dense that even Garshab wouldn't have him. "If we stop them at the wall, we don't have to worry about where they want to go next."

"Barmayon," said the commander, "do I have to explain to you that it's not our wall?"

Everyone chuckled, even Barmayon. "Well, of course we can't stop them from coming through it. Gate opens from their side. But we could stop them from going one step farther. They can only send, what, twenty through those gates at a time? So let them face forty of us. Or, better yet, let our archers pile them up till they can't climb over the bodies anymore."

"That's an excellent idea," said the commander politely. "If they come through the wall, we'll certainly do as you suggest. But that may occur to them as well, so instead of coming through the gate, they'll probably make their way through the foothills beyond the wall, where they can maneuver for their own tactical advantage. In those hills their infantry will have the advantage over our chargers."

Faces all around the table scowled, but no one

could deny it. The Sendar had built the wall to tax wagons on the Great Trade Road, not to stop armies.

"But that brings up another point, Commander Merahb." Hormaz's voice was smooth in the sullen silence. Jiaan's neck prickled. Hormaz was one of Garshab's most loyal followers. "If the Hrum can bring an army through the foothills, so can we. If the Kadeshi hadn't kept us busy, we could have taken Sendan ourselves anytime in the last hundred years."

"The Kadeshi—and the fact that every gahn who has taken up the simarj banner has bound himself to truce with Sendan," said the commander dryly. "A truce they have never broken either."

"Yes, but that can hardly be said of the Hrum," Hormaz objected. "Surely the warrior's way is to keep them from ever setting foot in Farsala. We circle around through the hills and ambush their camp on Sendar soil. Or, even better, split the army in two—send one half through the hills and the other around by sea to hit them from both sides! We could smash them beyond recovery and send their weeping survivors home to their emperor, to beg him not to send anyone else to die at our hands."

Enthusiasm rumbled through the room like distant thunder. *So that's Garshab's plan,* Jiaan thought with a shudder. It was like him. Flashy, complex, and impractical. Thank Azura the commander was still in charge.

"That's an interesting idea, Hormaz," said the commander. "Except for two things."

"The only requirements I can see are the mighty arms of Farsala's deghans, and a commander with the steel for it," said Hormaz. "Which of those do you think we lack?"

"Oh, I wasn't thinking about might or steel." How could he sound so calm, so assured? "But judging by the last few weeks' maneuvers, this army couldn't coordinate a two-pronged attack on this forge. What will you do if your half an army comes thundering down out of the hills and finds that the other half's ships hit a contrary wind and are two days late? Or you're bringing your men up the coast and suddenly realize that the horsemen had to go around one too many canyons and that they're still a day's ride away?"

Hormaz opened his mouth, but the commander

lifted a hand to cut him off. "Yes, I know you can send out scouts and messengers to try to keep your forces coordinated, but do you think the Hrum have no scouts or messengers or spies? They'd march out to meet the army, the half army, nearest to them, defeat it, and then defeat the other half. And in Sendan they could bring us to battle at a time of their choosing, on ground that favors them. Not to mention that their supply lines would be close and solid, and ours wouldn't."

"A good commander, with the heart for a bold plan, could deal with all these things," Hormaz insisted. But this time only Barmayon looked enthusiastic, and all around the table gazes lowered.

In the maneuvers the commander had run over the last few months, the deghans had shown themselves to be skilled and courageous fighters. As individuals, Jiaan thought dryly, he'd be terrified to face any of them. As a group, they had little more discipline than a herd of stampeding cattle.

Most of the warriors didn't see that, Jiaan knew. To them, a battle was simply to charge the enemy, wound or slay him, and move on to the next. But the high nobles in this room, who were trying to make the proposed battle plans work, were beginning to see the weakness that sprang from the Farsalan inability to fight as a unit.

"Our deghans," said the commander gently, "are the best and bravest fighters the world has ever seen. On our chargers we are invincible . . . as warriors. But none of us is Sorahb reborn, and we've been fighting Kadeshi raiders for too long. To fight an army like the Hrum's, we have to fight together, to share the battle between us instead of snatching for glory like greedy children.

"But there's an even more pressing reason than that to let the Hrum pass the wall. Because only after they've attacked us, on our soil, does their time limit begin. After the first battle in Farsala the Hrum commander has one year to conquer this country; if he fails, they will never attack us again."

"What?" Jiaan wasn't certain how many voices chimed in. His might have been one of them.

The commander smiled. "This is the advantage of good intelligence, my friends. The Hrum try not to let it be known among the lands in their path, but their commanders are given a time limit—one year from the day of the first battle. If at the end of that year they do not control all cities, large towns, and most of the countryside, their army is withdrawn, and negotiations begin for the country they attacked to become an independent, allied state."

"An allied state? What in the name of all djinn is that?" It was Garshab himself, startled out of his appearance of neutrality.

"It's just what it sounds like," Commander Merahb replied. "The Hrum are a straightforward people in some ways. As an independent, allied state, we would retain our own rulers, levy our own taxes, and our laws would prevail, just as they do now. That's the independent part. Alliance means that we allow the Hrum to move their armies through our borders, in order to extend their reach beyond us."

"But if we allow them—"

A single lifted hand imposed silence on the babble of questions. "No, they will not attempt to attack us again. When the Hrum pass through the lands of an allied state, that's all they do—pass through. And in exchange for passage of their troops, they offer marvels of engineering and increased trade. And the right to levy taxes on the Trade Road would still be ours, though whether goods that went on to their army would be taxed is something the gahn would have to negotiate.

"On the other hand, if we choose not to admit their forces, they'd take ship along the coast, land on Kadeshi soil, and not trouble us with their passage. I've been told several of their allied states chose that alternative for the first few decades after they defeated the Hrum, and the Hrum abided by their decree . . . until they saw the advantages the alliance brought to those who trusted the Hrum and agreed to allow passage through their lands."

"This has to be a trick," Hormaz snarled. "A lie fed you by some paid informant, to get us to relax our guard so they can . . . can . . ."

"If it's a lie, it's an ill-designed one. It assures that we'll fight like lions for at least a year." Jandal had been silent till now, at the commander's request, Jiaan suspected. But it was hard to silence a man whose troops comprised almost one tenth of the army—the best-trained tenth. Jandal's lands were on the Kadeshi border.

"Where did you get this . . . this farrago?" Hormaz demanded.

"From merchants on the Trade Road," said the commander. "Men who had traveled through the empire, both conquered states and allied states, for many years, and who—"

"Merchants? Lying peasants! Bribed by the Hrum, beyond doubt."

"I asked every merchant I could seek out." The commander's voice grated with irritation. "For six years I've been asking. There were hundreds of merchants, and they all told the same tale. I don't think they were all in the Hrum's pay. And as Jandal says, why devise a lie that forces them to fight us for a year? Why not something that would persuade us to surrender at once?"

"But why quit after a year?" It was Gafrid's deep voice. "Why not just keep on till they conquer us?"

"I asked the merchants that question," said the commander. "They didn't know. A few had heard that one of the first states the Hrum conquered resisted so long, and so fiercely, that though the Hrum prevailed, their army was all but destroyed, and it took the land decades to recover. They said that long ago the emperor decided that it wasn't worth it and to . . . well, to pick only the fights they could win."

A ripple of contemptuous laughter swept the crowd.

"Don't underestimate them!" said Merahb sharply. "The Hrum have conquered twenty-eight countries over the last few centuries, and there are only *four* allied states. Only four in thirty-two have managed to resist them for just one year. The commander they send against us, whoever he is, will be very aware of his time limit. My friends, we are in for a year of the most bitter fighting imaginable. The Hrum can draw on the resources, the manpower, of twenty-eight lands. They are vastly experienced in conquering others, and all we've had to fight off were the forays of Kadeshi warlords. The traders even say that the Hrum have swords made of steel that is far stronger than ours."

His eyes swept the silent crowd.

"But I say a sword is only as strong as the arm that wields it. I say that no man afoot can stand against the might of our chargers. I say that other lands build walls of stone, but Farsala has a wall of warriors—warriors who will shatter any who come against them like surf on rock. We are Farsala's wall!"

Cheers rebounded off the rafters. The deghans pounded one another's shoulders and stamped their feet. They would follow him anywhere now. But it occurred to Jiaan that a weapon-smith might have something to say about the relative strength of steel. And a sword that breaks is useless in the mightiest fist.

"So you see," said the commander when the cheering finally died, "it's to our advantage to have the first battle on our soil. To attack them elsewhere would be to waste our strength before their year is even started. And especially, it is to our advantage to fight that battle on ground of our choosing, on ground that would give our chargers the advantage."

There followed a spirited discussion of tactics and terrain as the deghans debated what type of ground was best for a charge and how to bring the Hrum to battle at the place they chose.

Garshab was surly and silent, but Jiaan, watching him, remembered something.

"Sir?" He cleared his throat, hesitating. The other deghans ignored him, but Commander Merahb turned, drawing the others' attention as well.

"Yes, Jiaan?"

Jiaan took a deep breath. He'd never dared to speak up in conference before, but at least he sounded like a deghan. The commander had visited him often as a child and, when Jiaan was five, had decreed that he be tutored by a local clerk, not only to read and write, but to speak without a peasant's accent. He'd hated it as a boy, pulled from hunting lizards in the fields to sit in a stuffy office and repeat sentences. But he'd blessed his father for it a thousand times since.

"Sir, it occurs to me that if we could send men by sea and through the foothills, to attack from both sides, the Hrum might think to do the same."

"Nonsense!" Barmayon snorted impatiently. "The only place they could land would be Dugaz, and those swamp ruffians would make short work of them!"

The deghans laughed, and even the commander smiled. "Perhaps, my friend. But given what I know of Dugaz ruffians, they might just as easily decide that they don't fancy the odds and let the Hrum pass unhindered. The boy's right. I'll send Markhan and Kaluud to speak with the city governor and make certain that if the Hrum do land on our coast, at least we'll get warning."

Several nodded, and Jiaan made a note, concealing a deep and ignoble satisfaction. Neither Markhan nor Fasal had forgiven him for their embarrassment at the flags-and-lances match, and their attitude had infected Kaluud and most of the rest of the commander's aides. Having two of the worst offenders sent off to the swampy, fever-ridden rathole of Dugaz would make his life much simpler.

When the meeting ended, the deghans had a precise description of the terrain they wanted and had decided to send out scouts to find numerous places that might suit them for the first battle. Plans to lure the Hrum to the site they chose were a bit more nebulous, but the commander said they needed to scout the countryside first, anyway. Almost every foot of the Kadeshi border was known to Farsala's army, but it had been centuries since they'd fought on the western side of the realm. And they needed better intelligence about the Hrum's movements and plans, and they needed . . .

It occurred to Jiaan that it would be easier for the Hrum to choose ground that would put Farsala's chargers at a disadvantage, and then force the deghans to meet them there, than it would be for the deghans to force the Hrum to do anything. The deghans had to defend the cities, after all. The Hrum could choose their targets at will. But the commander knew that, so Jiaan said nothing.

Eventually the others filed out into the cold drizzle, still arguing enthusiastically, eager to begin the fight—the glorious year of war that would win them the honor of being the fifth land to defeat the Hrum. What marvelous advantages, what wealth would come to the rulers of an allied state?

The commander sat on the anvil, letting his weariness show as he watched Jiaan tidy his notes and roll the maps. "You look worried, lad."

"Well," said Jiaan, "it occurs to me that while there are four allied states, there are twenty-eight conquered ones. I wonder how many of them were certain that they could defeat the Hrum."

"All of them, probably," said the commander. "It's a warrior's greatest strength, to be certain he can win. You're not certain we can beat the Hrum?"

"No, sir," Jiaan admitted. Thus proving that he was a peasant, not a warrior, just like Fasal and Markhan had claimed.

"Thus proving," the Commander sighed, "that

you're smarter than all these boneheaded deghans put together." He laughed at Jiaan's expression. "The certainty that he can win may be a warrior's greatest strength, but it's a commander's greatest weakness. *I'm* worried about the Hrum. That's why it's so important that I be in command, not Garshab. But between my caution and the others' boneheaded toughness, we will beat them. I promise."

Jiaan nodded and smiled. But he couldn't help but wish that Farsala's previous gahns had provided them with a few stone walls.

CHAPTER TWELVE

SORAYA

SORAYA LEANED HER HEAD back in the tub and felt the ripples lapping around her shoulders. It was smaller than a proper bath— indeed, her knees were tucked up so high, they poked out of the water—but it was warm, and relaxing, and she was alone, which made her morning bath one of the best moments of the day.

She was in the tub earlier than usual this morning, for she'd awakened, as she almost always did, to the noise of Golnar stoking up the fire, pushing the bath kettle nearer to the flames, and beginning the day's baking. Eblis, the djinn of sloth, had no hold on Golnar. Soraya had finally become so accustomed to these sounds that she could usually go back to sleep, but not this morning. She knew the woman was already being as quiet as she could, but since the hearth was open to both her room and the big room that served for kitchen, dining, and all household work space, sounds carried through.

At least rising early meant she got the first bath. Soraya disliked soaking in water the others had used, even if they did wash themselves in the basin and rinse with tepid water, just as she had, before stepping into the steaming tub. But she also disliked waiting for over a mark while Golnar heated sufficient water to fill the tub afresh, so rising shortly after Golnar started work wasn't a bad . . .

Light bloomed on her eyelids, and they snapped up as the bathhouse door opened. She and Behram, the older of the two boys, stared at each other. The young lout hadn't even tapped! And it wasn't as if this was a public room, where anyone might enter unannounced.

Soraya grabbed the sides of the tub and rose, ignoring Behram's widening eyes. He was only thirteen. Who cared what a servant thought? She reached down, seized the basin of dirty, cooling rinse water, and hurled the contents at his face.

Her aim, she was pleased to observe, was as accurate as a deghass' should be. Behram yelled and stumbled back into the snowy yard. His hair dripped, and water ran down the front of his brightly embroidered shirt. Soraya stepped out of the tub, careful of her bare feet on the roughly sanded planks, and closed the door.

She climbed back into the tub gratefully, for the midwinter chill had raised goose bumps on her damp skin, despite the brazier in the corner. Sometimes Soraya thought the cold that came with the strange, frozen snow of the mountains wasn't as deeply chilling as the cold that came with the damp, winter drizzle of the lowlands. She actually liked the blizzard winds that screamed around the eaves, though she missed lightning and thunder. Of course, winter's slow drizzle seldom carried thunder with it either, and there were enough human storm sounds to make up the lack.

In many ways, Behram was like his father. He was growing into the same stocky, muscular build, with the same dour temperament. But where Behras was dour and silent, Behram bellowed like a bull ox.

"Ma, look what that . . . what *she* did to my shirt. And it was clean! All she had to do was ask me to go."

"Well, you should have been knocking, you great lump, and you know it. It's not like we've only family in the bathhouse these days. She's probably not used to sharing a bath at all."

In fact, Soraya shared the bathhouse at the manor with her own family and all the lesser members of the household, like her father's noble aides and the cousins who attended her mother. She had no objection to her servants using the tub—*after* she had done so.

"Aye, but this isn't being some great manor," Behram protested. "And she's not a great lady. Not anymore."

Soraya winced. *True enough, djinn take him.*

From the sound of the smack, and Behram's howl, Golnar had gone for an ear. She defended Soraya's exalted status in a way that was almost as wearing as Behram's attempts to ignore it.

Soraya found she couldn't recapture her earlier contentment, so she rose, dried herself, dressed, and went into the house. Behram had already gone, but Behras and Hejir were still at the table, eating the flat honeycakes that Golnar made in the morning. There was no scent of cooking meat, which meant they were out again. Well enough.

"I'll hunt today," Soraya announced, taking her place on the bench nearest to the warm hearth. It had become clear after just a few weeks that if there was to be meat on the table more than one day in five, it would be up to Soraya to provide it. Behras and Behram had tried, but they were hopeless. Hejir had been hopeless too, until Soraya started taking him along as her game carrier and taught him a bit.

"Can I go with you?" he asked now, mumbling around a mouthful of flatcake with the mannerlessness of any eleven-year-old boy. He was something of an imp, but he was also the only person in the house whose company Soraya enjoyed. Sometimes.

"Not today. I'm going down to the desert, so I won't be back till dark—perhaps not till late night, since the moon's almost full. That's too long for you."

Golnar sighed in a mixture of relief and disapproval, and Behras' tight lips echoed the same emotions. They disapproved of her going off by herself, understandably, since they were paid to look after her. On the other hand, they didn't trust her to look after Hejir properly, either. And everyone appreciated the game she brought back.

"But I could—"

"No." Soraya spoke with enough autocratic finality to silence him. Hunting was the only time she could be alone, and she wasn't in the mood for Hejir's chatter.

He scowled and turned back to his plate, and the meal ended in disapproving silence. Soraya didn't care. She'd long since taught both Golnar and Behras the futility of arguing with her.

It was as good as being married—maybe even better; though when Soraya wed, she'd be able to live in a wealthy man's manor, as well as run her own life. Surely her father wouldn't choose a husband less indulgent than he was himself. That is, if he managed to win his war and get back to her before she turned into a wrinkled hag.

After breakfast Soraya gathered up her bow, quiver, and the rest of her hunting gear and went to the stables to get a big satchel. Golnar had supplied enough bread, soft cheese, and dried fruit to feed a big man for days, but hunting made Soraya hungry enough that she'd eat most of it. And when she returned, with any luck, the bag would be full of game.

Hejir followed her out. "You certain you won't be taking me, Lady? I could carry for you."

"Not this time." She chose a satchel and pulled it off its peg. "I want to go alone."

"You never take me to the desert," Hejir complained.

He was right, so Soraya said nothing. Hejir sighed. "Is it true that in the flags-and-lances arena at the gahn's palace they're moving the trees and streams, and even the hills, about between matches?"

"Of course. How can it be difficult or exciting if everyone knows the best ground on which to fight or take shelter? Mind you, they're small hills. And the trees are small, with their roots in pots."

Hejir sighed again. "I'd like to see that someday."

"Perhaps you will," said Soraya. "Someday."

When the Hrum are defeated and Father comes for me. It had become almost a prayer, that phrase. A promise that soothed her heart and helped her endure.

"I'd like to see the desert someday too," said Hejir with the soulful longing of a child who wanted his way.

Soraya laughed. "Perhaps. *Someday.*"

But not with her.

She packed and made her way through the snowy forest, avoiding the deeper drifts with a determination born of having floundered in them. The only time she disliked snow was when she had to wade through it.

Soon she reached the entrance to the canyon that had led her up into these mountains months ago. It was a good way to go down, with only a few sheer bits—though far from fearing heights, Soraya loved them. She paused on one, placing her booted feet carefully on either side of the trickle that ran down the path here, and gazed out over the spires and rugged, mazelike gullies of the badlands. But mostly she noticed the space, endlessly open, stretching out beneath her like an invitation to take flight.

She couldn't, of course, but the desire sang in her heart.

Descending to the desert lightened her mood in other ways, for the seasons seemed to be reversed here. In the mountains all the world was frozen in sleep. In the plains where she'd grown up, the grass was brown and fallow, awaiting the warmth of spring. But in the desert, where the storms that were strong enough to scale the mountains produced rain instead of snow, it was as if spring had come with the onset of winter. The low grass that had been brown and parched when she first saw it was now green and growing. Even the prickly plants, for which she had no name, were putting on new growth. The canyons echoed with the sound of water racing down their narrow bottoms; the trees beside the new streams had new, green leaves. And everything was blooming.

Soraya had shed both her short cloak and her sheepskin vest by the time she reached the desert floor—one of the reasons she'd wanted a large satchel. Her skin was sweaty under the leather guard that protected her left forearm from the bowstring, but Soraya was accustomed to that. Up in the mountains it might be cold, but here it was more like a brisk spring day than early winter. And if it was this warm now, how hot would it be with the summer sun blazing down? Soraya sighed. She'd probably find out, not only this summer, but perhaps other summers to come. *Until the Hrum are defeated and Father comes . . .*

She missed her first shot, at a rabbit, but the arrow struck a soft patch of sand, so she was able to retrieve it intact. The nearest fletcher was in the nearby mining camp, and Behras grumbled about the price he charged. Not that it was Behras' money.

She wandered through the red-and-gold-walled valleys, keeping out of the muddy streambeds. She was careful to mark her backtrail, either with clear footprints or with a triangle of stones or twigs. Not that it was possible to become really lost, with that towering cliff to the south, but her father had taught her huntcraft, and she wouldn't shame his teaching by losing her way.

Eyes on the ground was the rule for both a hunter's footing and for tracking, but Soraya almost stumbled with astonishment when she came across the deep-cut, recent tracks of half a dozen gazelle. The graceful antelope of the desert were far smaller than the gazelle of the plains, but just one of them carried more flesh than dozens of rabbits. Enough to keep meat on the table for weeks! She'd seen their tracks before, but they were never recent enough to be useful. She could catch this herd.

Her father had taught her that excitement had no place in the hunt. Soraya took a deep breath, let her tension flow out with it, and began the stalk.

It took longer than Soraya expected to catch up with the herd, for they climbed easily up slopes that were difficult for her—especially since she was trying to be silent. But patience was part of the hunt too. She even took a moment to stop and wolf down some bread and soft cheese.

When she finally came upon the gazelle, they were grazing in a small gully, with one of the new, spring streams trickling down it. Crawling on her hands and knees, trying to avoid the prickly plants, Soraya slowly made her way toward a thicket of low, tangled trees. The gazelle's ears twitched occasionally at the small sounds she made, but when they became restless, Soraya stopped and waited till they quieted. Her bow was stronger than many women could pull, but it was far weaker than a man's—which meant she had to get closer to her prey. With rabbits, who froze in place when danger approached, it was easy. To get this close to a herd of gazelle was more than most men could manage. Soraya reached her blind and settled behind the thin screen of brush, watching the herd, picking her target. Some hunters went for the biggest, strongest buck, the meatiest doe, but her father had taught her to hunt as a predator hunts, taking the old or injured so the herd might thrive to produce more game.

Choosing a target was easy in this case; one doe limped on a leg that was visibly mangled. She was thinner than the others already, but not so thin as to be worthless to a hunter. Not yet.

Moving slowly, Soraya strung her bow, then nocked an arrow and sighted down it. She needed a clear path through the brush — and, at this distance, a bit of height — to allow the arrow to fall to its target. She followed the doe with her arrow for long moments before the shot came clear, then she drew back the arrow, feeling the pull in her shoulders and back as the bow flexed, and loosed.

Too high! She knew it the moment the arrow left the string, and she bit her lip in helpless regret as the arrow hissed over the doe's striped back and shattered on the rocks behind it.

The gazelle jumped at the snap of the string and the crack of the arrow, skittering in all directions, looking for the source of the sounds.

Soraya froze, bow in hand. She was downwind. If she didn't move, they wouldn't see her.

A long time passed before the herd settled and

still longer before their wariness faded enough that Soraya could draw and nock another arrow.

Not so high this time, just a few inches above the crippled doe's shoulders. Now wait till she turns broadside . . . wait, wait. Not yet, brush in the way.

The doe tore up a mouthful of grass, chewed it, took a few limping steps, and turned to the left. *Clear shot! Now!*

The arrow leaped from the string and hurtled across the distance to pierce the doe's side, knocking her over, feet thrashing.

The time for stealth was past. Soraya jumped up and hurried to her prey.

It was probably dead by the time she reached it, but its legs still twitched, so Soraya drew her knife and cut its throat. Blood spurted, but not in rhythm with a beating heart. *Dead. Good.*

Soraya had hunted with girls, and even grown women, who flinched and squealed at death, but she had no patience with them. Where did the silly things think meat came from, anyway? Still, she grimaced as she turned the doe so that she could reach its belly. She'd refused to clean game at first. That was for servants. But having servants to do it meant she had to bring at least Hejir with her, and her privacy was worth the sacrifice of some dignity. She'd let Hejir teach her to clean game, just as she was teaching him to track and stalk, and she'd become almost accustomed to blood on her hands and clothes, though the messiness of it still disgusted her.

More blood than usual this time, Soraya realized. A desert gazelle might be smaller than one of the plains, but it couldn't possibly fit in her satchel. After some thought she finished cutting through its throat and severed its head—why carry more weight than she had to?

She let the gazelle's corpse bleed out as much as possible while she put on her sheepskin vest. Not only would it pad her shoulders, but she'd gotten chilled waiting for her shot. She packed her bow and quiver, then lifted the doe onto her shoulders with an unladylike grunt of effort. *Weeks* of meat for the table. But not so heavy that she couldn't get it back up the trail.

Soraya bent carefully to pick up her satchel and set out. One of winter's truths, in both the desert and the plains, was that the days were short. She had perhaps two or three candlemarks before darkness fell, but as she'd told her keepers, the moon would be near full tonight. Even in the woods, it would shed enough light to let her make it home. It would be cold in the mountains after dark, though. *So step up the pace.*

Soraya walked briskly. She had no need for silence now, and she could take easier routes around obstacles she'd been forced to climb in pursuit of the herd, so she made good time. Between the noise she made and her focus on haste, it was some time before she noticed that she was being stalked.

What sound had reached her, she never knew. She simply froze, listening for something beyond the whisper of wind and her heartbeat. There! A jackal's grunting cough.

Not a howl, so the ones he spoke to are close. Keep moving, but don't run. If you run, so will they.

Jackals seldom attacked people—and only if their pack was very large—for they preferred smaller prey. They sometimes took a peasant child, but even a smallish woman should be safe. *Except,* Soraya thought grimly, *for smallish women who present themselves to jackal packs covered with blood.*

It was the gazelle they really wanted, and she'd let them have it when the time was right.

Now that she was listening for the sounds, Soraya could hear occasional snorts and the scrape of claws on rock. Surely her imagination was magnifying their number. There couldn't be as many as it sounded like. Soraya swallowed, but her mouth remained dry.

Here it was, the straight-walled, rocky canyon she remembered. The jackals would be forced to come into the open there, and they'd all be behind her.

Starting into the canyon, Soraya heard the scuff of their claws as they balked at revealing themselves. Or perhaps they were gathering their number for the charge.

She'd only gone a few dozen yards when they swarmed after her, yipping with excitement now that the chase had begun. There must be thirty of them! No matter. Soraya dropped the gazelle's carcass and ran for the other end of the canyon, fear driving her pounding feet.

They would—surely they would—stop for the fresh, bloody kill instead of chasing her down. She had to look back, even if it cost her a precious fraction of her speed.

She saw the first of the pack reach the carcass

and stop, just as she'd prayed they would. Almost all of them stopped, but a handful left the gazelle to the rest of the pack and came on after her.

Soraya hadn't thought she could run any faster, but she did, flying over the sandy canyon floor, splashing through the stream without pause. But the jackals ran also, faster on four feet than she could ever be on two. She wasn't going to make it, not even out of the canyon. She'd have to climb, but . . . There!

Soraya dropped her satchel. Maybe they'd think it was another carcass and stop to investigate, but she didn't look back to see. All her focus was on her racing feet and the ledge, perhaps five yards above the canyon floor. But the rock face below it was almost sheer! She couldn't—

She heard their panting behind her—too close! Soraya flung herself up the cliff, scrambling desperately for handholds, footholds, any way to reach the ledge.

Rocks snapped and crumbled under her boots, but not before lifting her a few precious feet. Claws scrabbled on the rock below, sending her swarming up the cliff like a lizard. Soraya dragged herself onto the ledge and rolled to the back of it, facing out, ripping her knife from its sheath with shaking hands.

No snarling faces appeared. She took a shuddering breath. Her whole body was shaking, but she twisted forward till she could peer over the edge.

Seven jackals sat on their haunches, watching her with the alertness of hounds who've treed a squirrel. They couldn't climb the rocks. She was safe.

Soraya dropped back and lay with her eyes closed, waiting for her heart to stop hammering. The ledge, as she'd already observed, was about twice the width of her body at its widest point. It narrowed sharply as it stretched farther up the rock face.

Only now did she notice that her hands and fingers stung. Opening her eyes, she saw they were bruised and scraped—bleeding in places.

"Wonderful." Her voice was cool and ironic, not quivering with terror, and that gave her the strength to sit up and take stock of her situation.

The jackals stared up at her. Soraya wondered why they weren't with their brothers, who were tearing at the gazelle farther down the canyon. Perhaps they were lower in status—the last to be allowed at the kill. And therefore hungrier. *Hungry, peasant jackals. Joy.*

Well, if she couldn't go down, could she climb up? Not from where she was. Directly over her head was a smooth outcrop of sandstone. Soraya rose carefully to her hands and knees and crawled up the ledge as it angled across the canyon wall.

Below, the jackals rose to follow her.

After a few yards the overhang vanished, but there were still no handholds, and the ledge had narrowed to the point that she could no longer crawl along it. In the other direction the ledge narrowed even faster.

Soraya sighed and crawled backward to the widest place. She sat and looked down at the jackals. She'd have to wait them out. Even the most foolish hound grew bored with a treed squirrel eventually.

She wished she still had her bow and quiver, but she could never have reached the ledge burdened with her satchel. In fact, looking down, Soraya wondered how she'd done it even without the satchel. She couldn't see any knobs or cracks that might support her hands or feet. She had to be five yards above the canyon floor. Too high to jump down without breaking an ankle at the least.

Oh well, she'd worry about that when the jackals left.

Soraya wished she had some food or, better yet, her water-skin. The race to the rocks had made her thirsty.

The sun had vanished behind the great cliff some time ago, and now Azura's light was draining from the sky. Soraya opened the front of her vest and wrapped it around her tucked-up knees. Azura be praised that her father had sent her into exile with rough, boy's clothes instead of a deghass' silks. If she were a boy, she could piss on the watching jackals. In the spirit of defiance, she tried to do that anyway, but she didn't have the range.

Soraya rearranged her clothes, awkward on the narrow ledge, and waited.

The jackals waited.

The canyon grew dark, but not so dark that Soraya couldn't see the shadowy forms beneath her. The rest of the pack finished with the gazelle's carcass, and most of them left, but four added themselves to the group below her. Soraya shivered. *That's only a superstition,* she told herself firmly. *Just because there are eleven djinn, that doesn't make everything that comes in elevens unlucky.*

Still, why had only four chosen to join their friends?

And why had she told her servants she wouldn't be back till after nightfall? They wouldn't even start looking till dawn. Could they follow her to this distant canyon? Hejir was the best tracker among them. Soraya sighed. The jackals had to give up, eventually.

The moon rose above the great cliff, but it took some time to reach into Soraya's canyon, filling it with silvery light and black shadows.

The jackals howled.

"You're not frightening me with that," Soraya told them, and herself. "Make all the noise you want—I'm up here and you're down there, and that's not going to change till you've given up and gone home."

They watched her in ear-pricked silence for a long moment. Then a chorus of yips broke out and rose once more into a full-throated, eerie howl.

Soraya clapped her hands over her ears. "I'm not listening!" Then she grimaced. That was something Merdas did. His nurses said he'd probably outgrow it by the time he was four.

The jackals howled again, sounding for all the world like parents shouting down a stubborn toddler. Soraya lowered her hands and cursed them for the spawn of Borz and Gudarz, the djinn of greed and cruelty. The sheer childishness of it made her feel better. The jackals went on howling, but she shouted louder.

Suddenly they fell silent, their heads turning toward the end of the canyon. Soraya looked too.

Pale shadows drifted like ghosts over the canyon floor. Realizing they'd been seen, they stopped, as eerily still as the jackals. Then they charged, shouting and hurling stones. The jackals fled, yelping when the stones found targets.

The ghosts resolved themselves into a handful of Suud. Their hoods, blown back in the heat of the chase, revealed faces as pale as the moon overhead, as pale as the djinn armies Rostam had fought. Soraya wished they would use the spears they carried on the jackals, instead of stones.

Most of them ran on, chasing the jackals out of the canyon, but one tribesman stopped and came to the base of the cliff beneath Soraya's ledge, looking up.

The moonlight on his pale skin showed his

features clearly. He was young, perhaps her own age. Tangled, silky-looking hair fell to his shoulders. His robe, open at the front, displayed a lean, hairless chest and no more clothing than a strip of cloth wrapped around his hips and a pair of sandals. He should have been freezing, even in his robe, but perhaps he was accustomed to wearing next to nothing in the brisk night air. By the standards of his own folk, he was doubtless properly clad, and she was feeling gracious anyway.

Soraya smiled. "Thank you." Was there any chance he'd understand her?

"You not trouble." He grinned at her widening eyes. "I talk you Faran good good. Mother, Father, me trade you people. You scared scared, climb big up!"

Was he laughing at her? "I was not 'scared scared,'" said Soraya. "Climbing up was the only sensible thing to do."

His brow wrinkled. "Sen-si-ble. Smart? Climb smart," he agreed. "Climb rock . . ." He paused, obviously at a loss for words, then he slapped the cliff face with both hands. "Not smart. Climb up you. Climb down?"

He *was* laughing at her, djinn curse him.

"You're right," Soraya admitted coolly. "I can't climb down. I will require you, and the others, to assist me."

The others were returning as she spoke. There were seven more of them, and three were women. Underneath their robes most of them wore simple, short tunics that left their legs bare from midthigh down, even two of the women. The third wore no more beneath her robe than the rude boy did.

"What?" the rude boy asked, his brows knitted in puzzlement.

"Bring me down," said Soraya, choosing simple words and a commanding tone. "You"—she gestured to the approaching group to make the plural clear—"bring me"—now she gestured to herself—"down." She pointed to the ground at the boy's feet. *There, that should do it.*

He evidently understood, for he stepped back a few paces and studied the rock face. Then he shrugged. "Not do. Big . . ." His hands moved, describing the steepness of the cliff. "You big scared scared climb up. We not scared scared. Not climb up. You talk rock. Talk rock, climb down."

"Talk rock?" she echoed. What was he trying

to say? "I can't climb down. You have to come get me. Or bring a ladder."

He frowned in bewilderment. "Lad-der?"

"Ladder." Soraya mimed climbing rungs with her hands. "Ladder."

His expression cleared. "Climb. Yes. Talk rock. Climb down."

"I don't know what you mean, talk rock." Soraya's voice was rising. "I can't climb down. You. Bring. Me. Down!"

His scowl this time was not from puzzlement. Some of the others were frowning too. "Not yell. Yell like jackal girl. Talk —"

"I can't talk rock!" Soraya yelled. "I can't climb down by myself. I need your help, you barbarian buffoon!"

He probably didn't understand half of the words, but her meaning evidently got through.

"Rude," he said clearly. Then he turned and walked back down the canyon the way he'd come.

The others followed. They moved swiftly, as silent as the ghosts they'd first seemed to be.

Soraya's jaw dropped. "Wait a moment. Get *back* here, you stubborn spawn of Eblis. Come back! I *order* you to come back!"

They didn't even turn their heads.

Soraya sank back onto the ledge, hissing with fury, groping for a rock to throw, but there was nothing larger than gravel. *How dare they!* When her father came for her, she'd tell him about this, and the whole Farsalan army would descend on the desert and wipe those insulting, arrogant savages from the face of the earth!

Except that her father had sworn never to take an army into the desert again.

Then she'd get the boy when he and his parents came to trade! He'd said he went with them. She'd circulate his description to every city, offer a reward . . . Except that she didn't know how to describe him in a way that would differentiate him from any Suud boy in his teens.

Then she'd track him down herself! Hejir and his father and brother would find her and get her down. When she was warm and fed and rested, she would return. With weapons! And track him down and . . .

The fantasy kept her from crying, but eventually she had envisioned her tormentor's destruction in all the ways she wished.

The moon was riding high now, but winter

nights were long. And they were mostly dry here in the desert, though wishing for rain was silly no matter how thirsty she was. The Suud should have left her some water!

Soraya leaned forward and groped below the ledge, hoping to find some handhold she couldn't see. She'd gotten herself up here, after all. There had to be a way to get down. But she found nothing within reach.

Soraya tried to find a way to climb up again— and failed. She tried stretching down with her toes, then rolled back onto the ledge, trembling, when her feet skidded and she almost fell. At least five yards high. Maybe more. She'd certainly break an ankle, even if she jumped into the sand. She'd be worse off helpless on the ground than she was up here.

Hejir could probably track her. She'd give them a day to find her before she tried anything as risky as jumping.

But that left the rest of the night and most of the next morning to wait. So she would wait. With dignity. And not cry. She started to wrap her vest around her knees again and then paused. Someone was coming up the canyon. Humming, though the tune was low-pitched and strange.

"Help!" Soraya called. "I'm up here."

"I know." It was a woman's voice. "I come."

The tribeswoman strolled up to the foot of the cliff below Soraya's ledge and looked up. Her face was creased like a withered apple, and it wrinkled even further as she grinned. "You do have a problem, jackal girl."

Soraya scowled. "The rude boy sent you, I see."

"Abab? Rude? Maybe." Her Faran was accented, but it was far better than the boy's had been. Perhaps that was why they'd gone, to get someone who could translate.

"I can't get down," said Soraya. "I need a ladder."

"Abab said 'ladder.' We not have one. So I come." She laid her hands on the rock below the ledge and closed her eyes.

Soraya sighed. Of course they had no ladder — and probably no rope long enough to stretch from the top of the cliff, where it could be tied, to the canyon floor. Even Behras didn't have that much rope, but the ladder that went to the barn loft was tall enough.

"I need to send a message," said Soraya. "To my servants, so they can bring a ladder."

"Silent," said the old woman. "I am speaking."

Soraya frowned. The woman hadn't been speaking. Perhaps she meant she wished to speak now. Soraya waited, peering down. The old woman laid her weathered cheek against the rock and said nothing.

"Look, I just need some—"

"Silent. Shh."

"Oh, very well." Soraya leaned back. How like the rude boy to send her a woman so old that her mind was enfeebled. But at least she spoke decent Faran. When she stopped petting the rocks, Soraya could offer a reward to whoever would go to the croft and bring back her servants and a ladder. And perhaps they could bring a water-skin and some food as well. Soraya heard the snap of breaking rock and leaned forward to speak—then yelped and lurched back as the woman's face appeared before her.

The woman smiled cheerfully and clambered onto the ledge to sit beside Soraya. The legs displayed by her short tunic were veined with age but firm and muscular. "There." She pulled out a damp-looking, skin bag. "Thirsty?"

"Yes, thank you." The water tasted leathery,

but no worse than the water in her own flask would have tasted by now. Soraya hadn't let herself realize how thirsty she was. She drank half of it before she stopped to breathe and ask the question: "How did you do that?"

"I climbed." The woman shrugged. "Like you did. Ready to go now?"

"I can't climb down." Exhausted tears rose in her eyes, but she blinked them back. "There are no handholds. . . ."

If there were no handholds, how had the old woman climbed up?

"I will help," the woman offered. "Here." She put the water-skin back in the pouch slung over her shoulder, turned, and crawled back off the ledge as easily as a lizard or a spider. As if she did it every day.

Her calm face vanished below the rim, and Soraya leaned forward to peer at her hands and feet. "How are you *doing* that?" There were no handholds under the woman's fingers that she could see.

"Turn and give me your foot. I will show you."

Remembering her near fall, Soraya hesitated. But if an old woman could do it . . . She turned and carefully reached down with her toe.

"Other foot."

Soraya complied, and firm fingers gripped her ankle, pulling her leg slowly down till her foot touched a small chink in the rock. It didn't feel big enough to support her, but somehow her toe stuck there, so when the woman took her other ankle and pulled it down, Soraya allowed her weight to slide slowly off the ledge. The first foothold held, and her other foot was guided to another cleft, which felt even smaller. But with the old woman's hand on her ankle, her foot adhered.

"Very good." The old woman climbed up so her body was between Soraya and the drop. What in Azura's name was she using for handholds? "Now let this hand go." She laid her small, rough-skinned palm over the back of Soraya's hand till Soraya lifted it.

"Good. When I move foot down, hand to footplace."

"But . . ."

The woman was already descending, and Soraya felt her foot being pulled from the rock and slowly lowered. She drew a deep breath and let her body sink, groping for the chink her toes had occupied.

The woman guided her slowly down the cliff. *She must be the most skilled rock climber in the tribe,* Soraya realized, with the small fraction of her mind that wasn't engaged in clinging desperately to the smooth stone. There were a few crevices, apparently, and the old woman found them all. Soraya was just imagining that at times there was nothing but the woman's small hand bracing her foot on the rock. And when her palm was flat against the surface, with the woman's on top of it, well, there had to be some sort of fissure under her fingers, or she would have fallen. Besides, those strange moments passed too quickly for her to be sure of anything; the climb down seemed to last forever, but in only moments her feet touched the canyon floor.

Soraya's knees wobbled like wet leather. She stepped back and gazed up at the sheer wall below the ledge. She could see a few small holds, but not nearly enough. "How did you *do* that?" she repeated, turning to her rescuer.

Her father had scoffed at the tales that claimed the Suud were djinn or descended from them. He'd lived among them, and he said their only powers were their knowledge of the desert and their mastery of the skills they needed to survive there.

The woman grinned like a girl. "You climbed up. Why not climb down?"

"But . . ." It was true. So much for magical powers. Soraya took a deep breath and went to find her satchel. The jackals had been at it, eating her food, biting through her water-skin. And they'd fouled what they couldn't eat. Soraya let the stinking thing drop. "Thank you."

"Little trouble. More trouble to have you bringing jackals from all ends of the world to here."

"I didn't bring them," said Soraya tartly. "They were here already." She turned and started out of the canyon, toward the trail that led up the great cliff. She'd had enough of the badlands to last her for quite a while.

To her surprise, the woman followed. "I know, girl. I am . . . teasing? We just came here. Our hunters will thin that pack. More than ten is dangerous to the camp and to every hunter goes out." She grinned again. "We will eat jackal for weeks. It tastes . . ." She grimaced, and Soraya laughed.

"It tastes musty," Soraya said. "Or so I've been

told." At the moment she'd be delighted to eat jack-als, no matter how they tasted. "You don't have to come with me. I know the way."

"Little trouble," the woman repeated.

She escorted Soraya all the way to the top of the great cliff. Soraya watched her climb the trail, slowing her own pace when the woman fell behind. She walked up just like any other strong, elderly woman, doing nothing in the least bit odd. She was even a bit breathless when they reached the top.

"You'll be well now," she puffed. "Not so large a pack in the forests."

"The sun will rise soon." Soraya gestured to her white-skinned face. The cold breeze off the mountain snowfields ruffled the silky, pale hair. "Will you be all right?"

"Probably be back to camp in time," said the woman. "If not, I have robe. Cloth thick enough." She turned to go.

"If you come home with me," said Soraya, "you can stay inside during the day. And I'll reward you for your help." What Golnar would think of a tribeswoman spending the day in her house was Golnar's problem.

The woman just waved and walked on down the trail. She was surefooted, but not extraordinarily so. Ignoring Soraya's wishes seemed to be a habit with the Suud, but that changed nothing. She would have to return to the desert after all. A deghass recognized a debt of honor.

SAMAN WAS ENRAGED *when he discovered that Tahmina was carrying Rostam's child. He decreed that when the babe was born, it would be cast out in the mountains to die. But Tahmina defied him, swearing that if the child was abandoned in the mountains, she would go with it—that if her babe was put to death, she would die too.*

Saman's love for his daughter proved stronger than his hatred for Rostam. He promised that the child would live and that Tahmina could keep it. But in return for his forbearance, he made one demand: that the child should never be told of its father's true identity. Tahmina wept, but to save the child's life, she agreed.

Saman held to his word, even when Rostam led

Kay Kobad's army to drive him out. Saman and his family were forced to flee into Kadesh, where he swore service to a Kadeshi warlord and was granted an estate.

So Sorahb, son of Rostam and Tahmina, was born in Kadesh and raised in the service of his grandfather's overlord.

When he came to know his laughing grandson, Saman repented his anger. He gave the boy a grandfather's love, and as Sorahb grew Saman taught him all he knew of the warrior's arts. Sorahb was so quick to learn, so strong of arm, and yet so modest and noble of demeanor that even the Kadeshi marveled at him.

When he asked about his father, Sorahb was told that he had been a warrior in Saman's household, who had been killed by Kay Kobad's warriors when Saman was driven from Farsala. So Sorahb came to hate the warriors of Farsala and hoped to avenge the death of the father he had never known. But he never spoke of this to his gentle mother, for he knew his warlike desires would make her fear for his safety.

When Sorahb was sixteen, the Kadeshi warlord his family served resolved to make war upon Farsala. Sorahb begged to be allowed to fight with them, and such was his courage and skill at arms that all men agreed he should go, despite his youth.

The night before he left with his grandfather's forces, Tahmina called him to her room. "You know this amulet that your father gave me?"

"Of course I do. You showed it to me when you spoke of his courage and your love for each other, and I have never seen you without it."

"Well, now I'm giving it to you," said Tahmina, taking the amulet from her neck for the first time since Rostam had placed it there. "I ask you, for love of your father and of me, to wear it at all times, that it may keep you safe in the battles to come."

Thus Tahmina sought to protect him without breaking her oath of silence, for she knew that if Rostam saw the amulet, he would recognize it, and that would keep her son safe indeed.

Sorahb promised, and she laid the chain over his head so that the gold amulet showed clearly on his chest. Azura's sun shone upon it as Sorahb rode off to war, lightening his mother's heart.

But young men riding to war for the first time do not care to be constantly reminded of their mothers. Even as a youth, Sorahb had too much of his father's farr to break his word. But he saw no harm to his oath when he lifted the amulet and dropped it inside his shirt, where none but himself might know of it.

CHAPTER THIRTEEN

SORAYA

ON THE EVENING OF THE FIFTH day after her return to the croft, with the moon just past the full, Soraya was ready to set out. She had napped in the afternoon, having already packed gear to camp in the desert and foodstuffs to pay off her debt.

Her first thought had been to hunt for the tribe, but they could hunt for themselves, and she was wary of carrying game until she was certain the jackals would no longer be a danger. Her next thought was to give the Suud the kind of goods they traded for in the markets: cloth, iron pots, steel knives, and spearpoints. But the croft had little to spare, and the peddler who might bring such things wouldn't come again till spring.

The one thing Soraya's household had in plenty was dried foodstuffs: beans, grain and flour, dried fruit and vegetables. Little could be grown in the desert, so perhaps this would be the best repayment. In any case, it was all she could offer, and she stuffed several satchels, despite Golnar's disapproval.

It was dusk when she left, ignoring Golnar's final frown; Soraya had told the family that it might take her several days to find the tribe and not to come looking for her till four days and nights had passed.

The burst of joy she felt, striding down the path to the canyon, made the heavy satchels seem lighter than goose-down pillows. At home she could never have given an order that would win her four days of freedom. Even married, in her own house, she wouldn't be able to give such an order unless her husband was gone. Exile had some advantages.

It took longer to make her way down from the cliff top burdened with two heavy satchels, and Soraya had to stop several times to rest her shoulders. The moon, in its clear sky, gave her plenty of light, and the night had barely begun when she reached the canyon where she'd been trapped. A shiver passed over her skin as she looked up at the ledge. It really was as high as she'd remembered. But there must be some handholds, or she couldn't have gotten up in the first place.

The tracks of the Suud hunters' sandals going into and out of the canyon were plainly visible, and after some deliberation Soraya decided to follow the outbound tracks. It had been close to the middle of the night when they found her, she thought, but only a few candlemarks had passed between the time they left and the old woman's arrival. Presumably, they had gone back to their camp by the swiftest route and sent the woman back. Presumably.

In the sheltered canyon the tracks were fairly clear, despite the passage of five days and the shadows where the moonlight didn't reach. Outside the canyon the wind had had more play. Soraya often had to drop her satchels at the end of the trail and cast around for a long time before she found another track. Azura be thanked it hadn't rained, or she'd never find them.

She was following a clear set of tracks that had lingered in the mud beside one of the streams when she spotted a girl even smaller than the old woman creeping around the side of a boulder. Walking backward?

"Hello," Soraya called softly. This Suud might guide her straight to her tribe's camp, if she could make her desire understood. "Do you speak Faran?"

The girl spun—a girl in truth, not more than ten or eleven years old, Soraya guessed.

"Shh!" the child hissed.

Soraya snorted. She was a Suud, all right.

The girl continued walking backward until she reached a patch of rock, then she turned and came toward Soraya; but now she jumped from one rock to another, never stepping on the soft ground . . . where she might have left tracks.

"You were making backward tracks!" Sure enough, the ground where the child had walked backward was muddy, her footprints clear.

The girl stopped, perched on a rock about two yards from Soraya. "Ebok addu lahasaha?"

Soraya sighed. "You don't speak Faran."

The answer was a string of bouncing, incomprehensible syllables.

"All right, you don't want to leave tracks? Let's try this." She smiled, hoping her good intentions would show, and approached the rock where the child perched. The girl tensed, but she didn't run. Soraya turned her back toward the girl and pulled the satchels aside. "Hop on." She patted the small of her back, looking over her shoulder.

The girl's brow wrinkled in puzzlement.

"No tracks," said Soraya, pointing to the child's muddy sandals. "Just my footprints." She pointed to her own booted feet. "I carry you home." She patted her shoulder this time.

The girl's pale face lit with comprehension. Giggling fiercely, she swarmed onto Soraya's back. The thin legs that locked around Soraya's waist were surprisingly strong, but the small arms embraced her neck without strangling her. The girl was lighter than she'd expected, though added to the weight of the satchels, she was burden enough. Sudaba wouldn't have approved of a deghass carrying a Suud urchin—she didn't like it when Soraya played horse for Merdas. But Sudaba wasn't here. If it got Soraya to the Suud's camp, that was what mattered.

"Where to?" she inquired, setting off at a slow walk.

The girl giggled.

THE REINING SYSTEM they finally settled on wasn't too bad, though it did leave Soraya with a certain sympathy for horses. Small, warm hands pressed her cheeks to turn her right or left. After one experiment with the girl pulling back on Soraya's throat, they settled for a tug on Soraya's hair to signal for a stop, and the child's forehead nudging the back of Soraya's neck set them in motion again.

Soraya's arms and legs grew weary, but she began to enjoy the game—for whatever it was, it hadn't stopped. The girl guided her over rocky stretches, in and out of blind gullies, and looping around spires, just like the Suud guides who'd taken Soraya through the desert in the first place.

Soraya only hoped that her small rider would take her faithful steed home instead of abandoning it when the ride was done; having seen her in action, Soraya wasn't sure she could track this child if the girl didn't want to be tracked.

But, no, it seemed the horse was to get its oats. Soraya caught the scent of smoke on the breeze and soon saw firelight flickering on the tall slabs of rock in front of her.

The Suud encampment was tucked in the broad, sandy bend of a stream, a bigger stream than any Soraya had seen in the desert. Judging by the green density of the trees and brush on its banks, it might run year-round.

The babbling conversations broke off as Soraya and her rider entered the camp. The Suud turned to stare, and then they began talking even faster, but Soraya cared little for their interest.

The camp wasn't very impressive. Round structures that looked like a cross between a hut and a tent were scattered about—perhaps a score of them. Made of flexible sticks, covered with skins, and topped with patterned, oiled silk, which had obviously been purchased in Farsalan markets, the largest hutch couldn't have been more than nine feet across, and not even a Suud could stand upright in it.

Most of the hutches had fires in front of them, with pots and the Suud's rather beautiful baskets scattered around. Roughly in the center of the encampment a couple of men were erecting a spit made of iron rods over a crackling fire.

Though Soraya was obviously of considerable interest, no one approached her. On the other hand, no one reached for the spears that were propped against the tents or stuck into the sand. Good enough.

The child squirmed to get down, and Soraya knelt and released her. She ran, chattering, to a woman who picked her up and eyed Soraya warily. So much for a pail of oats.

"I'm looking for the old woman." Soraya kept her voice carefully calm. "The one who helped me."

"You want to do it over?" The aged, ironic voice came from behind her. "I think one time for the jackals is plenty enough."

Soraya turned, gratefully dropping the satchels. "Good, you're here." She rubbed her shoulders where the straps had pressed. "I was afraid I'd have to follow you from camp to camp."

"Why follow me at all, jackal girl?"

Soraya grimaced. "I wish you wouldn't call me that."

"Then tell me your name. And why you come."

"I'm Soraya. And I came to repay you, for helping me."

"So-ray-ya." The woman tested it on her tongue and nodded. "Good. Now you ask my name."

Soraya frowned. She didn't care what the woman's name was, but . . . "Very well. What's your name?"

"Maok."

"Fine. I came to—"

"Say my name. If you say it wrong, I will tell you."

Soraya scowled. "May-ok."

The woman nodded. "Good. I did not ask you for repay."

It took Soraya a moment to track the conversation back. "You didn't have to ask. It's a debt of honor."

"Ah." The old woman regarded her for a long moment, her wrinkled face unreadable. Her eyes were very bright. "We have no same word, honor. We call it a debt of the spirit. The word for spirit is 'shilshadu.' It means 'the heart of a thing.'"

"Don't you want to know what I brought?" asked Soraya.

"Say shilshadu."

Soraya sighed. "Shilsadu."

"Shil*sh*adu."

"Shilshadu."

"So what repay did you bring, for your shilshadu debt?"

"Not a great deal," said Soraya. "Some dried food. I thought it might be something you didn't see much of." She knelt and began unpacking the satchels as she spoke. The Suud, no more immune to the lure of gifts than anyone else, gathered round. The flour and grains were greeted with nods of recognition, the dried fruit and beans with exclamations of delight. She'd guessed well, it seemed. Debt paid. She could be back at the croft by morning. Soraya sighed.

"Stay," said the old woman . . . Maok. "We will have your joining feast."

"Joining feast?" Soraya asked.

Maok nodded. "A big feast, with what you bring."

Soraya looked around. The camp was primitive. Of course, so was the croft. The camp was *more* primitive. "I don't think —"

"We will eat jackal." Maok's ancient eyes danced.

Soraya grinned. "All right, I'll stay."

"Good." Maok clapped her hands sharply and

rattled off commands. The Suud laughed and scattered—all but one boy, who stood staring at Soraya. The rude boy. But he had sent the old . . . Maok back for her. Perhaps he hadn't intended to be rude.

"I thank you," said Soraya, "for sending Maok to help me."

The boy smiled. "Little trouble. Maok talk rock best."

Talk rock. Did he have "talk" confused with "climb"? But he'd used the word climb, hadn't he? "Well, I thank you," Soraya repeated. "Though I wish you'd told me you were sending someone. I was . . . I didn't understand that."

The boy's grin faded; his gaze fell, then lifted again. "Sorry not talk about Maok. You scared. I know. Should have talked."

Soraya frowned, trying to work this through. "You mean you deliberately didn't tell me you were going to send help? Why? I was . . . concerned."

The boy sighed. "Scared. I know. But *rude.* Make me angry. So not talk about Maok. Sorry."

"I was not rude," said Soraya.

The boy scowled. "'Barbarian buffoo,' you said."

273

"You know those words?"

"Barbarian. Talk barbarian big, Farsala people."

Soraya sighed. "I see." Perhaps he had been provoked. "Very well, I accept your apology."

"Apology." The boy nodded. "Good. Now you apology."

"I accept your apology," Soraya repeated patiently. "I just said that."

"No, you apology," said the boy firmly. "About you rude."

Soraya's jaw dropped. "You want me to apologize? You were the one who stamped off and left me without a word. Why should I apologize to you?"

The boy's skin was so pale, his flush of temper was visible even in the moonlight. A babble of words erupted. His hands gestured emphatically.

Soraya had no idea what he was saying. Oh, she knew it was insolent, but without knowing the precise content, she couldn't reply in kind.

"I don't understand you," she said clearly, talking over his tirade. "If you want me to und—"

The boy turned and stamped off.

Soraya snorted.

"Men." The amused voice came from behind her.

Soraya turned to meet the sparkling eyes of a girl about her own age, though she must have been a full handspan shorter. Soraya had been eye to eye with the rude boy, and he was tall for a Suud.

"Not men, really," the girl went on. "Still boy. But finished bao'ok, so thinks man. Very . . ." Her hands waved, as if groping for the word she couldn't find.

"Touchy?" Soraya suggested.

"Touchy?"

"It means quick to anger. Quick to take insult."

"Yes! Boy just finished bao'ok is touchy."

"What's bao'ok?" Soraya asked, struggling with the unfamiliar syllables.

"Bao'ok is hunt-track thing," said the girl. "Important hunt-track. Boy makes man, girl makes woman."

"So it's some sort of hunt," said Soraya. "And it's also a test you must pass to be considered an adult?"

"Yes!" The girl nodded emphatically. Her pale hair, a bit shorter than most Suud women's, bounced. "Adult. My name is Elid."

"Elid," Soraya repeated. She had no desire to rehash the conversation she'd had with Maok with every member of the tribe. "My name is Soraya. What makes this bao'ok different from any other hunt?" And why did passing it make boys so touchy?

"Most hunt, hunt animals," said Elid. "Bao'ok, hunt adult."

Soraya's skin chilled. "You mean you have to kill someone?" Perhaps she should leave.

"No, no," said Elid hastily. "Not *kill*. Hunt-track."

It took a while, but Elid managed to make it clear that in bao'ok, a teenager would attempt to track several of the tribal elders, who did their best to elude him. When he, or she for that matter, succeeded, he was considered an adult. But this ritual was evidently more important for boys, since after bao'ok they would leave the tribe into which they'd been born and move into another tribal group, where they would ultimately take a wife.

"So the rude . . ." Maok had said his name. Abab? "So Abab is from another tribe?"

"All men start other tribe. But come here, make our tribe."

"I see," said Soraya, though she didn't, entirely.

As they talked Elid showed Soraya around the

camp, where the meal was being prepared apace. Watching the ugly woman who tended the spit, Soraya feared the end product wouldn't match even Golnar's efforts, much less that of her mother's cooks. On the other hand, she really wanted to eat some jackal.

The pack, Elid told her, had already been thinned to the point that even a child could roam at will.

There were children everywhere. Some were helping—or, in a few cases, hindering—their elders, but most of them dashed about in childish games. Soraya saw some playing what looked like a hiding game and wondered if it was an early form of bao'ok, but she wasn't interested enough to ask.

Elid showed her the inside of some of the round hutches. Small and very primitive compared to a deghan's pavilion, but they seemed snug enough, with their blankets rolled up against the walls. Moonlight, glowing through the oiled-silk roofs, even shed some light inside them.

Preparations for the feast were crude, by Farsalan standards, but they were fast. Only a few marks after she'd reached their camp, the food was ready.

The Suud ate with their fingers, though they had daggers to cut their meat, like a civilized person would. And Maok presented Soraya with hot water to wash her hands and face before she ate.

The style of service was also strange. Each fire had a pot or a roast or a dish of flatbread beside it, and each tribesmember had a bowl. But instead of any order of courses, they just wandered from campfire to campfire, ladling what they wanted into their bowls.

Soraya, going from pot to pot under Elid's gregarious tutelage, met most of the tribe, though she stopped remembering the names she repeated after the first few. She looked for the Suud couple who had guided her through the desert, but they weren't there—at least, she thought they weren't. She had only a vague memory of their faces. Had she even heard their names?

It was wearing, trying to communicate with people who didn't speak her language. Soraya didn't much like the food either—too little salt and flavored with unfamiliar herbs—but she was hungry enough to eat it. The jackal, smoked and seasoned with something spicy and sweet, wasn't as bad as she'd feared.

In time all the diners settled at one fire or another. Hands and faces had been washed again and the bowls carried off, presumably to a similar fate. Judging by the position of the moon, it was well after midnight, and Soraya's afternoon nap seemed far in the past. No one was speaking Faran now, but the alien babble was lulling. Soraya leaned against a soft-woven basket, stuffed with something even softer, and let her eyelids drift down.

SHE AWAKENED TO THE SOUND of drums. They weren't loud, but she hadn't seen them when Elid showed her around. Packed in the baskets? Soraya opened her eyes. She had rolled onto her side, and for a moment the bizarre image before her seemed to be tipped at an angle. *That's all right, in a dream,* thought Soraya hazily. Because she had to be dreaming.

Maok was dancing in the fire. The Suud had removed the spit from over the central campfire and had raked the coals into a long bed. The rest of the tribe stood around, some of them clapping in rhythm with the drums, but they all watched Maok as she stamped and twirled, her face creased in a smile. The embers simply glowed in most places, but flames spurted up around the old woman's feet, curling around her ankles, leaping to her hands as she stroked them.

The children were watching too. Some of the older ones crouched at the edge of the fire pit, stretching out their hands and then snatching them back. Giggling. The girl Soraya had carried into camp was one of them.

Soraya realized she was sitting up, with no memory of having risen. Sand clung to her arm where she had lain on it. Her mouth tasted odd, as it did after sleep. Her heart was pounding. She wasn't dreaming.

Maok was still dancing on the coals. The flames, flames that rose nowhere else, leaped around her like romping puppies.

Someone walked between Soraya and the dancer, and Soraya lurched forward and crawled around pale legs till she knelt beside the children at the edge of the river of fire. She could feel the heat on her face a yard away.

She looked at Maok's feet. They were bare, landing squarely on the coals, sometimes sinking in so that the embers drifted over her toes. She must be entranced—ensorcelled! Her feet would be burned to the bone!

They didn't look burned in the clear, red light. And though her expression was serene, Maok didn't seem to be entranced. She was humming along with the drums, but she looked up when someone called to her and made a laughing reply. Then she spun her way off the coal bed.

She scuffed her feet in the sand, as if to cool them, before moving out of the crowd a bit to examine the hem of her tunic. Looking for scorch marks?

Soraya swallowed, trying to control her breathing. She was awake. But she couldn't have seen what she thought she'd seen. Djinn magic? Soraya had spent most of the night watching the Suud eat dinner and play with their children. She couldn't believe they were djinn. She rose and made her way through the crowd to where Maok stood.

"May I look at your feet?" Her voice was strange in her own ears. Humble. She wasn't sure which she dreaded more: horrible burns or their absence.

Maok's brows rose. "I thought you were

asleep." She frowned, then shrugged and turned, grasping Soraya's shoulder for balance as the girl knelt. She lifted one foot so Soraya could examine the sole.

It was small and square, the skin on top subtly wrinkled and marked with the veins of old age. There were no burns anywhere, not even on the tender skin between the small, squarish toes. Some calluses, as if Maok went barefoot often, but nothing that might have saved her from the kind of burns she should have borne. Her skin was warm to the touch, not icy, like a djinn's was supposed to be. Not a djinn. A sorceress.

Soraya let Maok's foot fall back to the sand and looked up at the withered face. Somehow it felt right, that Soraya was on her knees. "You work magic."

Maok shrugged. "Your people would call it that, I think. Magic is like honor—we do not have a word for it. I talked to the fire, to its shilshadu, and told it not to burn me."

"Like you talked to the rock," Soraya whispered. "And told it . . ." Not to let them fall? Absurd. Insane. *Magic.* "You must be a mighty sorceress."

Maok laughed. "Not so mighty. I'm a good All Speaker, but anyone can do it. Look."

Soraya's eyes turned back toward the fire and widened in astonishment. The ugly cook was walking across the coals. She didn't dance, as Maok had, and no flames leaped to dance with her. She was frowning in concentration, but she clearly wasn't being burned either. And as she stepped off the embers the rude boy, Abab, stepped onto them, walking slowly and steadily.

Soraya rose to her feet, her mouth opening, though she didn't know what she intended to say. Before she could make a sound, Maok's knuckles cracked on the back of her head.

"Don't talk to him," said the old woman sharply. "He doesn't talk fire easy as some. You don't interrupt."

"You didn't have to hit me," Soraya muttered, rubbing the back of her head. "Could you . . . Could you teach me your magic?"

If it hadn't been for the rude boy, who was stepping off the coals, looking proud and a bit relieved, she wouldn't have dared to ask. But if *he* could do it . . .

"I could," said Maok, studying Soraya with

old, unreadable eyes. "You always get what you ask, don't you?"

"Mostly," Soraya admitted. "But if you say no, I'll accept that." Not even she was foolish enough to argue with a powerful sorceress.

A shadow passed over Maok's face. "I will teach you, if you learn. If you want. But it takes time to find the shilshadu of things. Time to find your own shilshadu, first. You must come back and back."

Soraya would have to spend many nights here, she realized. Perhaps live here for a time. Worse than the croft. No one was walking on the coals now, but the children were still holding out their hands and snatching them back, giggling.

"Maybe," Soraya murmured. "If I can."

CHAPTER FOURTEEN

JIAAN

JIAAN LOVED RIDING Rakesh; he was as smooth and strong as the wind, and his manners were so good that they almost made up for the bad manners of the human members of the company. Almost.

Half a score of noble aides had chosen to accompany the grooms who were exercising the horses today, riding their fathers' chargers, or even their own, for most of them would fight in the charge themselves. When the Hrum came.

Jiaan scowled at the thought. Though he'd rather have died than admit it, he was grateful that his father hadn't dared to promote him to fight like a deghan. This would be his first battle—the first time he would raise his bow to shoot a man. To kill. Jiaan wasn't sure if he was more frightened of disgracing himself by being unable to shoot them or of them shooting him, but either way he was afraid. And he was only an archer, who would fight from a distance instead of riding straight into the Hrum's too-strong, deadly swords. Swords that had conquered half the known world. No, he didn't envy the young deghans who rode beside him. But that didn't mean he liked them.

The others hadn't been quite as vicious since Markhan and Kaluud had been sent to Dugaz, but the underground war was still going on.

It doesn't matter, Jiaan told himself. *It's the battle that matters. They'll charge, and I'll save their hides with my archery. Or not, if they annoy me enough.*

But of course he'd do his best for them. All Farsala would fall if they failed. And almost worse, he would have proved that his father was wrong about him.

They were nearing the ground they'd chosen for that first, crucial battle—or, at least, one of the battlegrounds to which they hoped to lure the Hrum. Plans to do that were still a bit vague, since they all depended on the enemy's cooperation. If the Hrum didn't cooperate, the Farsalan army would be at a huge disadvantage. Jiaan knew the deghans were far better organized and disciplined than they'd been when winter began. The long months of muddy, freezing drills had been good for something. But even now, any tactical plan more complex than a well-supported charge tended to come apart when they tried it. And for a charge to work at its best, they needed an open, level field to charge across.

At least the weather was helping. All the last week had been like today, overcast, with a cold wind blowing, but no rain. Jiaan shivered. Spring was almost upon them. The saturated earth was drying out, and all the intelligence they'd managed to gather indicated that the Hrum would attack as soon as the ground was dry enough.

It seemed to Jiaan that everything was happening too fast. Even the peddler who'd been commanded to deliver goods to the lady Soraya's hiding place had rushed through his rounds at nearly twice his normal pace. Jiaan would have bet that they'd never see the man again, but he'd stopped at the camp just last week, trading this and that with the troops, slowly working his way up to the commander.

He reported that the lady was well when he saw her, just a month ago—though he claimed she'd struck up a friendship with the Suud, of all things. The commander had raised his brows at that, but he'd been pleased, too; he said that if the Suud were keeping her safe, no one would ever be able to find her.

A burst of hoofbeats pulled Jiaan's eyes to one side. One of the grooms, who led a string of horses behind him, had goaded them into a canter. Jiaan frowned. The commander said that strings of horses shouldn't be run together, for the chances of an accident were greatly increased by their enforced proximity. But perhaps the deghan who commanded this groom had other ideas or simply cared less about—

Jiaan felt the tug on his saddle, but it was Fasal's whoop that sent him spinning to the other side. Fasal's pretty, gray mare wheeled away, with all the agility of a good flags-and-lances horse.

Fasal held Jiaan's bow high, like a lance. He didn't even look over his shoulder as he galloped off toward the rolling hills. *Arrogant ass.*

For a moment Jiaan considered letting him go, thus sticking Fasal with the problem of how to return the bow without losing pride. But the wind was cold and fresh on his face, Rakesh could catch any horse alive . . . and the others were watching.

Jiaan clapped his heels to Rakesh's dappled sides, gripping hard with his knees as the gelding broke into a gallop, letting his own body sink into the rhythm of the stretched-out stride. He wasn't the rider his father was—he wasn't as good as Fasal, for that matter, who seemed to be glued to his saddle—but anyone could handle Rakesh's smooth, ground-eating gallop.

Fasal looked back at the sound of hoofbeats, his hair whipping over his face so Jiaan couldn't see his expression. But he turned the mare, away from the level ground and around the slope of a high hill, out of sight.

Jiaan smiled grimly. The deghans had practiced their charges in the wide valleys. But because the commander wanted Jiaan's advice about the placement of archers, Jiaan had covered the terrain with the scouts, searching through the hills around the flat, open fields. He turned

Rakesh to go around the other side of the hill. The gelding shook his head in protest, for he wanted to continue the chase, but he obeyed.

"Soon, my friend," Jiaan murmured, though even Rakesh's sensitive ears couldn't have picked up his words over the rushing wind. "Soon."

The hill was big, but Rakesh was fast. Jiaan had to pull him in, stamping and snorting, as they drew near the mouth of the small valley on the hill's other side—the valley that Jiaan had explored and Fasal hadn't.

They wouldn't have to wait for long. With Rakesh slowed, Jiaan could hear Fasal's mare pounding toward him . . . closer, closer now!

Jiaan loosened the reins and urged Rakesh to run once more. He grinned when Fasal came into sight, for the fool was peering behind him, over his shoulder. He held Jiaan's bow down by his thigh, but he hadn't dropped or hidden it. Good. Jiaan waited for just the right moment and then whistled.

Fasal's head shot up, his face a mask of astonishment as he saw Jiaan galloping toward him. He didn't have time to stop his mare and turn her before Jiaan would be upon him, so he did just what Jiaan had known he would: He leaned to the left and sent the little mare flying into the mouth of the small valley, so conveniently available, that looked like such an excellent escape route but that turned into such an excellent, dead-end trap.

Jiaan slowed Rakesh as he followed, despite the gelding's protesting pull on the bit. Unlike Fasal, he knew how swiftly the low ledge appeared after you went around that blind turn.

The staccato stamp of hooves told Jiaan when Fasal encountered it, and he laughed. It would serve the young fool well to disgrace his horsemanship with a tumble over his mount's ears—though if he broke his neck, it would be Jiaan's turn to face the commander's wrath. So Jiaan wasn't too sorry when he heard the mare's hoofbeats a moment later, pounding irregularly up the trail at the far side of the sudden shelf that gave access to the rocky, narrow upper gully.

Rakesh, running at an easy lope, made nothing of obstacles, weaving in and out of the boulders like a shuttle through the warp. But soon the ground grew too rocky for Jiaan to risk the gelding's legs, and they finished the last quarter league of the chase at an anticlimactic walk.

By the time Jiaan came up to Fasal, the young deghan had realized he'd been trapped. Straight black hair blew over his face, but his smile held anger and arrogance instead of defeat.

Here the gully's sides were too steep for any horse to climb. The only way out was past Jiaan.

Jiaan pulled Rakesh to a stop, turning him to block the exit. "Thank you. That was very enjoyable. May I have my bow back?"

Fasal's smile widened. "Come and get it."

Jiaan frowned. Fasal was two years younger than he was, and smaller, too, but he was a deghan; for all the commander had taught Jiaan, there was no doubt Fasal would be the better fighter. He wouldn't dare damage the bow — it was too expensive. But Jiaan's whole spirit rebelled at the thought of standing aside and letting Fasal ride back into camp with his bow as a trophy.

On the other hand, if he tackled the idiot, the bow might be damaged, and they'd both get in trouble for fighting each other instead of —

A horse whickered to the north, soft and questioning, as if it scented Rakesh and the mare. It sounded like it was just on the other side of the hill. A herdsman?

"Ah, you don't want it back, perhaps? But without this"—Fasal gestured with the bow—"you'd have nothing to do in the battle, would you?"

Jiaan had been hearing comments like that all winter. They still stung, but . . . Most of the gullies between these hills were like the one he stood in: rocky and barren. Bad grazing. And they'd left the army's horses almost a league behind.

"What's the matter?" Fasal frowned at his lack of response. "Nothing to say to the truth? I—"

"Be quiet," said Jiaan softly. "There shouldn't be horses over there."

Even as he dismounted and started climbing the hillside, he felt like a fool. It would be a local herdsman. Or a stray horse. Or a trick of sound and no horses on the other side of the hill at all. But he climbed quietly.

After a moment, to his astonishment, he heard Fasal following him. Quietly.

He still felt a fool, especially when he neared the top and lowered himself to crawl the last few yards till he could peer over the edge. . . .

All thought of how he looked evaporated. They were Hrum—perhaps two dozen of them. They wore cloaks of peasant brown, instead of scarlet, but the matching, brimmed helmets and breastplates were impossible to mistake. Even their boots matched.

Fasal crawled up beside him. The young deghan's breath hissed as he saw what Jiaan had seen.

But why were they here? Not scouting, or they'd have been fewer in number and better disguised. They even had their shields with them— curved, wooden rectangles almost a yard tall— though now most of them lay facedown on the ground or leaned against the rocks, for the troop was clearly at ease. They gathered in small groups, conversing, though softly enough that Jiaan couldn't hear them. A few were eating.

There were too few of them to attack anything but the smallest village . . . unless there were more troops hidden in these deserted hills. The back of Jiaan's neck prickled. No, surely a whole army couldn't have gotten past the guards the commander had posted. Were they waiting for something? Someone?

Fasal tugged Jiaan's tunic and slithered back, very quietly. Obedient to the silent signal, Jiaan followed.

"I think they're waiting for something," Fasal whispered, his mouth close to Jiaan's ear. "That gives us some time. Maybe. You keep watch here. I'll go alert the commander."

Whatever the Hrum were doing, the commander had to find out about it as soon as possible.

"Take Rakesh," Jiaan whispered back. "He's faster."

Fasal nodded and started off before Jiaan could add any more advice. He left Jiaan's bow where he'd been sitting, though without the arrows, which lay in the quiver on Rakesh's saddle, it wouldn't do him much good. Jiaan snorted softly and watched Fasal trying to move swiftly and silently down the slope. He did a good job, Jiaan had to admit, with only a few stones shifting under his feet, and those too softly for someone on the other side of the ridge to hear. He also had the good sense to take his mare with him and to walk Rakesh out of the gully instead of setting off at a noisy gallop.

He'd doubtless look very heroic, thundering into the camp on a panting horse, bearing the news. *Curse him.* But looking heroic was a deghan's job.

Before returning to his post, Jiaan took a moment to scan the ridge, this time selecting a small pile of rocks that he could peer around, exposing as little of his head as possible. Pity there was no brush on the ridge top—only tumbled stone and the flattened brown grass of winter, with green coming on underneath it.

There were twenty-one Hrum, Jiaan noted, now that he'd had time to count them—twenty soldiers and a man he thought was an officer. They weren't as relaxed as they'd first appeared. The men's eyes would sweep around every now and then, scanning the ridge top and the valley in each direction. The man Jiaan thought was in charge paced, whenever he forgot his duty to stand still and look calm and commanding. He was less inclined to join the others in conversation, and his gaze was even more restless. *Expecting company?* Jiaan slowly concluded that Fasal had been right, for once. They were waiting for someone.

Their alertness made Jiaan grateful for the rocks—and for his peasant-brown hair, only a shade darker than the dry grass. And he was grateful when the groom, who'd crawled up the hill behind him in total silence, touched his ankle for attention instead of crawling right up beside him. The soft grip on his ankle was startling enough.

Jiaan crept down to meet him, out of sight.

"The young deghan, he sent us to be helping you, sir," the groom whispered. He was an older man—some deghan blood, perhaps, but his accent proclaimed that he'd been peasant-raised. "There's six more of us, back that way." He gestured toward the valley where Jiaan had chased Fasal. He'd had the sense to hold the others back, to approach Jiaan alone. Good. "The deghans, they all went with the lord Fasal."

So the whole troop of them can gallop heroically into camp. Jiaan sighed. He was probably better off without them, but . . . No matter.

"With any luck, all we'll have to do is watch," he told the groom. "It looks like the Hrum are waiting for something, and our job is to see what it is. Still . . . Are any of you archers?"

"Two." The man nodded. "Sanji and Bid. The rest of us are just grooms."

"That's fine, for what I want," said Jiaan slowly. "Look, if we're lucky, whatever the Hrum are waiting for will come, then our army will arrive and capture them all. But if we're not so lucky and our army arrives before what they're waiting for comes, then we'll capture them and ask them about it. Nicely."

The ferocity of the old groom's grin would have done justice to a deghan.

"But if we're not so lucky," Jiaan went on, "what they're waiting for will come before our army does. If that happens, we need to try to keep them from leaving—or at least slow them down."

"You and seven grooms, sir?" The man's brows rose. "The young deghan said there was near twenty of them. And he didn't talk to me about anything but watching."

"Twenty-one," said Jiaan. He had to admit, it sounded like too large a number for an aide and seven grooms to handle. "But I don't intend to fight them. How many horses do you have with you?"

After a few more moments of whispered conversation the groom went back down the hill, shaking his head and muttering. But he'd promised to send the archers up to Jiaan, and he'd said he'd do his best to find a place near the entrance of the Hrum's smaller valley to conceal the horses as well as might be. Jiaan hoped they'd be within earshot, or his tentative plan would fail completely. Even as he'd given the orders, he felt foolish. With any luck, those orders would never be needed—Azura knew it wasn't much of a plan, and Jiaan dreaded exposing himself to the other aides' mockery. But letting the Hrum escape would be even worse, and Jiaan didn't dare rely on luck.

He'd made certain the groom knew what to do well enough to tell the others, and he'd gotten all the archery support he could. But he'd forgotten to tell the groom that the archers should bring him some arrows! Oh, well, he'd borrow from the others. Hopefully, they'd never need to shoot.

Jiaan returned to his watch. He still felt vaguely embarrassed—half-born peasants weren't supposed to come up with battle plans. And this plan was lame enough to justify that rule. But if the Hrum finished their business and started to leave, he had to stop at least a few of them so they could be questioned.

Embarrassment didn't stop Jiaan from stationing the two archers in good positions on the ridge and borrowing a quiver of arrows.

The Hrum soldiers chatted. Their commander paced, caught himself, stood calmly for a while, then paced again.

The grooms probably had their horses in position by now. Jiaan wished he'd been able to post them at the other end of the Hrum's small valley, to drive them toward the plain where the army camped. But he hadn't enough men, and—

A man, wearing the bright-dyed tunic and trousers of a Farsalan peasant under his brown cloak, came down the valley. He approached from the border side, Jiaan noticed. His heart began to race.

If the Farsalan army didn't arrive soon, Jiaan would have to make a decision. A command decision. His hands were trembling. *Just prebattle nerves*, Jiaan assured himself. He kept his eyes on the newcomer.

From his station on the ridge top, Jiaan had seen him before the Hrum did, but within moments, the man had walked right up to them. Was it only because of the wind that he kept his hood up, concealing his face? Several of the Hrum had their hoods raised, and Jiaan's own ears were cold, but still . . . *Come on, let's get a look at you.*

It seemed Azura wasn't sending luck Jiaan's way. The peasant-clad man—the spy?—went straight to the leader and began to speak without so much as touching his hood. If he'd just turn and look up . . .

The Hrum commander held out a purse. The man reached out with his right hand, then changed his mind and took the purse with his left. *Payment! So soon?* Jiaan's breath hissed. *A traitor instead of a spy, Arzhang take him.* A wasted curse, for the demon of treacherous ambition clearly owned this one already.

The soldiers were beginning to stir, packing up, preparing to leave. Having been paid, the spy would give his report. Then the Hrum would depart, taking with them the knowledge they'd come for. It might take marks, but it might take only moments! Jiaan had to interrupt them now, before information could pass.

Jiaan nocked an arrow, drew his bow, and fired into the dirt at their feet. They jumped, all eyes turning toward him.

"That was a warning shot. The only warning you'll get." He tried to make his voice sound deeper, calm and commanding. But it came out tense and breathless and sounded very young, he feared. *No matter, keep on.* "We have this valley blocked off at both ends and archers on top of the ridge. Throw down your weapons and move away from them now, and those of you in armor will be treated as prisoners of war."

The traitor would die, but most soldiers cared little for those who betrayed their people to the enemy, even if they were the enemy in question.

"Stand down now—"

A dozen arrows arced toward him in answer, clattering into the rocks he sheltered behind. He hadn't really expected them to surrender. *All right, time to supply some persuasion.*

Jiaan put his fingers to his lips and whistled twice, praying that Azura's wind would carry the sound instead of killing it. He loosed another arrow, and the rest of the archers fired with him, but their shots went wide since none of them had had a chance to find the right loft or to see what happened to the wind down in the valley.

The soldiers had snatched up their shields and helmets when Jiaan began to speak. Even as the first shots hurried toward them, they scrambled into formation, a rectangle four men deep and five wide; its lines were so precise that Jiaan's eyes widened in amazement.

Even as he raised the third arrow, the officer

dragged the spy into the center of the formation and snapped a command. The rectangular shields rose into position, the men on the outside of the rectangle holding theirs edge to edge to form a wall and the ones on the inside lifting theirs overhead to form a roof.

Two arrows, one Jiaan's, hit the shields and skittered off. One struck more squarely and lodged in the wood but couldn't break through. The Hrum were enclosed in an impenetrable box, so perfectly aligned and swiftly constructed that Jiaan's jaw sagged in astonishment. It took Farsalan officers a quarter mark of shouting to get the deghans and their support troops to form a sloppy line!

He studied the shield wall, looking for chinks he could send an arrow through, but he saw none. The other archers, down the ridge, had reached the same conclusion. They looked at Jiaan, a question in their eyes: *Now what?*

"Wait for the charge," Jiaan commanded, raising his voice to carry to the Hrum below. "Then we will all open fire."

As bluffs went, it was a thin one. The Hrum had already started moving toward the other end of the valley, still maintaining that perfect rectangle, when the sound of galloping hooves reached them.

Their formation wavered to a somewhat ragged stop, and the shields wobbled as the men beneath them did something Jiaan couldn't see. When they fled before the horses, their formation would break. Shields would drop, and the archers could surely hit enough of them that some would still be there to tell their tale when the deghans finally arrived. What was taking them so long? Had Fasal stopped to comb his hair and change his clothes before riding into camp?

But instead of fleeing, to Jiaan's surprise, the box started moving back, toward the oncoming horses. The men beneath the shields had turned around—that had caused the movement he'd seen. But what were they doing? Did they think they could fight a Farsalan cavalry charge? On *foot*?

Evidently, they did. The box of shields marched back to the wider place where the Hrum had been waiting and stopped, listening to the hoofbeats pounding closer.

Jiaan signaled his archers to be ready and nocked his own arrow. Now that the fighting had begun, his hands were steady. His focus was on the center of the formation, where, presumably, the leader and the traitor would be standing when the shields came down.

What were they waiting for? They'd need time to lower those big shields into fighting positions, to get weapons in hand, to —

The horses burst into the valley and thundered down on the Hrum. Jiaan, expecting it, looking down from above, saw at once that they had no riders, no men with them at all except the grooms who drove them from behind.

As Jiaan had ordered, the grooms turned and fled back down the valley as soon as they saw the Hrum. But the horses, enjoying the run, hurtled onward.

In a movement so precise that it stole Jiaan's breath, the Hrum's shields dropped, now positioned to protect their bodies from a cavalry lance rather than arrows from above. The last two lines held their short swords low; the first line canted them upward, above the horses' backs, seeking the riders who weren't there.

Jiaan fired arrow after arrow, as rapidly as he could nock, pull, and aim.

Some of the horses, those usually ridden by

the support troops, skidded to a stop in front of the Hrum's line, unwilling to trample the tight-packed men. But the chargers, true to their training, galloped on, knocking the Hrum off their feet, smashing their wondrous formation.

But there were no deghans to follow up on that confusion, to spear and slash at the soldiers in their stumbling disarray.

The Hrum began to laugh, even as several arrows found their mark and men cried out in pain. Jiaan drew an arrow and pulled back the string, holding it ready, his gaze on the milling mass of men and horses. The leader was in the middle—judging by the look on his face, he was swearing instead of laughing. Too many horses bucked and pranced around him for Jiaan to risk a shot.

But where was . . . ? There! The traitor hadn't fallen under the lashing hooves, but had taken advantage of the swirling confusion to escape, scrambling up the slope of the low hill on the valley's other side. Jiaan's first arrow missed, thudding into the earth below the man's feet—feet that suddenly became swifter. The man swarmed up the slope like a fleeing rabbit.

Jiaan only had time for one more shot, so he timed it, waiting till the man crested the ridge, silhouetting himself against the windy, gray sky.

Jiaan's arrow leaped from the string, hurtling through the empty air, arcing down. . . . Too high! So near a miss, it caught in the shoulder of the spy's cloak, but from the way it shifted with the movement of the cloth, Jiaan knew that it hadn't lodged in flesh.

Swearing himself, Jiaan turned back to the Hrum, but they'd already driven off the masterless horses. The shields were rising again, and several arrows whirred in Jiaan's direction, forcing him to curl tight behind the sheltering rocks. He got off only a few more shots before the Hrum marched out of the valley, in good order, carrying their wounded with them.

OVER A CANDLEMARK PASSED before the Farsalan army arrived.

"They got away," Jiaan told the commander calmly as the panting horse slid to a stop before the boulder where Jiaan sat. The commander wasn't riding Rakesh now; the gelding was probably winded by all that galloping back and forth. The rest of the squadron cantered past, following the Hrum's trail, but Jiaan knew their lead was too great.

While he waited for his army's arrival, Jiaan had recognized how little time had actually passed since Fasal had left and how far the relief force had to come. He didn't blame the young deghans for their late arrival. Much.

"So the grooms told me," said the commander. He sounded like Jiaan felt, calm laid over a seething cauldron of fury and frustration. "They're still trying to round up the horses. Probably be at it for days."

Was he angry at Jiaan? If so, Jiaan deserved it. He should have found a way to stop them. A better plan of attack. A real deghan would have . . . "I'm sorry."

The commander's brows rose. "About the horses?"

"About the Hrum. I should have stopped at least a few of them."

"With two archers and five grooms? I don't see how," the commander said. "It's impressive enough that you tried. If you'd succeeded, I'd turn the army over to you and resign."

Jiaan's lips twitched, despite his angry depression, and the commander grinned. "Come on, lad, no one could have stopped them with a handful of servants and a ruse. They may not be deghans, but they're . . . professionals. It's too bad we couldn't interrupt their business, but it's not surprising."

"Well, I think we did that much at least." Jiaan sighed.

"What?"

"The spy, the *traitor*, only had a few moments to give his report before I interrupted them. Though it might have been a short report," Jiaan finished gloomily. So much for his battle plan. The other aides would laugh their heads off.

The commander leaned forward, his face intent. "Tell me, exactly, what happened here."

Jiaan told him. It didn't take long. "But since he escaped, it probably won't do us much good," he finished wearily. The anger was fading, taking his energy with it. The frustration remained. "He'll just meet them somewhere else, and they'll get the information anyway. So I didn't accomplish much, did I?"

"Not necessarily." The commander's voice was gentle, but his gaze was still intent. "If he really is a traitor instead of a spy, well, he's been paid. Now that he's got his money, he might not take the risk of seeking them out. At the least, you probably delayed them getting the information, whatever it was. And at the very least, you followed the order you were given—the only order, which was to keep watch."

The commander's face was unreadable. Jiaan's gaze dropped. "I sort of exceeded that, didn't I?"

"Yes," said the commander, "you did."

"I'm sorry," said Jiaan softly, "if I've . . . disappointed you." Did the commander understand that Jiaan was speaking to his father now?

A slow smile spread over the commander's face. "You have no idea what I think of you, lad. But you will. Oh, yes, you will."

He reined his horse away abruptly, to organize the pursuit, the return when pursuit failed, and all the other things that needed organizing. Jiaan gazed after him, brows knit in thought. Had *he* been speaking to Jiaan as a son, instead of as an aide? Jiaan didn't know. He never knew.

HE DIDN'T KNOW UNTIL that night, in the commander's pavilion, where the high deghans of the army gathered in their silk-lined robes. The commander made Jiaan stand before them and repeat his report in excruciating detail.

When all the snarling "why didn't he's," "why didn't you's," and "they should have's" had been repeated several times, the commander held up his hand for silence. He got it quicker these days than he used to.

"We're all at fault," he said firmly. "Yes, it would have been good if the watchers posted in the mountains had gotten word to us that the Hrum were coming. That they got a squadron of twenty past the wall without us hearing about it means either that our border guards are asleep on their feet or that we don't have enough of them. I'll be addressing that myself. And, yes, it would have been nice if the Hrum hadn't taken the Trade Road, where their tracks were lost. It would have been nice if djinn had risen from the pit and seized and held them while we took our sweet time arriving. But for a moment let's focus on what we learned."

No one spoke, but the room rustled with small, uncomfortable movements.

"We've learned that the Hrum are engaged in active scouting—and that we need to do something about our border watch. As I said, I'll take care of that myself.

"We can assume that if they're scouting in

force, they intend to cross the border and engage us, probably as soon as the ground is dry enough for easy marching. But they might think that's what we're thinking and come sooner, to take us by surprise. They might not be here for several months, but they might come tomorrow. And if they do, judging by our performance today, they will catch us with our trousers around our ankles."

The room was utterly silent now.

"We need to be ready for them," said the commander. "We *have* to be. So let me start by asking why it took ten of our young aides to bring word that the Hrum had crossed our borders?"

Jiaan breathed again. He wasn't being scolded. At least, not yet.

"Fasal and Jiaan made good decisions," the commander went on. "One to carry the news and one to stay and watch—both needful tasks. Fasal then went a step further and had the good sense to send the grooms back to support Jiaan, while he rode on with the message. But why didn't the other aides go with the grooms? If they had, Jiaan would have had a real force at his disposal—near parity of numbers. Though parity of numbers hardly matters when the disparity of intelligence is so great."

Jiaan's eyes were on the ground, his face as hot as if he were the one being reproved. He'd have felt sorry for the other aides if he hadn't also felt their resentment, beating like sunlight against his skin. And besides, the commander was right.

"You think it's beneath your dignity"—the commander's voice was ominously soft—"to lie in the dirt on a hilltop instead of dashing about on a charger? Well, you're wrong. As of this moment all of you who accompanied Fasal into camp— except for Fasal himself, who had seen the Hrum and was the proper person to report his findings— all you others will fight on foot, as support for your commanders, from now until I believe you've learned to think with your heads instead of your horse's hooves."

A babble of protest arose, not from the silent, red-faced young men, but from their fathers. "A deghan's honor . . ."

"Silence!" the commander roared. "A deghan's honor is to fight for the gahn—on foot, on horseback, on your belly in a dung heap, if that's what it takes to stop the Hrum for one cursed year! You'll do as I say, the lot of you, and I don't want to hear about it from your fathers either! You'll walk with the support troops till I say otherwise. Except for two: Fasal, whom I'm appointing one of my personal messengers to carry my orders during the battle, thus putting his speed and focus to good use; and Jiaan, who will ride behind me and carry the standard. Anyone who can come up with a plan with so few resources will react flexibly under any circumstances, which is what I need in a standard-bearer.

"And now we're going to address the subject of how long it took this army to assemble a single squadron and get it moving. . . ."

The lecture continued, but Jiaan heard none of it. Carry the standard? *He* was to carry the standard, not only of his father's—his *father's*—house, but of Farsala itself! He would ride in the charge. Like a real deghan. So what if his palms were moist and his mouth dry with fear. So what if the glares of the other aides, the noble born who had been reduced to take a common trooper's place, were vicious enough to promise months, perhaps years, of retribution. To ride into battle as his father's son—that was worth any price he had to pay in the future. Any price.

CHAPTER FIFTEEN

KAVI

KAVI STOOD OUTSIDE the door of Patrius' tent and waited for the guard to announce his presence. Lamps had been lit within, making the heavy canvas glow faintly as the last of the gray light faded from the sky.

"Good. Let him aru." Aru? Enter? Kavi had spent the winter seeking out every trader he could find who spoke Hrum. He understood it fairly well now, though he didn't intend to let Patrius know that. He had come to know Patrius somewhat and believed him to be a good man — but he was an officer first. And only a fool would be careless around Strategus Garren.

Even the common soldiers seemed more wary today. Kavi had to show his identifying tattoo to two different sets of guards to make it this far, but he'd long since realized that Patrius' claim that it would get him "straight to the officer in command" had been . . . overstated.

On the other hand, he'd been right that it wouldn't instantly identify Kavi as a Hrum spy. The five interlocking diamonds curved around his shoulder like half a bracelet—*purely decorative, sir.* Only if you were told about the symbolism behind it would you realize that it represented a double image of the emperor's five-pointed iron crown.

The arrow that had cut into his shoulder two days ago had missed the tattoo by inches. Kavi prayed that no one but him would ever understand that particular irony.

Patrius looked up as he entered, but he didn't rise from the scroll-covered traveling desk where he sat. He didn't smile. He generally took a serious approach to life, Kavi had learned, but he looked more serious than usual tonight. "I wasn't certain I'd see you again."

Kavi went to the brazier in the corner, holding out his hands to the warmth. Winter was fading, but it wasn't over yet. "Since I'd been paid, you mean? I'm a merchant. I keep my bargains."

Patrius' lips pressed together in annoyance. "It wasn't that. Not entirely. One of my men thought he saw those cursed archers get you as you went over the ridge."

"They almost did," said Kavi. "I should charge you extra. I had to mend my cloak and tunic."

In fact, the arrow had sliced though skin and muscle so deeply that it left a scar, but it wasn't severe enough—Time's Wheel be praised—to stop him from delivering his report. That was all Strategus Garren cared about. That Kavi had been hurt, that he'd spent months living in nearly constant fear would mean nothing to Garren.

"You should have stayed with us," said Patrius. "You'd have been safer."

"Really? I heard they chased you up and down the Trade Road and all over the countryside."

"We're here," said Patrius calmly.

"And so am I. But I'm not doing that insane 'secret meeting' thing again."

"It seemed like a good idea," Patrius admitted. "Since we were taking a scouting party over the border anyway."

"A scouting party is more likely to be finishing their scouting if they aren't a walking signpost: 'we are the Hrum.' Fewer men, better disguised."

"I wanted to see the terrain myself."

"So go by yourself. In a better disguise."

"Substrategi must always have an escort of at least two deci in enemy territory," said Substrategus Patrius. "Their swords keep me safe."

Kavi still wanted a closer look at those swords; he wanted to see one being forged even more, but he knew better than to ask. He'd already been chased out of the smith's tent, and all the man was doing at the time was making shovel heads.

"Their swords, their matching armor and helmets, and those cursed matching haircuts almost got you killed. Not to mention me."

"I saw terrain. We're both still here. And speaking of the terrain, I'm most interested in your report."

It was an order, however courteous the phrasing. Now that Kavi was marked as theirs, his loyalty assured, he was hearing more orders and fewer seductive promises. At least Patrius took the trouble to be courteous.

"As you know, the army consists of the deghans and their support troops. The deghans ride chargers and are the . . . the core of the army. Everyone else, the half-blood bastards and a few poor relations who can't afford their own chargers, either follows the charge on foot to clean up whatever's still standing after the deghans go over it or they're serving as archers, to soften up the enemy before the charge gets there. They also keep enemy archers from taking the deghans down as they approach. I watched a few practice charges when I was in their camp."

"Indeed." Patrius didn't sound as concerned as Kavi would have preferred.

"Yes. It took the officers half a mark to line them up properly and get them moving. They pick fights over stupid points of honor, like who's riding closer to the banner. They're arguing forever about whose horse is best and whether gold-embroidered barding is appropriate on a practice field. They look like total buffoons," said Kavi. "Until the charge. They were fighting each other, horseman against horseman, so they were fairly well matched. But I tell you now, no foot soldiers, no matter how well trained, could possibly withstand them."

They were arrogant and foolish, and most of them treated a wandering peddler worse than they treated their livestock, but there was no question they could fight. It was all they were good for, as far as Kavi was concerned.

"How many deghans, and how many foot soldiers and archers?" Patrius picked up his pen. He looked tired, but he still didn't look worried.

"Six hundred and eighty-four deghans," said Kavi. "The grooms who feed the chargers knew the exact count. All the mounted men were supposed to bring at least three archers and six footmen in support, but many of them brought more. They double as servants, you see. Over seven thousand fighting men, I'm guessing."

Patrius did smile then, at Kavi's glum expression. "Would it make you feel better to know that we have ten thousand men? And can summon more, if we need them?"

"No," said Kavi. "Not after seeing what unmounted chargers did to your formation in that valley."

Patrius shrugged. "That was a . . . different circumstance. What have you learned about their plans?"

It was Kavi's turn to shrug. "Only what the cooks and grooms knew. They've been scouting for large, flat fields, preferably where there's some cover for their archers nearby. I heard rumors that they plan to lure you to some place like that, but they can't quite figure out how to do it if you won't oblige them."

Another smile lightened Patrius' face. "I know the feeling. Where, exactly, are these fields they're considering, and how do they plan to bring us there?"

"How should I know? I'm reporting to the commander about his daughter. He'd probably get suspicious if I started asking about his battle plans, don't you think?"

"Probably." Patrius' voice was cool enough to remind Kavi who was in charge. "But that's what we need to know, in order to bring them to ground of *our* choosing. So you'll have to go back and ask."

Kavi rubbed his face. "I knew you'd be saying that. What excuse am I supposed to give for showing up again, when I should be going on with my rounds?"

The deghans might be arrogant, but they

weren't all stupid. Kavi refused to admit, even to Patrius, how much they frightened him.

"One that doesn't get you killed, I'd suggest. Or, worse yet, caught."

"Worse for you, maybe."

"Worse for everyone, peddler. But especially you. You can't have any illusions about what the Farsalans would do to a traitor."

Kavi had no illusions where deghans were concerned. He shuddered.

"Your only hope would be to turn on us," Patrius continued. "And we're no more merciful to traitors than anyone else. You might live for a few more weeks, or months, if you betrayed us, but once we caught up with you, your fate would more than make up for the respite. You might survive, as a half-crippled slave, but that would be the best you could hope for." His voice was as cold as Strategus Garren's.

"I'd figured that out already," said Kavi. "But thank you for explaining it."

The pause lasted long enough to make Kavi realize that sarcasm might have been a very bad idea. Then Patrius sighed.

"I'm sorry. You've done nothing to deserve

threats. It's just . . . I've been working hard lately. And the stakes are very high here. Higher than any one life." This was the man Kavi sometimes glimpsed behind the officer.

"Why else do you think I joined the game?" Kavi replied. "I'll go back. But next time I'll be coming to find you on *this* side of the wall."

Patrius leaned back in his chair. "When you come into camp more people see your face."

"I'll keep my hood up."

"The country folk will still see you, and they'll remember you if you're asking around for the army."

"You're not that hard to find. And this side of the wall, who cares who sees my face?"

"By the time you have your information," said Patrius, "this army might be on the other side of the wall."

Kavi's heart contracted. "That soon?" No wonder Patrius looked tired.

"It could be. That's why it's so important that we get your information. Soon."

"I'll try to get it for you, though I can't promise to succeed. Just as a matter of curiosity, do I get tortured to death for failure as well as for treason?"

"I'm sorry," Patrius repeated. "And, no, the empire is in no way that unreasonable. If you fail to learn their plans, you'll be paid less, but that's all. But if you succeed, you'll be very well rewarded."

The carrot and the stick, for a balky mule. The Hrum's favorite method. And is that so bad? "Then I'll have to do my best, won't I?"

Kavi nodded farewell and left the tent. One of the things he liked about the Hrum as a whole was that they didn't insist on a lot of bowing and groveling—Garren was an exception.

Perhaps the way the Farsalan chargers had crashed through the Hrum's shield wall had frightened the substrategus more than he cared to admit. Kavi hoped so. There was no human society that could keep a secret mark secret for very long. The meaning of that tattoo on his shoulder would be exposed, sooner or later. If the Hrum didn't hold Farsala when that happened, Kavi would die, for he knew better than to believe that the Hrum would take him with them if they lost. No, Kavi had no illusions. Peasants couldn't afford them. At least, not now. Someday, when the deghans were gone, that might be different. It had better be. Kavi had staked everything on it.

SO SORAHB WENT FORTH to fight against the army of Kay Arash, who had inherited the simarj banner from his father, Kay Kobad. Kay Arash accompanied the army, but it was led by Rostam, who had been Kay Kobad's champion, and who was still the greatest warrior Farsala had ever known.

This pleased Sorahb. He might not be able to fight against the same gahn whose armies had killed his father, but at least their high commander was the same. Sorahb hoped he might face his father's killer in the field, even unknowing, and so resolved to defeat any man who came against him. And such was the power of his arm, the energy of his youth, and the strength of his resolve that he did so, overthrowing all who came against him in the first day of battle.

The army of Kay Arash wondered at him; except for Rostam, they had never seen a warrior who was his match.

On the second day of the battle Sorahb attempted to fight his way to Kay Arash, for to take the gahn would bring great honor, and he felt it would be a fitting way to avenge his father's death.

The gahn was surrounded by a guard of Farsala's finest warriors, and no Kadeshi had ever come close to taking him. But Sorahb fought so fiercely and well that Kay Arash's guard was nearly defeated, and they were forced to gather all their numbers to keep Sorahb from breaking through to the gahn.

Kay Arash fled the field with just two of his men to escort him and his standard-bearer at his heels. When the gahn's banner departed, the Farsalan deghans took it as the signal for retreat, and they, too, retired, thus ending the second day of battle.

Rostam, whose troops had been winning on the field, was sorely aggrieved. "Who is this Kadeshi who dares to think he can force a gahn to retreat—and succeed! Tomorrow I will fight this man."

So on the third day Rostam sought out the young Kadeshi warrior who had won all his battles so far, and Sorahb crossed swords with him willingly. Sorahb knew that if a legendary warrior like Rostam had killed his father, he would have been told of it. But he also knew that to fight so mighty a champion could bring nothing but honor to his house and his lord—especially if he won.

For one full afternoon they fought without cease. Slowly, both the Farsalan and the Kadeshi warriors abandoned their own struggles, by mutual accord, to watch the duel between the legendary Rostam and an unknown Kadeshi youth, who, though he could not win, would not be beaten.

As Azura's light fled the sky and night came forth, the trumpets of both sides called for retreat. Rostam and Sorahb both drew back, and each saluted the other with his sword.

"Never have I fought a warrior so strong and skilled," said Rostam in astonishment. "Let the two of us end this war. If the Kadeshi will send you as their champion, I will fight for Farsala, and whichever of us wins, that side may carry the conflict with no further bloodshed."

In token of his intent Rostam dismounted from Rakesh and drew the circle of challenge in the earth around his feet.

CHAPTER SIXTEEN

SORAYA

AFTER SO MANY MONTHS of practice, finding her own spirit, her shilshadu, was easier for Soraya. She still had to meditate to reach that bright, still place within her, instead of just opening a mental door and stepping through, as Maok did, but she could find it. She sat in Maok's hutch, cross-legged, as the old woman had taught her—not that anyone could have stood under the low ceiling—and tried once more to speak to fire.

Touching the fire's spirit wasn't too hard, for fire called to her in its bright, hot dance. It was a hungry spirit, Soraya had discovered, its only will to consume and burn—to consume so that the glory of its world-dance-heat might go on, for the moment it stopped eating, it died. The difficulty lay in convincing something so mindlessly self-centered not to eat her.

Not me, Soraya willed. Her spirit, matched and melded to the fire's, carried her will. Her skin felt hot. Her body was hunger—hunger to feed the glorious heat. *But I am you,* Soraya told the small pile of embers glowing dully on the cupped stone that sat before her. *I am your heat. I am your hunger. You don't eat me.*

She felt it respond, yielding in the way of mindless things. *We are one. You don't eat me.*

Slowly, holding her breathing steady, keeping their spirits melded, she reached out and touched the coals . . . and felt heat sear her skin, eating, burning.

Her shilshadu-va, her spirit trance, crashed like a pile of kicked blocks. She snatched her hand back, swearing, and plunged her fingers into the pot of cool water she'd placed ready. *Curse the stupid stuff! I can talk to it. Why can't I persuade it?*

"Fire's hard," said Maok placidly.

Soraya had become accustomed to the way her teacher addressed her thoughts, even though

Maok swore she couldn't read minds. "I know this," Soraya said carefully in her clumsy Suud.

When Soraya had decided to return to their camp, Maok had insisted she learn Suud. Soraya had agreed, as long as she was able to learn magic, too.

She had spent most of the winter with the Suud, and she'd made enough progress in the language that she could understand almost everything that was said, even if she couldn't always find the words she needed to reply. She wished magic had been as easy.

"I know," she repeated with a sigh. "But this is last other chance I can try, talking to fire." Azura knew she'd tried often enough before.

Maok grinned. She often did, after Soraya spoke. "You've done very well in such a short time, my girl. Many can't even talk to fire for months. Some never can. And you've mastered water. Do you want that colder, by the way?"

"Yes, but I do myself." Soraya gathered the remnants of the trance and sought her shilshadu, waiting till her vision seemed sharper and the homely objects in Maok's hutch grew vivid and distinct. Then she reached for the water, for its delight in even the small movement it made around her fingers. She reminded it of melting snow, of ice, of cold streams and deep lakes. The water around her scorched fingers was frigid now.

"A babe can work water," Soraya grumbled. Water loved to change; all you had to do was remind it. Not like fire at all. Or, still worse, stone, whose spirit she couldn't even find, though Maok swore it had one. "At least I never will take cold bath again." Not that she'd ever taken a cold bath. Even living with the Suud, she only needed to wait till Maok or one of the other All Speakers went to the bathing pool, and then she joined them.

"Fire's hard," Maok repeated. "It has too much will, too much need, to yield easily. And unlike an animal, it has no mind to be changed."

"You do it," said Soraya. "Abab does it."

Maok laughed. "But Elid can't. Amark can't. Many can't. You have a spirit that matches well with fire. It will come to you. Eventually."

Soraya scowled. "Do you must leave?"

"You know we must." Maok's voice was gentle.

Soraya did know it. The game was well thinned—not just the jackal pack, but the gazelle, the rabbits, even the big lizards that had proved so tasty when she'd finally brought herself to try one.

331

The root plants along the stream bank and the bushy herbs were nearly all harvested. The Suud had planted more, and they'd be big and ripe when the tribe returned again, but that would be many months in the future. Now they had to move on.

"I think it will take much days for me to persuade fire," said Soraya. "Big much." She knew how foolish she sounded, but the Suud had eight different words for "many," depending on how much more or less than twenty they were talking about. Since the day she'd told the camp cook that there were more sweet roots in the stew than there were stars in the sky, she'd settled for the silly-sounding but safer, "much" and "big much."

"Well, you won't do it tonight," said Maok. "Take a break. I'd send you out to play tracker if it wasn't moon dark."

Soraya grimaced in agreement. She loved "tracker," though that simple word was a poor translation for something as complex and important as bao'ok. To the Suud, bao'ok was more important than magic.

At first Soraya had thought it was because so much of their existence depended on hunting. She was a fair huntress herself, better than most deghasses, but having seen Suud trackers at work, she'd been unsurprised to find that she wasn't nearly as good as they were.

She'd been lucky, when she first found the tribe, that she'd chosen a gift of food to pay her debt. After passing bao'ok, a boy brought food to the tribe he sought to join, in token of the skills he would use to support them. Of course, Soraya hadn't passed bao'ok, but Maok had considered her action to be a sign that the tribe should accept her for a time. Aside from that initial gift, however, Soraya couldn't offer the tribe much support— compared to the Suud, her hunting skills were laughable.

It wasn't that they worked magic to hunt either. You could talk to the spirit of an animal, certainly. It was far easier than reaching the spirits of inanimate things, for even the smallest and least-significant living creature was self-aware. This had amazed Soraya; who could have imagined that butterflies *knew* they were beautiful? They did. Their whole existence centered on flashing their lovely wings before mate after mate but never showing them to predators. And she'd thought *she* was vain. Soraya had knelt in the flower-studded grass beside the bathing pool, laughing in delight, and the Suud, understanding, had smiled and let her be.

They could have used magic to hunt. You could convince an animal that you were a member of its herd or flock and lure it right to your hand. But once you touched a creature's shilshadu, it was very hard to kill it. Soraya understood why the Suud generally used their magic only on plants and inanimate things.

But bao'ok, as she'd soon learned, wasn't about hunting animals—it was about hunting men. She hadn't understood why for some time. She'd watched the toddlers playing their hiding games. Watched the older children tracking one another. She'd gone out with Elid and some of the others near her own age, and she'd helped—or hindered—them as they stalked one another through the rocky maze, setting small, embarrassing traps and ambushes. But she hadn't really understood bao'ok until the night she went out gathering kiok with Sulib, the girl she'd carried into camp that first night.

Sulib pointed to a series of rusty-looking streaks on the rock face that towered above them. "That's what they come to get," she said.

"What who come get?" Soraya asked slowly. She wasn't certain she'd understood all the words.

"The kula of dirt," said the little girl. The streaked rock was the hard granite of the great cliff, not sandstone.

"What is kula?"

The child frowned, searching for words Soraya might know. She shrugged. "Kula. This is kula." She knelt by a sandy bank and began digging like a badger. "To move the dirt. To take it away and make a muob."

"Dig," said Soraya. "Kula is 'digging,' and muob is 'hole.'"

Sulib looked baffled.

"Kula makes muob?" Soraya asked, to be certain.

The girl's face brightened. "Yes. You dig to make a hole."

"They who come." Soraya found a kiok bush with several ripe fruits on it and began picking, careful of the thorns. "They dig the dirt? Miners? You mean this is what the miners come for?" She'd switched to Faran in midsentence, and Sulib gave her an exasperated look.

"Ayan," said Soraya. Sorry. She said the word for "sorry" a lot these days. Curious, she put down the basket and climbed up the slope of loose scree at the bottom of the cliff. She still couldn't reach the streaks, several yards above her outstretched hands. They didn't look like much. Nothing glittered in the moonlight, as gold or gems might. What was it her father said lured miners into the badlands? Some kind of better iron? No, iron ore that would make better steel. That was it. She shrugged and went back to picking fruit.

But that night she had mentioned the incident to Maok and was astonished when the woman's expression darkened.

"Sulib shouldn't have shown you. It was lahu'uash. Girl, you must not speak of this to your own people. Ever."

"I won't," said Soraya, startled by the intensity in Maok's voice. Then she felt something brush against her mind. Not pressure as much as something that wanted to be pressure, like the feeling that made horses run before a storm. Soraya's first impulse was to flee, but she knew to the bottom of her soul that Maok wouldn't hurt her. Her teacher had never touched her mind before, but Soraya didn't sense Maok's spirit, just that soft, questing touch.

"It's worth luabu *money*," said Maok, using the Faran word for "money," since the Suud had none. Soraya didn't know exactly how much luabu was, but she knew it was a *lot* more than twenty.

"It is nothing for me," said Soraya honestly. "I have big much *money*."

The sense of pressure in her mind seemed to ease, though the touch was still there.

"You are your father's daughter," Maok murmured.

"You know my father?" asked Soraya, startled. He had said he stayed with the Suud for a time, but none of the others had mentioned him. "I assumed that he stayed with another tribe."

"He did," said Maok. "But word gets around. If the diggers of dirt come, we will probably have to kill them. That's why this is important."

"Kill them? But . . ." Soraya found it hard to picture her new friends killing anyone. Then she remembered something else her father had said. "The miners, the diggers in dirt, they kill you, don't they?"

"Not in the beginning," said Maok. "At first they steal our men and force them to dig. And the younger women, to faru. But it comes to killing, in the end."

"I understand," said Soraya, chilled. "I won't talk anyone of this thing. I . . . I *swear* it."

She didn't know if Maok understood the Faran word, or if what she learned from Soraya's mind reassured her, but the strange not-quite-pressure vanished.

Soraya had let the topic go then, but she soon realized why bao'ok, the hunting of men, was so important to the tribe. After that, when the trackers took her with them, she understood that it was an honor, that she had been included in the tribe's defense. Like a boy who had brought his food gift to the tribe. Like a warrior, instead of a girl. It was a lot of fun—and something her mother would never have permitted her to do, which made it even better. If it hadn't been moon dark tonight, Soraya would have abandoned her last chance to talk to the fire and gone with the trackers.

"It's bad I can't persuade my eyes to let me see in the dark, like you the tribe can." The first time Soraya had gotten a close look at a Suud's eyes in dim light, she'd been amazed at how wide their pupils could expand. She'd long since become accustomed to their djinn-pale hair and skin, but those huge, black pupils still looked unnatural. Almost inhuman.

Those eyes let the Suud roam the inky night almost as if it were broad daylight. Soraya, who could barely see her hand in front of her face if she walked away from the fires, was restricted to the campsite after dark.

Maok snorted. "You can only talk the body into fixing what's wrong, not changing what's right. Your eyes are the way they're supposed to be, day-dweller."

It was a mildly insulting term for Farsalans. They had others that were worse. And Soraya had become so accustomed to staying up at night and sleeping in the sunlight that on the rare occasions when she went back to the croft to check in with her keepers, she yawned through the days and had trouble sleeping when darkness fell.

"But there's so much you can change, can heal. Like Oluk's . . ." Soraya searched for the right word: *Infected? Fevered? Bad?* "Like Oluk's fever-bad thumb. Or Dumud's hurt knee. These things could be killing or . . . or *crippling* in my people." Even for deghans, who got the best medical care, doctors couldn't work the kind of miracles she'd seen in this camp. "If you use magic for my people, you could get *money*. Big much than for baskets. There is a fever that kills people who work in the . . . the wet places. They go to harvest silk, they make big much *money*, but the fever kills them. What would you do about the fever of the wet places?"

"I'd tell them to stop living in the swamp," said Maok, and shooed a laughing Soraya out of her hutch.

Soraya wandered between the fires. The signs of the coming move were subtle. When she'd first arrived, at the beginning of the winter that was now so near its end, she wouldn't have seen them at all. But baskets that had been scattered in friendly groups around the various work areas were now beginning to gravitate toward their owners' hutches. The game squares the children had marked in the sand with stones and sticks were falling into disarray, neglected by their small creators. A stew pot, supported by three carefully leveled stones, bubbled over the central fire. It had been stew more and more lately, as the game thinned out. They might be here for another month but probably not two.

The croft was going to seem very boring

now—and restricted, even if Golnar was afraid to argue with her. She would have to become a deghass again. Of course, it would be nice to sit in a chair instead of on the ground.

Soraya strolled to the central fire and poked the stew with the wooden ladle. Not only short on meat, but the vegetables were fewer than they had been. A double handful of the dried beans she'd given them made up the difference, but still . . .

She dipped up a ladle and tasted, wrinkling her nose. She'd never liked—

A stinging slap on her wrist sent the ladle splashing into the pot.

"Ow!" Soraya glared at Rumok, the homely camp cook. "Why did you do that?"

"If you take food without the cook's permission, you get your hand slapped, just like any baby," said Rumok smugly.

"You let other people taste," said Soraya, rubbing her hand. "I see them taste much times."

"They ask permission first."

"No, they don't. Not . . ." *Not often. Very seldom. Hardly at all.* She didn't know how to say any of that in Suud, and Rumok spoke no Faran. "Ask little much," said Soraya. She hated sounding so stupid. Most of the Suud spoke at least a bit of Faran, but Rumok never even tried.

"If they didn't ask permission, they had probably gotten it earlier." Rumok stepped up to the pot, made a great show of tasting the stew, and then added two pinches of belish.

"You are doing that because you know I not like belish," Soraya snapped. "It tastes plenty much bad of belish before." And the cook hardly ever adjusted the seasonings after she added them. Anger surged. Rumok had disliked her from the day she arrived, and Soraya had never done anything to deserve it.

"You are mean, a selfish bitch." *And very ugly, too.* Soraya even knew the Suud words, for once, but she didn't say them.

"And you are a nasty, spoiled brat, with no more manners than a toddler," Rumok replied. She turned her back on Soraya and stirred the pot. She loved the power of being the camp's chief cook, of being the one who determined how the roast would be seasoned, what vegetables would go into the stew. Abab, who often got on her bad side too, had once told Soraya that if Rumok was angry and knew there was a spice you didn't like, it would turn up in every dish served for days.

Perhaps it was good that Soraya was leaving. She contemplated overturning the pot into the fire, but that would punish more people than just Rumok. People she wanted to think well of her. People she was going to miss.

Hissing with frustration, Soraya stalked away. If the cook had understood Faran, Soraya could have vented her rage, but her stupid, halting Suud just wasn't sufficient. She could have hurt her anyway! She could have told the bitch how ugly she was, with her thin mouth and her lumpy nose and her fish-belly-pale skin, pocked with the scars of some long-ago disease.

But Rumok was aware of all those things. It was probably why she disliked Soraya, for being beautiful when the cook wasn't. But that wasn't Soraya's fault!

Still, she had no desire, even at the height of her fading anger, to hurt someone in a way that would . . . well, hurt. She had a hot temper (unladylike!), but she never . . . *Hot. Hurt.* Could she somehow make the fire's shilshadu understand pain? Make it reluctant to hurt her?

Soraya hurried back to Maok's hutch and

crawled inside. The coals she'd used before had burned themselves out, so she swept them into Maok's ash jar and took a pot out to collect new ones. Returning to the hollowed stone Maok had given her for this exercise, she tipped out the new embers. Away from the fire, their glow was already fading from brilliant gold orange to deep red.

Soraya shut her eyes and took a deep breath, letting her anger, her sadness at the tribe's departure, flow out with it. It took several breaths before she felt calm enough to reach within herself, into the bright darkness where her spirit dwelled. When she opened her eyes again, the plain, clay ash jar and the light blankets of Maok's bedroll had become objects of marvelous complexity and wonder.

Maok had only to reach out with her mind to see the world like that. Maok could do it for marks, even days, at a stretch if she wished. Soraya couldn't hold the trance and walk at the same time. But she could reach out to the coals, to their heat and their need, and the will that struck chords against the heat, need, and will of her own spirit.

She offered the concept of pain, in all its varied forms, physical and emotional. The fire's shilshadu held no response. Fire knew no pain, even when water doused it. Only hunger, unsatisfied, and darkness, and the end of the dance.

Soraya reached deeper. *Doesn't the end of the dance hurt?*

No, it only ended.

Does the hunger hurt?

No. The fire's hunger was need, not pain.

Death? The cold end of the spirit itself?

No. It was. If it was not, it would not know. Pain was a thing of food. A human thing.

But you are mine. You should know my pain.

Soraya started to reach deeper yet . . . then stopped. She already owned the fire. It wasn't working. Suppose she let the fire own *her?*

She opened the gates of her spirit to the fire, and it flooded in—hot, greedy, seeking. Its dance was her, and she was the dance. Its hunger was her hunger. Its joy, her joy. And her pain would be its pain.

Slowly, she reached out and touched an ember with the tip of one finger. Its texture was that of rough paper, and she could feel the heat wiggling under her touch.

Soraya laughed and gathered all the embers into her hands—as alive as newborn kittens.

"I knew you could do it," said Maok quietly behind her. "I'm glad it was now. This isn't something you should try without supervision until you've mastered it, no matter how well your shilshadu speaks with fire."

"I can't imagine not doing this," said Soraya. But speaking, even in Faran, made the melding of spirits ripple like disturbed water. Fire didn't talk.

She returned the embers to the hollowed stone, gently, as if they were as alive and fragile as they felt, and brushed her hands together. The skin of her palms was hot, but of course there were no burns. Fire doesn't eat itself.

"You could come with us," said Maok. "You'll miss us, and I'll miss you."

The trance was sliding away. Soraya's heart pounded out a dance of triumph, but . . .

"Why did you teach me?" How many times had she wondered this and not dared to ask lest Maok change her mind? She knew she hadn't been the easiest pupil, lashing out even at her teacher in frustration at her own ineptitude.

Maok shrugged. "In part, because I wished to learn from you. But mostly because you remind me of my sister."

"Your sister?" Soraya frowned. Among the Suud it was the men who moved on to other tribes. The women stayed.

"She was not quite a year older than I," said Maok reminiscently. "But we were as different as darkness and daylight. Her spirit, like yours, spoke best to fire and storms and predators. And she was always flirting with the boys."

"I don't flirt," said Soraya.

"Of course you don't." Soraya's eyes fell, and Maok grinned. "But my spirit spoke best to stones and trees, and neither of us had any luck mastering the other's abilities . . . until we taught each other. I wouldn't be an All Speaker if it wasn't for her." The old woman fell silent.

"Did she die?" Soraya asked softly.

Maok snorted. "She loved drama too. Especially at your age. No, she fell in love with a widower with young children who was fixed in another tribe. She's a good All Speaker herself and has four children and grandchildren coming soon. The point of the story is not that I'll miss you, but that you, too, have something to teach."

"Something to teach?" Soraya blinked in astonishment. What had she to teach anyone? The thought enticed her, but still . . .

"I can't go with you," said Soraya. And if the part of her heart that had learned how not to be a deghass regretted it, she didn't let it show. "Staying here for a few days, even weeks, is one thing—a messenger from my father would wait that long. But months on end . . . No. It's spring now. The snow is melting on the roads. My father will defeat the Hrum and come for me. And when he does, I'll be there."

CHAPTER SEVENTEEN

KAVI

I T TOOK KAVI EVEN LONGER to work his way through the guards to Patrius this time. The first set he encountered, as he approached the Hrum camp at dusk, almost skewered him before he could show them his tattoo. He couldn't blame them. They were in enemy territory, after all.

He'd known the invasion was coming for months, but somewhere in his heart lurked the childish belief that Farsala could never be conquered. Even though he'd been working toward that end himself, Kavi had been astonished when he heard from a frightened carter that the Hrum had crossed the border. "Came right through Sendan's northern gate, they did. Set up camp in the fork of the Trade Road. Arrogant bastards. They'll be paying for it when our army reaches them."

Instead of taking Kavi to Patrius' tent, the final set of guards had chosen to detain him and send for the substrategus. Kavi felt conspicuous, with his hood raised on this mild spring evening, but the busy men who passed the alley between tents where they waited paid no attention to him. The fewer who could identify Kavi as a spy, the better — even among the Hrum. Perhaps especially among the Hrum. Captured soldiers might offer any information, to appease their captors.

Kavi noticed that all the tents around the square held the same positions as before: the surgeons', the cobbler's, the smith's, but the Hrum's mania for order wouldn't save them if the Farsalan chargers broke their ranks. Kavi might have shivered if his cloak hadn't been so warm.

Patrius hurried across the square, without escort in the midst of his own camp. Kavi thought that was sensible — why drag men around at your heels just for the show of it? But several of the guards shook their heads, and one muttered something about "not proper," and "not caring about . . ." *Rank?* Kavi guessed. *Dignity?*

"I'm glad to see you, peddler," said Patrius, walking up to them. Even in the dim light, Kavi could see the fine lines that had formed between his brows. "It hasn't rained for over a week now."

And not much in the weeks before. Never, even after the wettest winters, the muddiest treks between villages, had Kavi been so aware of the earth drying underfoot. There was no mud now, except in the hollows and in a few seeps that were soggy year-round. Planting had already started, but these men had something else in mind.

"I have the information you're wanting," said Kavi. "But I had to offer up all you paid me and most of my wares to pay the bribe to get it." He wished he'd been able to offer more, for his heart still flinched at the sickened guilt he'd seen in the foot soldier's eyes.

He'd been raised by his aunt and uncle, he told Kavi. He'd told Kavi everything, desperate to justify what he was doing. His aunt had been injured in an accident—had almost died and had needed temple healing to save her life. The neighbors had offered what they could, and the village women had pitched in to care for the children,

351

but his uncle had fallen so deep in debt to the temple that his farm would be forfeited at the year's end. A landless farmer with an invalid wife and three small children . . . His uncle had gone south to the swamps, to harvest silk cocoons, and hadn't returned. Whether that was due to fever or to the lawless men who ruled the area hardly mattered. The soldier was the only adult family member left besides his aunt, who still walked slowly, with the aid of sticks. He didn't dare take his uncle's path.

Kavi understood that. He also understood that selling his comrades and his honor for gold would destroy this man . . . unless Kavi made good on his promise. If good healing was priced so that all could afford it, if peasants got the same justice as nobles, then the soldier would see that Kavi had been right. Then his guilt might become an endurable burden instead of poisoning his soul.

The Hrum's avowed intention was to keep the land, and the people who worked it, intact and taxable. But Kavi knew that the conquest of Farsala would hurt at least some people who weren't deghans. He had resigned himself to that.

He'd told himself that it would be worth it in the end, for everyone. He just hadn't realized how badly seeing another man's pain, causing that pain himself, would hurt him.

But the deghans would get what was coming to them. That was what truly mattered.

"You'll be reimbursed," said Patrius indifferently. Kavi felt a flash of pure hatred.

"He told me the where and when." Kavi kept his voice level. "The how and why I got in pieces from several people." One of them had been the commander's aide, Jiaan. He'd actually told Kavi less than most, but the deghans' inability to subdue their arrogance enough to work as a team frustrated him—and who cared what the commander's domesticated peddler might learn? Blackmailed with the threat of maiming, Kavi was helpless . . . or so Jiaan must have thought.

"Come with me," said Patrius. "The command council is assembled. You might as well report to all of us at once." He turned to the guards. "I'll take him," he said in Hrum. "On my own avoporos." *Recognizance? Authority?*

Whatever it was, Kavi was allowed to cross the square to the command tent with only Patrius escorting him. He'd have thought that a bit trusting of them if they hadn't already searched him for weapons from his scalp to his toenails.

The command tent's big front room was full of men this time. Garren sat in the comfortable chair at the head of the table, and Kavi guessed that the highest-ranking officers occupied the rest of the chairs, while lesser men stood. There was no empty chair for Patrius, he noticed. His mentor might have some power, but other men had more. This would be a very good time to keep his smart mouth under control.

Patrius stepped forward and saluted in the Hrum fashion, clenched fist over heart. "Sir, the spy is returned with information on the enemy's plans. I thought it *dideri* that he come here and report to all of us."

Kavi might not know what *dideri* meant, but he noticed the exchange of glances around the crowded room. Was there some disagreement here? Something Patrius thought his report might influence?

Garren's eyes narrowed. "Have you heard his report, Substrategus?"

"No, sir."

A glint of amusement lightened the cold eyes. "Evenhanded as ever. Very well, bring him forward."

Was Patrius arguing with the strategus? Joy. But Patrius' expression showed nothing as he gestured Kavi forward. "Kneel," he murmured in Faran.

No smart comments, Kavi reminded himself. And if the half step he took before kneeling put his knees on the softness of the rug instead of the cold canvas floor, no one could construe that as disrespect, surely. *The rug is new*, he thought. As was the beautifully carved and polished chest that held goblets and a wine pitcher. It looked like work from Desafon. Had the looting started already?

Time's Wheel has to dip before it can rise, Kavi told himself. And only the deghans owned anything worth looting. *No clever little comments*.

It was a promise that became harder to keep when Garren rose and paced forward to tug down Kavi's hood, exposing his face to every man in the lamplit tent.

"You may speak." Garren reseated himself. His Faran had improved.

"The Farsalan army is moving, even now," Kavi began. No one translated his words into Hrum. Had they all learned his language? And was that a good thing for Farsala or a bad one? *Never mind. Go on.* "Their intention is to camp at the west end of a large field that lies north of the village of Sindosh and perhaps a league south of the Trade Road. It —"

"How big is this field?" The speaker was a deep-voiced man with a ruddy beard. Kavi wondered why he was the only man in the tent who wasn't clean-shaven.

"It's about a quarter league long and half as wide at the widest," Kavi answered.

"About an imperial mile by half a mile," Patrius translated.

"The terrain isn't completely flat, of course," Kavi went on, "but there aren't any hills there — just slopes, I guess you'd call them. And it's grassy, with almost no rocks to trouble a charger."

For they intend to use their chargers. Are you listening to this, you arrogant, near-noble bastards?

"By stopping there," said Kavi, "they hope to lure you to take up position near the other end of the field." This was the part the foot soldier hadn't known, so Kavi had had to press deeper, dangerously deep into the structure of the Farsalan command.

"There's some ground there that they think

you'll like," Kavi continued. "A low hill on the western end that's got some steep faces behind it and a lot of big, scattered rocks. Defensible. A couple of streams. But most importantly, about a quarter of the way across there's a small creek. It's only two or three feet across, and in some places the west bank is about two feet higher than the one on the east. They're hoping you'll bring your army up to the other side of the creek, assuming that when their chargers have to jump it, their battle order will be disrupted and the riders thrown off, or at least unbalanced. In fact, the chargers can take something like that without breaking stride. And I've never seen a deghan who'd fall off at a small jump. You'd be lucky if they were unbalanced. And even if some did fall and their order was disrupted, it still wouldn't matter because the rest of them would hit you like an avalanche."

Again looks passed among the officers, but they didn't look worried, not nearly worried enough. Garren looked downright smug.

"They have a basic battle plan for wherever they encounter you." Kavi looked from one calm face to another. "They'll start out at a canter, with the archers riding in front—firing to soften you up if they can, but mostly their job is to keep your archers shooting at them instead of at the chargers. As they draw near your lines the commander will order the horns to signal, and the archers will stop, spaced so that the deghans can charge between them. When the deghans have passed through, the archers are supposed to ride around and hit your flanks, but at that point they're just a distraction. The charge will break your formation, but the deghans will go on, cutting as deep as they can. The foot soldiers will follow after them to take care of anyone they leave standing and make sure you can't regroup behind the deghans."

"Perfect," said Garren. "I think we'll meet them on the field they chose, just to be obliging."

Kavi set his teeth. *No sarcasm. But still . . .*

"Have you ever seen the charge of deghans? Their horses are trained to trample men. Horses are bigger than men. Horses are stronger than men." Irony leached into the last two sentences, despite his caution, and Garren's eyes grew cold. Kavi stopped talking. An ominous silence stretched.

"Oh, leave it," said one of the officers who stood. He spoke in crisp Hrum. "We have other

things to deal with. And he'd be right, if it wasn't
for the paregius."

Garren stiffened and glared, and several of the
other officers hissed for silence.

The officer who'd spoken looked chagrined.
"Sorry. But he doesn't understand Hrum, anyway."

Kavi did his desperate best to look uncompre-
hending, but it wasn't easy. *Paregius. What in the
name of all djinn were paregius?*

"Don't concern yourself," Garren told the officer. "Though I don't need to say that, do I? You
obviously have no concern for our military secrets."

The officer flushed.

Garren turned his gaze to Kavi and spoke in
Faran. "I believe you'll enjoy our hospitality for
the next few days, young spy. Until the first battle
is past."

"First battle's not all of it," said the officer with
the beard. It was hard to tell, in Hrum, but Kavi
thought he spoke with a faint accent. "First battle
may be the least of it, if you persist in taking the
way of fear."

"It's faster," Garren replied curtly. "I'll take
this land swiftly, and I will hold what I take." The
cool voice hardened to iron on the last words.

Kavi's heart sank at the thought of unloosing this man on Farsala. But Farsala had survived bad gahns before, and Garren would be checked by the Hrum's own laws.

"I'm just saying that a bit of mercy might be surer, in the long run." The bearded officer's voice was mild. "Not to mention more profitable." Kavi was impressed—he wouldn't have dared to argue with Garren just then.

"This has been settled," said Garren. "I will hear no more of it." He sounded just like a deghan himself, djinn take him.

The bearded officer shrugged and sat back, but he didn't look happy. *Fear and mercy?* Kavi was certainly afraid.

"You don't trust me?" Kavi asked in Faran, responding to the last thing said in that language. "If you lose, if the deghans even suspect what I've done, they'll kill me in a heartbeat. No, they'd condemn me in a heartbeat. The killing would take a long, long time. And sooner or later, the significance of this is bound to become known." He touched the tattoo on his shoulder. Sometimes it still seemed to ache.

"All the more reason for you to stay here," said

Garren, "until after the first battle. If it goes as you promise, you'll be richly rewarded. If it doesn't . . ." He shrugged.

Kavi's blood ran cold. He should ask *How richly?* like a proper, mercenary spy. But "We'll have just laws?" was the question that fell from his lips instead. "Based on local custom?"

Garren looked bored. "He's yours, Patrius. Take him off and see to him. And know that if he flees or if he's lying, it will come out of your hide."

"Yes, Strategus," said Patrius coolly. He turned to Kavi. "Come with me now, please."

Kavi had never been so grateful to leave any place in his life. Patrius could be dangerous, he thought, but not vicious. Not without cause. *Mercy versus fear.* The laws that restrained Hrum imperial governors would have to be ironclad to check Garren. Kavi shivered. He didn't have that much faith in anyone's law. But Farsala would be free of the deghans. That was what mattered.

"What was all the arguing about in there?" Kavi pulled his hood back up, trying to sound casual, as if he hadn't understood a word.

For a long moment he thought Patrius wouldn't reply, then the officer shrugged. "Strategus Garren wishes to complete the conquest of your country as soon as possible. Understandable, since he only has a year." His words were curt, but at least he'd answered.

"I've heard a bit about that," said Kavi. If he could get Patrius talking about this, maybe he'd talk more freely about other things. "I know it's being your law and all, but surely it often takes longer than a year to conquer a place. Suppose it's a big country or something?"

"It seems strange to most who don't know our history," said Patrius. His words came easier, now that he wasn't skirting the edge of military secrets. "Parapolis was the sixth country we tried to conquer, and after eight years of skirmish and siege we still didn't hold it. Our army was exhausted, far too many of our able-bodied men killed or crippled, and Parapolis itself so laid to waste that it was hardly worth taking anymore.

"In his old age Petronius saw the foolishness of our long war most clearly, so he decreed that no campaign should last for more than one year. Mind, if some allied state we've surrounded should turn and attack us, we'd have to subdue it. But none of them are quite that crazy," Patrius finished dryly. "And we give them no reason to take such a risk, for we still remember the blood-soaked streets of Parapolis and swear by Petronius' Compromise. We've also been known to say, 'Stubborn as a Parapoli,' but not usually in their hearing."

"I suppose that makes sense," said Kavi slowly. He'd heard pieces of this story from the traders he'd questioned but never the whole of it.

"The emperor's power is based on good sense," said Patrius. "There's more involved in conquest than warfare. It's not *practical* to make a man, or a state, into an implacable enemy—someone you'll have to fight for years and lose thousands of lives to defeat—when by taking a bit more time, taking the sure way instead of—" He broke off, his eyes flashing sideways.

Kavi followed his gaze to the empty carts that had held long, covered loads the first time he saw them. Even empty, they still stood behind the big tent with planks over its canvas sides, which he had learned was the armory.

At the moment Kavi wasn't interested in the Hrum's mania for organization. "So why is the strategus being in such a great hurry?"

Again Patrius hesitated, but in Kavi's experience the need to vent frustrations was generally greater than discretion.

"His father's a senator," said Patrius. "The senate is a council of retired governors who advise the emperor. They can even overrule him, if there's sufficient consensus among them. They have a lot of power. There was some question as to whether Strategus Garren should be placed in command of this campaign, but his father has already been . . . disappointed by the delay in his promotions. So the strategus has a great deal to prove."

"The Wheel may turn, but nothing's ever really changing," said Kavi softly.

"What do you mean?"

"The deghans believe djinn cause all their misfortunes, such as they are," said Kavi. "But my folk believe fortune turns on Time's Wheel. The Tree of Life grows and flowers for a time, then the Wheel turns and the Flame of Destruction takes you. But eventually it turns again, and a new Tree sprouts and grows. The aide I got some of the Farsalan plans from also has a father—and a great deal to prove, if I'm reading him right. Do any of you realize what will happen when those chargers hit your troops?"

Of course, what would happen to the Hrum would be nothing compared to what the deghans would do to Kavi if he was caught.

"Yes," said Patrius. "And I know that in battle anything can happen. But I'm not worried."

Kavi snorted. "Because of your *paregius*, whatever they—" He cut off the sentence, but too late. Talking loosened everyone's tongue, it seemed.

Patrius stopped, staring, and Kavi halted, too. "You speak Hrum."

When it's too late to lie, tell part of the truth. "I've picked up a few words, but I don't know that one. I hope *paregius* isn't some fancy way of saying 'courage' or 'honor' or some such thing, because none of that matters a snap to the weight of a warhorse."

Patrius laughed. "Didn't I just tell you we were practical? We have no illusions about that. You'll get what you bargained for, peddler. Within a year, all Farsalans will be imperial citizens, with just laws and fair taxes. No matter how . . . Despite my personal reservations about Strategus Garren, this will come to pass. I won't even tell anyone that you speak Hrum. I'd probably have learned it myself in your place."

There was also the fact that if Kavi got in trouble, Patrius' head looked to be the next one up to the chopping block, but Kavi decided not to mention that.

Patrius had told him the truth, Kavi thought. The truth, as he believed it.

He knew more about warfare than Kavi ever would, so he was probably right. The deghans would fall. Those who didn't die would be enslaved—and well they'd deserved it! The Hrum had conquered half the known world, and based on everything Kavi had been able to learn about them, they ruled well and justly. That was worth Kavi's risks, the sacrifice of a soldier's honor, wasn't it? Of course it was!

But later, lying in the small trooper's tent and watching the guard's silhouette, cast by flickering torchlight on the canvas wall, Kavi had a hard time getting to sleep.

CHAPTER EIGHTEEN

JIAAN

JIAAN GRIPPED THE LONG, polished staff that supported the gahn's standard with sweaty palms. He prayed it wouldn't slip. When he'd first been handed the banner, he'd stared at the gold-trimmed rainbow glory of the simarj—Azura's own bird, the symbol, always, of Farsala's gahn, no matter what house he came from. His father's leopard banner below it was made of plain silk, but to Jiaan, it mattered even more. The combined honor was overwhelming.

After less than a candlemark of carrying the awkward, top-heavy weight around the field in the commander's wake, the honor had faded to something that was almost irritation. It probably proved what he'd suspected all along: *I shouldn't be here.*

He should be with the archers, who'd already formed up in the cold, dawn light, not tearing around on Rama's back with a battle standard in his hands. Rama was his favorite mount, but she was an archer's horse, not a charger, and Jiaan wasn't a deghan. He realized now that he'd never wanted to be a deghan. Only a deghan's son.

Fortunately, all he had to do was hang on to the cursed staff. Jiaan set his teeth and listened to the commander explain for at least the dozenth time.

"I know your wife has ordered a proper hero's breakfast, but the Hrum are already in the field! They're not going to wait while your cook roasts fourteen saffron-be-cursed pheasants! Grab some bread, get your men in order, and get your ass in the saddle. Now! By Azura's arm, I swear I'm going to take this army out in a quarter mark even if there's not a deghan in it. The Hrum won't wait forever!"

They'd waited this long. They thought the terrain at that end of the field favored them, Jiaan knew. That was why the Farsalans had chosen it. If the Hrum grew impatient and marched on the enemy, they'd lose that advantage, but the disorder of the Farsalan camp must tempt them sorely.

The commander spurred Rakesh through the milling crowd, and Jiaan followed, swerving skillfully around a laundress, who stumbled along under a basket piled high with colorful silks.

The Hrum had arrived almost at sunset the previous day at the other end of the field from where the Farsalan army camped. They'd set up their own camp on the hilltop with astonishing speed, just as the commander had said they would. The hill was almost a fortress in itself, and over half their troops had guarded the camp during the brief disorder of setup. Not that the commander had ever intended to attack them there. The Farsalans needed a place where their chargers could run, and it seemed the Hrum were about to supply it.

They all knew that the battle would commence the next morning, so of course the deghans had spent most of the night in noble festival.

The Hrum had passed through the wall over a week ago—"Right through the gate, as if the bastards owned it!" one indignant deghan had complained. The commander had pointed out that they *did* own it.

Knowing the decisive battle was imminent, the deghans had sent for their families, "to witness and share in the glory, according to our ancient tradition." It was traditional for a deghan's family to accompany him to the field, bringing with them as much of the household's treasure as they could reasonably—or sometimes unreasonably—carry. This was supposed to show confidence in the army's invincibility, Jiaan supposed. It probably did. But it also made moving the camp to this site a logistical nightmare. Especially when you added in the fact that in front of their wives and children, the already difficult deghans became twice as proud and intractable.

The lady Sudaba had arrived, with Merdas in tow, despite not having been sent for. The commander ordered her home, stating flatly that he didn't have time to entertain his family in the middle of a campaign. He'd hoped her departure would encourage some of the other deghasses to do the same. It hadn't.

"Idiot!" the commander snarled to the next straggler. "You don't have time for a bath! You think you're dirty now, see what you look like by nightfall."

The tub was plated with gold. Jiaan prayed the Hrum had no way to tell what was going on in the Farsalan camp. On the other hand, if they did, they might laugh themselves to death. No, the Hrum were too professional for that. Jiaan sighed.

Even knowing battle would come, it had been a shock to see the rising sun glinting on thousands of spearpoints and helms. The Hrum's standards, replicas of their emperor's iron crown, supported by three crossed swords and mounted on a staff, traced scarecrow silhouettes against the sky.

Having watched one troop form up in the small valley where he'd witnessed their meeting with the traitor, Jiaan wasn't too surprised that they could turn out, in full battle formation, in the pitch dark. But having them just appear reminded him of the fabled djinn armies, which had been said to rise out of the earth itself. Clay golems that took no wound, while men bled and screamed and died. . . .

Jiaan shook himself awake and straightened the sinking staff. He would never forgive himself if he fell asleep and dropped it. He hadn't slept much last night, even after the sounds of revelry had faded. The veterans had told him that waiting was the worst part—Jiaan hoped that was true.

Fear of dropping the staff; fear of the Hrum, with their superior swords; fear, greatest of all, of disgracing his father by fleeing. He should be with the archers. The other aides were right. Blood told.

All you have to do is hold on to the stupid stick.

The only thing he wasn't afraid of was that the Farsalans would lose. However slow they were to assemble, however foolish they might look at the moment—and they looked ridiculous compared to the patiently waiting Hrum—on their horses, charging, they could smash any enemy. Watching riderless chargers break the Hrum's formation in the valley had told Jiaan that.

But the certainty that his side would win left him free to worry about other things, like the commander, his father, being wounded or killed. Not to mention Jiaan himself. This was different from practice. Different from his brief fight with the Hrum in the valley. Today he would follow the charge, right into the teeth of the Hrum's swords— and he wasn't suited for that by blood or training.

Just hold on to the stick.

It seemed to take forever, but the morning sun still slanted, casting long shadows before the chargers' hooves—a line of shadows stretching from one side of the field to the other. That same sun would blind the Hrum archers when the Farsalans approached. Jiaan knew that had been in the commander's mind too when he had chosen this place.

Rama stood quietly on the commander's left, but the chargers snorted and stamped with impatience. If the deghans didn't pound the earth with their feet, it was only because they were mounted. Anticipation, taut as a strung bow, hummed in the cool breeze.

The colorful banners fluttered, but they were hardly more colorful than the chargers. Barded in the same padded-silk armor the foot soldiers and archers wore, their coats ranged from pure white to jet black, passing through every possible shade of red and brown on the way. And though one white sock was thought to unbalance a horse's beauty, Rakesh wasn't the only horse who had one. Deghans might be fools about a great many things, but horses weren't one of them. In battle they rode the best horse, not the most beautiful.

The deghans themselves, their silk vests studded with steel rings, looked drab in comparison, even those who'd had the steel plated in gold. The rings on the commander's armor were unadorned, and when he'd promoted Jiaan to join the charge, he'd had rings sewn onto Jiaan's armor as well. Jiaan had been flattered, until he realized how much weight they added. And the round helmet that covered his old, padded cap was even heavier. But the rings would turn a sword, where padded silk alone might not.

The Hrum's shining breastplates were completely impenetrable, but Jiaan couldn't imagine how they could march or fight for long in anything that heavy. Perhaps that was why they waited with such ominous patience—they didn't want to march any farther than they had to.

Jiaan's father raised a hand, and the clarioneer, stationed on his right with Fasal and the rest of the message riders, lifted his horn and blew three wavering notes.

The cheer that rose from seven thousand throats was so fiercely exuberant that Jiaan found himself joining in without conscious intent.

The Farsalans set out over the field at an easy trot, almost entirely together after so many months of drill. The charge had to stay together, had to strike the Hrum lines at the same time. And setting off at this easy pace saved the horses' energy for the long combat to come.

Jiaan's helmet bounced distractingly with the rough gait. The commander's didn't, and neither did Fasal's. For all his skill as a rider, Jiaan wasn't a deghan. But his palms were dry now, though his heart hammered.

They stayed dry even when he heard the battle drums the Hrum used to send their signals beating out a slow, steady cadence. Jiaan knew nothing of Hrum signals, but the significance of this one was easy to guess: *The enemy approaches.*

They seemed to move very slowly, covering the two thirds of the field the commander had deemed the proper distance before the archers could fire. In the bright sun, with the bright banners streaming, it felt more like the show before a flags-and-lances match than the beginning of a fight to the death.

The commander called out, and Fasal pulled back and raced down the line to tell the left end to fall back into order.

Then the commander shouted to the clarioneer, and a staccato blast brought the archers cantering forward, dropping their reins and raising their bows to shoot. Jiaan knew in his bones the vibration as the string snapped forward, the need to compensate for his mount's movement. So what was he doing here?

Arrows hissed up like the whisper of death, and the Hrum's arrows arced out to meet them. The two flights wove through each other like threads on a loom, then the Hrum's arrows descended—toward the archers, Jiaan realized, watching them fall with practiced judgment.

They hurtled down like hail, but the Farsalan archers, who'd rehearsed this often over the past winter with blunted practice shafts, watched their fall and moved their horses into the clear.

A few mistimed it. Several horses screamed, and one man fell, twitching, into the grass. Jiaan prayed they could return for him in time.

The next flight was already in the air. The Hrum had raised their shields into the box formation Jiaan remembered, though now they broke it in places, so their archers could shoot. But the arc was too high!

Jiaan frowned as the arrows rose, knowing they would strike the archers again. Why, when the deghans were in range? Surely the Hrum knew the horsemen were the greatest threat.

The commander raised his hand and shouted, and the horn's screaming ululation was echoed in men's war cries as the deghans kicked their horses into a gallop.

The archers lined up as planned, with the precision the commander had struggled so hard to create. The chargers passed between them and swept down the remainder of the field like water from a broken dam.

The deghans still shouted, but the thunder of the chargers' hooves swallowed their cries, swallowed the world. If the drums still beat, Jiaan couldn't hear them. He yelled himself, just to hear the sound torn to shreds as it left his lips. He'd heard the crashing rumble of the charge before, but never from within it, from the very heart of it. The earth shook, and even the pounding of his own heart was lost in it. It was impossible to be afraid.

The horses stretched into a full gallop. The staff quivered and kicked like a live thing in Jiaan's hands as the simarj banner whipped in the wind, but he was an archer, accustomed to controlling his horse with his legs alone. The creek loomed before them, and Rama gathered herself and leaped, light as a foal. Jiaan slipped on the saddle and had to release the banner with one hand to grab the pommel and pull himself back into place. But he kept his station, at his father's side, only half a stride behind the front of the Farsalan charge.

So he saw, quite clearly, the moment when the Hrum's shields dropped. He was close enough to see the fear and resolution on their faces as the first rank raised their swords and the next three ranks raised lances. They were at least five yards long, the longest, thickest lances Jiaan had ever seen, impossibly big for stabbing or throwing. The Hrum swung them up, then down into position, ramming their sharpened butts into the earth like boar spears so that anything that struck them would be impaled. The first line of Hrum soldiers were now six feet behind a wall of glittering lance points—which were now only a few strides in front of Jiaan's galloping horse.

Rama wasn't a charger. She planted four feet and skidded to a stop, squealing in terror as another horse struck her hindquarters, pushing her closer to the lethal hedge of spears.

Already unbalanced by the awkward staff and the sudden stop, the shock of the collision sent Jiaan hurtling over Rama's head. He had time, as he fell, for a flashing moment of panic, for his mind to form the image of his body impaled on the lances, like a bird affixed by an arrow. He struck the ground with bruising force. Something in his shoulder snapped, and a wave of agony swamped him. His scream drowned out all other sounds, but when it died and he could hear again, other screams replaced it. Screams of men and horses, though the horses were louder, ringing in his ears, making his heart cringe sickly.

The banner! He had to raise the banner so the others would know that the commander lived, that they had to fight on. The command—was his father all right?

Jiaan dragged himself to his knees, gripping his left arm with his right hand, groaning behind locked teeth as broken bones grated. His helmet had fallen off.

The commander was fighting on foot, several yards away. He parried a Hrum's sword and launched a counterblow with a skill and strength Rostam himself might have envied. Rakesh stood behind him, blood streaming from a deep gash in his shoulder, one hoof lifted completely off the ground—not good, but at least he lived, unlike many other chargers who lay dead or dying on the broken lances.

The lances were down, now that they'd served their purpose. The Farsalan deghans, afoot, were fighting the finest infantry in the known world.

So let's get our own infantry into it!

Jiaan let go of his left arm, gasping as his shoulder moved, and groped for the staff. It was his collarbone that had broken, he realized. Like a boy falling out of a pear tree. Who'd have thought it would hurt so much?

He found the staff, half buried in the churned-up earth left by the chargers' hooves. It was a struggle to raise the heavy banner one-handed, but he managed. Then he used the staff as a cane to pull himself to his feet.

"To us!" he shouted. "To us!" His voice could no more penetrate the clamor of battle than a sparrow's chirp. All up and down the line men shouted in rage or pain. Metal rang on metal or thudded on the wood of the Hrum's shields. But Jiaan had done some good.

The Farsalan foot soldiers, as always, had fallen behind the horses. They could keep up at a trot, but not with the heat of the charge. They were running toward the battle, but when they saw the simarj banner rise, a cheer broke from them and they doubled their pace. Half a dozen men dashed past Jiaan and launched themselves at the Hrum line beside his father. Jiaan wouldn't have believed the battle could become louder, but it did.

Why was he standing here, holding a stupid stick?

The need to move, fight, strike back, fizzed in Jiaan's blood, but he couldn't abandon the banner! It was his responsibility—a responsibility he had to honor, to prove himself worthy . . .

The Hrum soldier in front of the commander fell, but two others stepped forward to take his place. The commander staggered back, slipping on the wet, torn grass. He recovered himself before Jiaan even had time to gasp, but he could have been wounded. Killed. It might have happened. It still might. *Djinn take the honor!* Jiaan was going to fight!

But he couldn't abandon the banner.

His dilemma was solved when a Farsalan soldier stumbled away from the line, blood streaming from a cut on his forehead. Jiaan walked to where he knelt, trying to wipe the blood from his eyes. Walking hurt his shoulder, but Jiaan didn't care.

"Here. Hold this." He pushed the staff into the man's hands. Did the soldier even know what he held? It hardly mattered, as far as Jiaan was concerned. His place was at his father's side.

It took long moments searching through the jumbled ground to find a sword. Jiaan wondered what had happened to its owner.

When he turned back to the battle, his father was winning. The Hrum line in front of him was beginning to fall back—not much, just a few inches at a time, but the commander was pushing forward.

The sword's smooth grip wasn't as familiar to Jiaan as his bow, but his father had taught him to fight with all kinds of weapons. With a broken collarbone, Jiaan couldn't have shot his bow anyway; with a sword, he could fight . . . if he could find a place to get in.

Jiaan stared in bafflement at the tight row of jostling backs. There was no space for him. Did real deghans ever have this problem?

Then a soldier cried out and fell back, clutching a bloody gash on his knee.

Jiaan yelled and threw himself into the man's place, cutting high, trying for the exposed flesh where the Hrum's neck met his shoulder.

The Hrum's sword swept up. The shock of the parry jarred the bones of Jiaan's arm, and sparked a fresh wave of pain from his collarbone, forcing him to blink back sudden tears.

The Hrum Jiaan faced was far older than he was, perhaps in his early forties, with a long, weathered face. His light brown eyes held nothing but professional attentiveness. If he was afraid, his expression didn't show it.

Jiaan hadn't realized he would see his opponent's face so clearly.

He tried again, this time a low strike at the man's exposed knee. The Hrum dropped his shield a few inches and blocked the blow. Jiaan remembered his training and let the rebound carry his sword up, sliding the Hrum's thrust away from his ribs.

They were coming back now, the lessons his father had taken so much time and trouble to impart. Jiaan slid his blade around the Hrum's with a screech of steel on steel and tried for the neck again, faster and harder than before. This time the Hrum's parry didn't jar his arm, though the two swords met with a ringing crash.

Jiaan stared at the handspan of blade that was

all that was left of his sword, shattered on the Hrum's blade like cheap bronze.

Their swords were stronger.

The Hrum laughed, genuine amusement in his voice, but there was a hard note beneath it. He raised his blade for a killing thrust. Jiaan barely managed to catch it on his hilt and shunt it aside.

But having blocked the blade, he had no way to protect himself from the man's shield as it rose and smashed into his face.

JIAAN NEVER LOST CONSCIOUSNESS, not entirely. His eyes were closed, his body limp on the trampled ground, but he could still hear the chaotic din of the battle. He heard the Hrum's signal drum begin to beat a different cadence, though he couldn't speculate on what that might mean. He was aware of feet stepping on him, of pain when his shoulder was kicked, but he couldn't move to save himself.

When his thoughts were clear enough to consider anything at all, he worked on movement, and eventually, on the fourth or fifth or sixth try, he opened his eyes. Light seared his brain, but before his eyes snapped shut, he saw that no one was fighting where he lay. No one had stepped on him for some time. But he could still hear the battle, not too far off.

His head ached even worse than his shoulder, and he couldn't open his eyes again. He had to do something, though he wasn't certain what. He had to clear his head. To think.

The stream. It wasn't too far back. Just the thought of cold water was enough to get his limbs in motion. Squinting painfully whenever he had to open his eyes, Jiaan dragged himself back, just a few inches at first, then a few feet. He stopped often, to rest his swimming head on the cool dirt, but finally his groping hand plunged over a lip of earth and down onto damp gravel. The streambed. Jiaan thrust himself forward with his knees and his one working elbow and slithered down the small bank and into the stream.

He laid the sore side of his face in the cold, shallow water. For a moment the pain that throbbed in his temples wiped out thought, but then it began to ease. He lifted his head and drank, then laid his face in the water again, and the pounding headache slowly diminished.

He could still hear the battle, but it wasn't

nearby. So where was it? Jiaan dragged himself to his knees and looked around.

The sun was high, which amazed him—surely at least a day had passed.

The Farsalans had been forced back, past the stream, almost to the point where they'd begun the charge. The field between Jiaan and the battle, several hundred yards away, was strewn with fallen weapons and armor, fallen horses, fallen men. Very few of them were Hrum. Jiaan shuddered.

The Farsalans were losing. Not surprising, since their charge had been broken. But the simarj banner swayed in the midst of the thickest fighting, so Jiaan knew his father still lived. What djinn had possessed Jiaan to abandon it and take up a sword? No, not a djinn. Battle fever. Just like a deghan. How absurd.

What could he do to help his father now? The commander had to get out of there, to retreat and gather the remains of his army. But with the Hrum pressing them . . . Horses. Many of the horses had probably survived, the archers' mounts at least. Jiaan had to find the archers and tell them to bring in all the horses so the deghans could escape. But how to find them?

Thinking made Jiaan's head ache again, and he lowered himself to the stream, splashing cold water on his face. Then he lay so that the water ran over his broken collarbone and swollen shoulder. As good as a cold compress, once the padded silk of his armor became soaked.

If he left the hollow of the stream, he'd never make it. Besides, the banks would give him cover from wounded Hrum returning to their own camp or from anyone searching for Farsalan survivors on the field. There were some hills to the south, where the archers might have sought refuge. Upstream.

The water helped. Jiaan took off his belt and strapped his useless left arm to his body. He crawled past two broken swords in the streambed, broken just as his had been. Their owners' blood flowed in faint pink wisps over Jiaan's hand, but he didn't have the strength to leave the water to avoid it. The banks grew higher as they approached the hills, but it seemed an eternity before the stream twisted behind the first low rise.

Gritting his teeth, Jiaan dragged himself to his feet and started climbing the shallow slope. Ordinarily, he could have reached the top in a handful of strides, but he was crawling again by the time he reached the crest and looked over it, down on the battlefield, now some distance away.

The Hrum were winning. Jiaan couldn't tell if the tide of combat had turned more swiftly as he crawled up the creek or if the change in viewpoint made the difference, but the Farsalan line, which had commanded the length of the field this morning, had been compressed into a single knot of men. All but a few wore the ringed armor of deghans; perhaps it was their armor that had let them survive so long.

The Hrum surrounded them, fighting on all sides, and the deghans were so outnumbered that for every Hrum who fought, half a dozen stood resting, awaiting their turn.

Horses! With horses, someone could break through to the embattled deghans, to the tall commander beneath the simarj banner, whose sword still rose and fell like a scythe. But Jiaan knew he couldn't find them in time.

Even as he realized this, the clarioneer sounded the long, low note of surrender. The clamor of sword against sword began to die as the surviving Farsalans stepped back, dropping their weapons.

But Commander Merahb did not.

Jiaan was too far away to make out the words he shouted, but then the commander took two long strides into the center of the ground the deghans had held so desperately and lowered the tip of his sword to draw a circle in the earth at his feet.

Jiaan's breath caught. No commander since the time of legends had declared himself his army's champion, staking victory or defeat on his own life or death. For combat of champions was always to the death.

His father had been fighting all morning—he had to be exhausted. But the Hrum commander had probably been fighting too—either that, or he was one of those who directed his men from some point of safety, behind the lines. He might not even have lifted a sword in years. And the Commander, standing alone, with Azura's sun waking sparks on the rings of his armor, was the same towering, invincible figure he had been in Jiaan's childhood. Jiaan's mind told him that any man could lose, could die, but his heart knew that the commander couldn't be defeated.

The Hrum debated for what seemed a very long time, though Jiaan's shadow didn't move over the grass. They were arguing. Did they know the significance of the circle? They fought in units. Did they even have a champion to send forth?

Jiaan was soon answered, for the five men who finally stepped forward held bows, not swords, and they fired from a distance.

The commander saw them coming, saw them nock their arrows and pull. He didn't move from the circle, didn't even turn aside as the arrows struck his chest, hurtling him to the ground. If he made a sound, Jiaan didn't hear it. It was Jiaan who screamed, but the sound was lost in the roar of anger from the remaining deghans, who dived for their abandoned weapons and hurled themselves at the Hrum.

But Jiaan's attention was on his father, struggling to stand. The arrow shafts protruded, obscenely, from his chest. Circles of red stained the silk around them. He rose to his knees, almost to his feet again. Then the second flight of arrows came, knocking him to the earth once more. This time he didn't rise.

Jiaan's vision blurred, and he let his head drop. He listened to the end of the battle, to the deghans' screams as the last of those still willing to fight died on the Hrum's superior swords.

Even if his father had fought, the sword in his hand had been Farsalan made. It would have shattered, like so many swords had shattered. Like the charge had shattered. He had never had a chance; he must have known it. And he had been Farsala's only chance.

Now it was over, for all of them.

ROSTAM AND SORAHB *fought from dawn to dusk for three full days. Neither Farsalan nor Kadeshi had ever seen such a battle, for it was Sorahb, in the glory of his youth, who was the stronger and the quicker. But Rostam had spent his whole life in war; his skill saved him again and again. And when his skill failed, Rakesh's did not.*

So neither could defeat the other—until the evening of the third day, as night stretched out its arms, and Rostam's mighty strength finally failed.

The next blow of Sorahb's sword against his shield loosened Rostam's seat on Rakesh's saddle. It was a small thing; a lesser opponent might not have noticed. But Sorahb saw, and he followed up his advantage with blow after crashing blow, until Rostam toppled from the saddle, his shield dropping from his numbed grasp.

"Now I will avenge my father," said Sorahb. "And all the brave Kadeshi warriors who have died on Farsalan swords." And he dismounted, to deliver the death blow to the enemy's champion.

But experience won out. As Sorahb dismounted, Rostam gathered up sand in the hand freed by the loss of his shield. When Sorahb stood over him and raised his sword, Rostam cast the sand into his eyes, then kicked his ankles, so the youth fell forward, onto Rostam's upraised blade.

Rostam rolled aside as Sorahb fell, his lifeblood already staining Rostam's sword.

The champion knelt beside Sorahb, gasping, astonished by his own survival. "Never have I met an opponent so able, so valiant," he said. "He has not earned death this day."

So in defiance of all tradition, Rostam took off his cloak and attempted to staunch Sorahb's terrible wound. Then he pulled his sword free and tore open the youth's shirt. The first thing he saw, as a warrior will, was that the wound had stopped bleeding. By this he knew Sorahb was dead, and regret smote his heart. He moved to replace the young man's shirt, in a show of respect for the body of the warrior who had fought so fiercely. Then he saw a glint of gold on the red-stained skin. Looking closer, Rostam recognized the amulet for the one he had given to Tahmina. And he knew the truth.

CHAPTER NINETEEN

JIAAN

JIAAN NEVER KNEW how long he lay, weeping, before the gentle touch on the back of his neck sent him spinning around—to stare up into Rakesh's bony face.

The horse jerked back at Jiaan's sudden movement, then he lowered his neck and lipped Jiaan's hair. *Pay attention to me.*

"Go away." Jiaan's voice was thick with anger and grief.

Rakesh didn't move, except to shift more weight off his injured leg. Caring for his father's horses had been part of Jiaan's duty for most of his life. He sat up and looked at the wound. The

Hrum lance had struck Rakesh's shoulder. Even from the ground, Jiaan could see splinters sticking out of the torn flesh. The lance head might still be embedded there. The Hrum were infantry. They'd have no use for a lame horse, even one as fine as Rakesh. They'd put him down.

Jiaan didn't much care if the Hrum killed him, but he couldn't let them do that to Rakesh. "Come on, old friend. We'll help each other."

Jiaan half crawled, half slid to the bottom of the slope. Only by clinging to Rakesh's good shoulder did he manage to haul himself to his feet. They walked together, at the same slow pace. Jiaan wasn't certain which of them chose the direction, deeper and deeper into the low hills, away from the battlefield, from the Farsalan camp with the deghans' golden bathtubs and the deghans' families.

The Hrum would sack the camp, Jiaan knew, but there was no one there he cared about. The only living creature he cared about walked beside him.

By dusk they had reached a shallow ravine, with a small creek flowing down the bottom. It was evidently popular with the local horses and cattle — Jiaan gathered dried dung, awkward with one hand, and built a fire. Peasant fuel, but there was little wood in the plains, and he was a peasant. He'd proved that. If the light attracted the Hrum, so be it; he needed light to tend Rakesh, and the horse would need the warmth. Jiaan wrapped Rakesh's reins around the base of a sturdy bush, unsaddled him, and set to work.

The lance head wasn't embedded, Azura be praised, and the long slivers that had lodged in the wound were easily extracted. Rakesh flinched when Jiaan pulled the splinters, but he didn't try to move away, and he barely stirred when Jiaan washed his shoulder with water from the stream. The exhausted gelding stood with his head lowered, too tired to graze. Jiaan wished he had a pail of oats and a warm stall or even a blanket.

He scrubbed his hands and arms in the stream, then he led Rakesh over to drink. After some thought he removed the horse's bridle. Rakesh would be more comfortable without it, and in the end, he might fare better if he did run off.

But the gelding stayed—perhaps the warmth of the fire felt good to him. Jiaan kept the fire going, even though bending over to collect more fuel made his head throb. Its light wasn't strong enough to draw the Hrum from their looting, but it did bring in others. First came a man who leaned on a broken javelin, limping on a knee swollen to twice its normal size. Then a horse whickered, and Rakesh answered, summoning an archer, unharmed, seated on a sound horse. He had his camp pack strapped to the cantle of his saddle, and he made a pot of tea.

Perhaps a dozen others straggled in as the night wore on. Jiaan didn't speak to them, even when one offered to try to set his collarbone, but he listened as they talked to one another.

The archers, circling around the Hrum's flanks, had met with massed arrow fire from the Hrum lines, fire thicker than they'd encountered at the front. It killed enough of them to drive them back, and then arrows started raining down from the hills behind them as well. But they'd still held position, firing into the distant army . . . until they saw what happened to the charge.

Most of the survivors were archers. Men Jiaan knew. Peasant-born men, who had fled, just as he had. The deghans were right, it seemed; peasants weren't suited for combat. Jiaan saw his own guilt in their eyes and looked away.

It was very late when Fasal staggered into the

camp. One side of his armor was torn open—by one of the Hrum's big lances, Jiaan guessed. It would have lifted him off his horse like a spitted cock. The blood on his ribs was dark and dry. A bruise on his temple, the exact shape and size of a Hrum boot heel, told how he had finished the battle. The line had probably passed over him, just as it had over Jiaan.

The Hrum had been ready for them.

Those lances weren't thrown together in some last-minute plan, not in these grasslands. They had been made weeks, probably months, ago and brought here for the sole purpose of breaking the Farsalan charge. With the pitiless clarity of exhaustion, Jiaan saw that his father had been wrong. It didn't matter how strong your arms or how courageous you were, or even how well-organized, if your enemy was smarter.

It wouldn't have mattered if their swords hadn't broken. Once those lances destroyed the Farsalan charge, the end had been as inevitable as sunrise.

The sun would rise in just a few marks. Jiaan shivered. Someone would have to do something then. But for now he could sit, with his mind as blank as he could make it, and watch Fasal start to reach for a mug of tea with his right hand, then wince at the pain from his ribs and switch to his left.

Images flashed behind Jiaan's eyes. The spy, reaching for his pay and changing hands. The peddler, reaching for his mule's bridle, a piece of firewood, a knife from his pack, and changing hands. Jiaan telling that same peddler, who hardly seemed to be listening, so casual had his questions been, that the commander was concerned about the deghans' lack of flexibility, that he meant to use the archers . . .

He moaned and covered his face with his hands. Was it all his fault? The lances, the shattered charge, his father's— No. Jiaan drew a shaky breath. No, those lances were the result of months of planning. The peddler—the traitor— visited the camp for the first time just a few weeks before the battle. No, the lances weren't Jiaan's fault. *But the ambush lying in wait for the archers was.*

He had traveled with that peddler for days. How could he have failed to recognize that mannerism when he saw it? His father would have recognized it.

His father had wanted to hold off the Hrum

army for a year. He hadn't held it for a day. Was that why he had drawn that circle in the earth, knowing he would die?

Jiaan hugged himself, weeping again. None of the men seemed to notice. Many had wept this night. Besides, they were listening to Fasal, who had put down his mug.

". . . hit them tonight." His young voice was low and intense. "They'll be exhausted, and the guards will be careless. Maybe even asleep."

Was he talking about attacking the Hrum camp? With what? There were hardly more than a dozen men gathered around the fire.

"Those of us on foot will take the guards," Fasal went on. Despite his obvious exhaustion, his voice held the authority of generations of deghans. The men around the fire looked at one another, but no one spoke. "Those who have horses will go straight for the slave pens. I think they're in the center of the camp . . ."

But what if he was wrong?

". . . but no matter. Wherever they are, we'll find them. All our survivors are there. The horses can break down the pens, then the survivors can take the guards' weapons . . ."

Unarmed, probably wounded, they'd take weapons from armed men?

". . . and they'll fight their way out. Then we'll all retreat into the hills and prepare for the next . . ."

None of the others spoke. Their eyes were on the fire, on their clenched hands. It was guilt that kept them silent, Jiaan realized, even in the face of this insanity. Guilt that they'd run to save their lives, while their comrades died. It was probably the same guilt that led Fasal to come up with this stupid plan. Jiaan felt it himself. It would be easy, right now, to die. Easier than living to face the sunrise. But it wouldn't be smart.

Jiaan's father hadn't been a fool. But for all his intelligence, for all his courage, he had fought by the old rules, the deghans' rules. And they had killed him. Jiaan was done with deghans' rules.

"No." It was the first time he'd spoken since Rakesh found him, and his voice creaked. It wasn't at all commanding, but Jiaan no longer cared how he sounded. It was what he said that mattered.

"What?" Fasal blinked, astonished at the interruption.

"No. We're not going to attack the Hrum

camp with a handful of exhausted, wounded men, with swords that break. A camp on a hill, in the dark, that we've never even scouted."

"Then what do you propose . . . peasant?" Fasal rose to his feet, sneering, though Jiaan could see that it cost him.

Jiaan thought about rising too, but he decided not to bother. Every man seated around this fire was a peasant, a fact that seemed to have escaped Fasal's attention. The rules had changed. Jiaan's job was to make them rules that would let the Farsalans win.

"We're going to wait till morning," said Jiaan. "Then those with horses will scout through the hills, gathering survivors. First we'll retreat to Sindosh, but only till we're all together. Then we'll retreat to a place I know in the mountains, a hidden place, where we'll gather more men if we can. Then we're going to figure out some place in this djinn-accursed land that we can hold for one solid year. And we're going to hold it."

"*You're* giving orders?" Fasal's voice rang with outrage. "Who do you think you are? Sorahb reborn?"

"No, I'm no Sorahb. I don't have to be. I'm

Commander Merahb's son, and I'm going to finish what he started."

It wouldn't be easy. Fasal's glare, as the men around the fire smiled in relieved acceptance, warned Jiaan what his first battle would probably be. But if Jiaan could do this, it would be enough. Almost enough. Once the Hrum were gone from Farsala, Jiaan would track down the peddler and kill him. That would finish it. That would make him free. But he still wasn't looking forward to sunrise.

CHAPTER TWENTY

KAVI

KAVI WANDERED THROUGH the Hrum camp unescorted, free to go wherever he willed, now that the Hrum had won.

The soldiers were celebrating, wild with wine and victory. But they weren't half so wild as deghans would likely have been. Kavi had been paid in full, since the deghans had fought exactly as he'd claimed they would. He'd left the small fortune in his tent without a qualm. Lawful people, these Hrum. They'd make good rulers—despite Garren! And they had no reason to wreak vengeance on Farsala, either.

Kavi had already peered into the surgeons'

tent—so few casualties they'd taken, inflicting so many.

The paregius, the long lances that had once occupied the carts beside the armory, had broken the deghans' charge like a flawed blade. The remains of the Farsalan army sat in the slave pens now, their high-born bitches and whelps with them. There was no more Farsalan army. No more deghans. Well, that was fine with him.

He didn't particularly want to see them. It was just that the slave pens were beside the corral where Duckie and the other mules were kept. He certainly didn't care who had survived or not.

The clerks, with their bright lanterns, were still processing the slaves. The Hrum were great ones for keeping records. Sacking the camp had taken almost as long as the battle—not because there was any fighting, but because there was so much loot. Gold dishes, glass goblets, even the tents were made of silk—how many poor, desperate men had died in the swamps, harvesting the silk that made those tents?

No, Kavi had no regrets. And the Hrum hadn't raped the women, either—a claim the deghans probably couldn't have made if their positions had been reversed. The women's faces were dirty and swollen with weeping. A few were bruised. But their glares were unbroken and full of hate. One glare in particular, which seemed to be directed at him . . .

He knew that face. But who . . . ? Of course, it was that Soraya she-bitch's friend; the taller, not so pretty one.

She obviously remembered Kavi. As she took in his freedom, his lack of escort, a grimace that made her downright ugly twisted her expression. She spat at him.

Kavi shrugged and turned away. Let her hate. It wasn't as if she'd be doing him any harm, not as a slave-servant in some far-off country. That's what she'd be now.

He reached the mule corral. Not many torches here. He slipped through the bars and called softly, and after a moment Duckie came to him, sniffing his hands for a treat. "Not tonight, lass. But then, I'm not packing you up tonight either, so that's fair."

Despite her disappointment, she remained. Kavi combed his fingers through the coarse brush of her mane and stroked her smooth neck.

Soon he'd be free to pack up and get on with

his life. A better life for everyone now, with no deghans lying in wait to take an honest man's goods or his labor.

The deghans might not keep slaves themselves, but they'd treated Kavi's people nearly as bad. The ones like that she-bitch, hidden in the mountains, didn't even regard peasants as people—just livestock, a bit brighter than their horses but less valuable.

No regrets, Kavi told himself firmly. How many of his people had died in the battle today because the deghans had spent less on their servants' armor than on their chargers' barding?

Kavi went to the tack box beside the pen, borrowed a brush, and began to groom Duckie, who assumed a look of idiotic bliss.

No, he had no regrets. No need for any. It wasn't like the deghans deserved better than they were getting. Not like they were his people. They weren't his people!

Kavi brushed harder, and the mule snorted. *They're not my people.* They meant less to him than Duckie did. Why should he care that they'd be hauled off as slaves. That was just how . . .

Just how they treated his people.

He was thinking like a deghan. As though the fact that they weren't his friends and kinsmen made them less than human. As though the fact that he cared more about Duckie than about them made them less valuable than Duckie in other ways.

And maybe they were right that peasants were different, deep down. For if he wasn't different, why should thinking like a deghan leave him leaning against Duckie's neck with tears running down his face and a cold hollow where his heart had been?

He couldn't do this. The battle, yes. Give the country to the Hrum to govern, gladly. But he couldn't allow anyone, even deghans, to be dragged off as slaves. The deghans didn't keep slaves, and if Kavi condoned it, if he allowed it, if he brought it about, then he had become one of them. The worst of them. And it wouldn't matter if they all died, for their essence, their ruthless indifference, would have survived in him. He had to stop this. He had to save them. But how?

The slave pens were closely guarded. Even if he could free a handful, what about the others? Even if he freed all here tonight, what about the rest? The ones who'd be taken when the deghans' undefended manors fell to the Hrum?

They'd take all the deghans' families as slaves. The empire's policy was to completely rid itself of the old government—though the Hrum army was still bitter about Garren's refusal to let the Farsalans surrender once it was clear they were beaten. Garren said that if they slaughtered the army, no one else would dare to resist. He was probably right. Death was a more potent threat than slavery. So speed superseded mercy. And profit, too, for strong fighting men made valuable slaves. But the Hrum army would probably make up that lost profit soon, when the few surviving deghans and their families surrendered.

The only way to save the slaves, all the slaves, is to keep the Hrum from conquering the country.

Kavi started to laugh, but Duckie's warm neck stifled the sound. All the risks he'd taken to give Farsala to the Hrum, and now he was thinking of trying to throw them out? But Patrius had told him that if the Hrum failed in their conquest within their time limit, one of the ways they convinced their erstwhile enemies to become allies was to return all they'd taken in the campaign.

All their looted goods. And especially all the people.

But how? There was no Farsalan army left, and even if there were, the thought of him leading an army made him snort. Peasants didn't fight, and Kavi was a peasant through and through. But Patrius had said that conquest involved more than fighting—so there must be other ways to resist. He'd find those ways. Make them, if he had to. Peasant ways.

Kavi finished grooming Duckie, checked her hooves, and made his way back to his own tent. He could face that bag of coins now, he thought. Maybe even count it. And then he would find a way to spin Time's Wheel till it dumped the Hrum on their heads.

He had to. If he failed, if he sent these people into slavery and left them there, he would never possess his own soul, intact, again.

CHAPTER TWENTY-ONE

SORAYA

SORAYA WAS YAWNING as she came back from her hunt in the late afternoon. She'd returned to the croft almost a month ago, but she still got sleepy during the day. At least her hunting skills had improved—four rabbits lay in the game bag over her shoulder. Yes, her hunting had improved. Her magic . . . Maok had said her abilities would grow even without guidance, but it would be slower. Slower meant a total standstill, as far as Soraya could tell. Of course, it was an unladylike occupation for a deghass.

Soraya sighed. One of the hardest things about returning to the croft had been being treated like a deghass again. She found she liked Golnar, and even Behras, a little better than she had, though Behram was nothing but an annoyance. And not even Hejir made up for the Suud's absence. She did miss Maok—and not only when she attempted magic. She missed Elid, too. She almost missed Abab!

But things were what they were. She was a deghass, of a proud house. But that didn't keep her from being . . .

The croft came in view, familiar now, with its peasant-garish, painted shutters. A strange horse was tied to the post beside the shed—not even the peddler's mule. Had her father come? Soraya's heart pounded, but the horse wasn't good enough for a deghan to ride. It must be a messenger, a messenger from her father. And if he was sending messages openly, then he must be almost ready to bring her home!

Soraya began to run, the rabbits thumping against her side.

Yes! Behras had gotten out the big handcart and was loading the family's possessions into it. But where was a horse for her to ride? And they'd told her that her father's aide had hired a wagon to

413

bring their things to the croft. Why wouldn't he do that now?

Soraya's steps began to slow, but her heartbeat didn't. She walked up to Behras. "What are you doing?"

The look on his hard face was not embarrassed compassion. It wasn't.

"I'm packing."

"I can see that. Why are you packing?"

Quick steps sounded in the house. Golnar appeared in the doorway, her embroidered apron twisted in her hands. Hejir clung to her skirts, wide-eyed, like a much younger child. A man stood beside her, dirty and unshaven. Under the grime and bloodstains, his tunic was the black and gold of the House of the Leopard.

Soraya turned back to Behras. She tried to sound confident, but her voice came out in a whisper. "Why are you leaving?"

He looked helplessly at his wife, then shrugged. "We're leaving because your da's not paying us anymore. Without his money, we can't live here, so we're going back to find a place we can farm."

"We'll take you with us, Lady, if . . . if you

like," said Golnar. There were tears in her eyes.

Soraya didn't need tears. She turned to the soldier, who sighed and straightened to face her.

"I'm sorry, Lady Soraya, but the high commander is dead, the army's dead, and the Hrum are coming."

"You're lying," said Soraya with certainty. This couldn't be true.

The man's tired eyes filled with the same embarrassed compassion as in the others'. "I'm sorry, Lady. I saw it myself. In the end, the bastards had surrounded them. The commander, your father, told everyone still standing to put down their weapons, that he'd end it. Then he drew the circle of challenge around him and waited for them to send out a champion. But the cowards sent archers instead and shot him full of arrows, like— Um, it was quick, girl. Lady. As quick as death in battle can be. The young commander, Jiaan, he told me where you were. Said you're to go with Behras and his family and hide yourself with them for a time."

"Which you're welcome to, I'm sure," Golnar added. "Though if you're to pass as one of us, you'd have to, well . . . Oh, Lady, I am so sor—"

She started forward, her arms outstretched. Soraya took a step back. Then another. Then she turned and fled, throwing the game bag aside when it hindered her.

It isn't true! It couldn't be true. Her father wasn't dead. The Hrum weren't coming, and—

She never knew what tripped her—a fallen branch, a stone. She hit the ground hard, skinning her knees and palms. The shock brought her back to herself, a bit.

A deghass didn't run in panic when given hard news. A deghass didn't lie to herself; in her heart Soraya had known it for the truth when the soldier described her father ordering his men's surrender. He cared too much to sacrifice his men in a battle they couldn't win. And he had too much farr to surrender himself. The Hrum enslaved their prisoners, didn't they?

Soraya blinked back tears. A deghass didn't weep. Besides, she had things to do.

She rose to her feet, ignoring the pain in her knees, and set out, walking purposefully.

She should make sure her father was buried properly. No, her mother would do that. If she could. Would the Hrum allow it?

Soraya spent some time envisioning the diffi-
culties her mother must have faced, arranging a
proper burial in the midst of a conquest. She fought
back tears again, because she hadn't been there.
Then she realized that the Hrum would have
taken Sudaba, and Merdas, too, as captives. As
slaves.

Soraya's breath caught, and she stumbled,
which wasn't good since she was halfway down
the trail to the desert, and the slope below her
ended in a sheer cliff.

Then that was the first thing she had to do.
She had to find Merdas and free him. He was the
sole heir of the House of the Leopard, and continuation of the house was a deghass' first duty. At
least she could rely on Sudaba to keep him safe,
until Soraya reached them. Yes. Sudaba was indifferent to the daughter she had borne, but she
loved Merdas. She would keep him safe, till
Soraya could find and free them.

Soraya rose to her feet and went on. In the forest you couldn't see clouds unless they were right
overhead. Here she could watch them gather, as
dark and rich as the sea.

Her next duty was to avenge her father.

Finding a way to hurt the Hrum might be harder than freeing Merdas and Sudaba.

In the moments when her mind functioned, she tried to come up with a plan to destroy, or at least damage, the Hrum army. But the moments her mind worked were getting farther apart, even as the thunderclaps grew closer and more frequent. So it was no wonder that she'd almost reached the Suud encampment before she realized she'd need help.

Of course! With the Suud's help, she could kill any number of people. And their magic would help her rescue Merdas, and her mother, too. That was why she'd come here instead of going back to the croft.

Soraya began to run again. The curves of the rock maze as she neared the camp were even more familiar than the approach to the croft.

They'd be asleep when she got there, for the sun was just setting, though the gathering storm made it seem darker. But Maok wouldn't mind being awakened early. Maok was wise. Maok would help her think and plan and . . .

Soraya burst around the last turn of the trail and then stared in shock. The Suud were gone.

The hutches were gone, the lovely baskets packed up and taken away. Only the fire pit remained, cold and filled with dry, dead ash.

They were gone.

Her father was gone.

He hadn't come for her. He had *promised*, and he hadn't come for her, the bastard. She was glad she hadn't said she loved him too. Glad, glad, *"Glad!"* she shouted to the empty rocks.

Thunder answered, along with a cold, rising wind. Soraya had always been able to sense the shilshadu of storms. This one surrounded her, opening itself as she reached for it. Closing her eyes, she grasped it whole—a violent, turbulent spirit that filled the boiling clouds above her. It began to shiver, a humming tension forming in its core. Soraya's mind touched the birth of lightning. With this, she could destroy—

She gasped as the thunderbolt blazed to life, yanking her mind back, pushing it away. It hit nearby, the crack of thunder like a physical blow. If she had kept hold of it, would it have struck her?

She wasn't a good enough Speaker to command storms. Or anything else. Destroy the

Hrum? That was a joke. She didn't know how to save Merdas. She didn't even know how to find him.

Cold rain pattered down, mingling with her hot tears. Soraya welcomed it, soothing her face, freezing her heart. Perhaps it would freeze her to death, if she sat and wept long enough, and solve all her problems.

But even as the rain embraced her, so did two warm, white arms. Soraya turned slowly, hiding her face in Maok's robe, and cried.

But as she wept out her grief, anger, and fear, her resolve hardened. She would find Merdas and save him. And then, somehow, she would find a way to avenge her father. The Hrum would pay and die. She was a deghass. She would see to it.

ROSTAM'S GRIEF *then knew no bounds.* "What djinn's trickery is this, that unknowing I should take the life of my own son? And such a son as would have gladdened my heart." *He rent his garments and painted his face and breast with Sorahb's wet blood.*

Both armies gathered, hearing his plaint and sharing his grief at the tragic end of the young champion.

But Rostam's grief was so deep, so strong, that mortal heart could not contain it. It grew past all earthly bounds and touched the heart of Azura himself.

"This is too piteous," *said the god. He descended to the trampled, bloodstained field, knelt beside the grieving father, and held out his arms.*

"Give your son into my keeping," *Azura said.* "Even I cannot wholly cheat death, but I can restore him. Not now. Not for many years. But when the *time has come, when Farsala most needs a warrior to lead it, then I will return to him the life so cruelly reft away. And Farsala will have a champion again."*

ACKNOWLEDGMENTS

Like any book, this one owes a debt to a great many people. My two faithful writers' groups, Wild Women of the West and a Few Good Guys, and the Denver Science Fiction Writers' Guild. My good friend Kara Schreiber, who gives me the best advice. My excellent agent, Irene Kraas, and my wonderful editor, Julia Richardson. I'd also like to acknowledge the debt of inspiration I owe to *The Lion and the Throne,* a wonderfully readable edition of Ferdowsi's *Shahnameh,* rendered in prose by Ehsan Yar Shatar and translated by Dick Davis. If anyone wants to read the actual ancient Persian myth of Rostam, Tahmineh, and Sohrab, I highly recommend this edition.

THE EPIC ADVENTURE CONTINUES. . . .

THE FARSALA TRILOGY BOOK 2:
RISE OF A HERO

CHAPTER ONE

SORAYA

SORAYA TRIED to urge the iron-mouthed mare to a faster pace, but the mare—who had probably pulled an ore cart before Soraya stole her from the miners—plodded stubbornly onward in the deliberate walk that seemed to be the only gait the worthless creature possessed. The sun was setting, painting the new spring grass that covered the low hills with mellow golden light. Soraya wondered if her home was still there.

She'd been forced to travel at night once she reached the Great Trade Road, for fear of encountering one of the mounted squadrons that scouted ahead of the Hrum army. Her rough, sturdy britches and sheepskin vest could have been worn by any peasant boy, but her straight, black hair marked her as the descendant of a long line of deghans—and the one thing all the rumors agreed on was that the Hrum were taking the deghans' families prisoner. She'd considered cutting it, but unless she shaved herself bald, her hair would still betray her. Though it wasn't a certain indication of rank. Soraya had seen girls with hair as straight and black as hers wearing peasants' gaudy skirts, and her own father had had curly, peasant-brown hair.

The messenger's account of her father's death flashed through her mind. "Shot full of arrows like a . . . It was quick, girl. Um, Lady."

Soraya thrust the memory away. She was a hunter herself. She had seen the death arrows brought. *Forget it. Forget it.* Merdas came first now.

Her father's death and the defeat of the Farsalan army, which he had commanded, left all Farsala open to the Hrum. But they didn't seem to have destroyed much so far. Even when she reached the Great Trade Road, where the Hrum troops were moving, most of the small villages she passed through, and the towns she skirted, were completely intact. Only occasionally did she scent the bitter stench of recent fire, or see townsfolk removing the blackened remains of some building whose owners, for whatever reason, had resisted the Hrum.

Of course, rumors abounded. Soraya sometimes stopped in the smaller villages, where she would purchase dinner from an innkeeper who had no idea that the meal served for her breakfast. There she learned what she could about the road ahead. She never had to ask for the whereabouts or doings of the Hrum—it was the primary topic of conversation: The main army was here, it was there. Setesafon had fallen. Setesafon had defeated the Hrum, and the leaderless remnants of the Hrum army were looting the countryside. The Hrum were besieging the capital city and negotiating with the gahn to leave Farsala forever, in exchange for all the gahn's treasure, for a yearly tribute of taxes, for half the populace to be carried off as slaves. . . .

Soraya cared little for the rumors, except for making certain there were no troops on the road in front of her. With her father dead, and all the deghans perished, Farsala would fall to the Hrum as surely as day fell to the night. The only question was whether she could reach her home and get

Sudaba and Merdas away before the Hrum found them. Or had her mother and brother fled already? Or been taken as slaves, or . . . No, they couldn't be dead. If they were dead, Soraya would have nothing left at all.

She had little enough, in truth. Golnar had left a pack, filled with food, in the house where Soraya had been hidden over the winter from her father's political enemies.

If her father had sacrificed her, as the priests demanded, might he have won the battle and survived? Soraya's heart contracted, and she pushed the thought away. She didn't really believe in propitiating the war djinn. No one did, not anymore. Especially not the political enemies who had cynically demanded her sacrifice, hoping to catch her father defying the gahn's order, hoping to take his command. But her father had outwitted them.

Soraya had gone into hiding, more or less willingly, for her father's sake, and to help him save Farsala from the advancing Hrum. But she would gladly hand Farsala to the Hrum on a platter, or the priests her head, if it would bring him back.

Tears blurred her view of the road, and Soraya wiped her eyes impatiently. She had wept too often in the last few weeks. But after she had wept out her first grief, she had resolved to do what her father would have wanted. *A deghass' first duty is the continuation of the house.* Soraya had to find Merdas and save him. He was only three years old now—two, when she'd seen him last—worth nothing as a slave. But surely even the Hrum wouldn't kill a child. Not out of hand, for no reason. Surely.

In the bottom of the pack Golnar had left for her, Soraya had found a small purse of smaller coins. It was generous of Golnar, the farmwife who had been Soraya's servant in the hidden croft where she'd spent the winter, to have left her any money. Soraya wondered if she'd had to argue with her husband about it. He was a practical man, with two sons to feed—it must have galled him to leave anything useful behind. On the other hand, Soraya's father had paid Golnar and her family to take care of Soraya. Oh, well. They'd left what they could.

It hadn't been enough to buy a horse, so Soraya had hiked to the nearest miners' camp and stolen one. She could repay them someday, she supposed. And she hadn't stolen one of their best horses, though that was more because she feared a good horse would make her conspicuous on the road than out of consideration for the miners. Deep in the mountains, the miners posted no guards. Soraya had opened the door to the shed that protected the animals from jackal packs, and selected a plain, sturdy-looking mare. She had saddled her and led her out without the slightest problem, though her palms had been slick with sweat.

It was only when the sun rose, and Soraya had tried to kick the mare into a canter, that she'd discovered the stupid beast wouldn't run if a lion were on her heels. But Soraya was almost there now anyway.

The lowering sun cast long shadows over the road. The ruts left by the winter's rains were still deep, but the mud only lingered in the lowest hollows. And even if the horse should pull a tendon, or be dragged bodily into the pit by Eblis, the djinn of sloth, it wouldn't matter, for the hills and fields along this stretch of road were as familiar as the lines of Soroya's own palm. She was less than an hour's ride from her father's manor, and after so many days of wishing the mare would hurry, it was sheer cowardice to suddenly wish that her steed would walk more slowly. *Merdas will be all right. He has to be.*

It had taken her two weeks to get home. Two weeks of hiding, of sleeping through the days in the brush, far away from the road. Of lying to everyone she spoke with, and feeling her heart beat more quickly when a man's gaze lingered on her face for more than a moment.

This was the hill that she and her father had so often raced their horses to when she was a child. But her father wouldn't have ridden around it with his eyes glued to the road to avoid the first sight of the house. He would have expected his leopard cub to have enough courage to look. Soraya lifted her gaze, and gasped.

Burned. The good stone walls still stood, but even from this distance she could see black streaks rising above the windows, telling of fire within. Soraya cried out and drummed her heels against the mare's sides. The mare jumped, and trotted for several paces before returning to her determined amble.

"Djinn take you!" Soraya flung herself from the saddle and began to run.

The road was rougher than she'd thought, but it was the growing stitch in her side that finally slowed her. Running was absurd anyway—no fires burned here now. Whatever had happened was long over. The Hrum had come, and gone. All that remained was to learn what they had done.

Soraya walked the rest of the way to the house, plodding as deliberately as the accursed mare, who followed her. She had to learn where Merdas and her mother, Sudaba, had gone. Or been taken. At least Sudaba loved Merdas, as she had never loved her daughter. She would keep him safe. Perhaps she had already fled with him to . . . to where? With the Hrum inside Farsala's borders, no place was safe. No place except with the Suud. But to get her brother to the Suud, Soraya had to find him.

She saw few signs of battle on the tough, outer walls as she approached the house. The ornamental bushes that some long-ago deghass had planted had been trampled, but their flowers still scented the air, warring with the stench of scorched timber. The outer gates that closed the long passage to the courtyard had been wrenched from their hinges and cast aside. A waste of good timber.

The stone-flagged passage was dark in the fading light, but it was empty and undamaged except for . . . What were those stains around the ceiling grates? Surely no one had . . .

Soraya walked forward and stood below the iron grid. It was too high for a girl who was small for her fifteen years to reach, so she knelt and felt the floor beneath the grating. Her fingertips came away rough with grit, and slippery with grease. Someone had poured hot grease through the grate as the Hrum soldiers passed below. That was what it had been designed for, in that long-ago time when the house was built, but . . . They must have been possessed! Surely they knew they couldn't defeat the Hrum, and angering them was the madness of the djinn of rage himself.

Still, Soraya found the corners of her mouth turning up. The House of the Leopard had fought to the last. Good for them! She knew that her father would have thought such helpless defiance a fool's gesture, but it lifted Soraya's heart.

She rose to her feet and walked on down the passage. The inner gates were still there, though their latch was broken, and one side sagged crookedly on a single hinge.

Beyond the gates Soraya could see the court-yard. The carved and polished railings of the second-story gallery were dark with soot and had been smashed in places, but Soraya could see that the rooms behind them were intact. Not all had burned, then. The central fountain seemed to be whole, though no sound of splashing water disturbed the stillness. That fountain had been the heart of the house. Its silence spoke of death, more clearly than even the shredded garden around it. Still, Soraya closed her eyes and listened.

No sound of servants cleaning and repairing damage. No scent of cooking. No footfalls. No childish voice, raised in laughter or indignation. They might have been hiding, but some other sense told Soraya clearly that Sudaba and Merdas weren't here. The house was empty, and had been for some days. Did her certainty come from the magic the Suud tribesmen had taught her? Perhaps, but what good were those shreds of domestic magic in the face of something like this?

Sudaba and Merdas were gone—but gone wasn't the same as dead. She needed more information.

Soraya reached out and laid her hand on the

gate, but it was only a gesture of farewell. There was nothing for her here but memories, and she was a deghass. A deghass didn't let grief stop her.

Soraya turned, and walked out of the passage and into the gathering dark without looking back.